likem

likemandarin

kirsten hubbard

DELACORTE PRESS

Text copyright © 2011 by Kirsten Hubbard
Jacket art copyright © 2011 by Ellie Landford

Visit us on the Web! www.randomhouse.com/teens
kirstenhubbard.com

Educators and librarians, for a variety of teaching tools, visit us at www.randomhouse.com/teachers

Library of Congress Cataloging-in-Publication Data is available upon request.

ISBN 978-0-385-73935-1 (trade) — ISBN 978-0-385-90784-2 (lib. bdg.)
ISBN 978-0-375-89750-4 (ebook)

The text of this book is set in 12-point Goudy.
Book design by Kenny Holcomb

Printed in the United States of America
10 9 8 7 6 5 4 3 2 1

First Edition

Random House Children's Books supports the First Amendment and celebrates the right to read.

to my mother
for showing me
the beauty in the badlands

before

The winds in Washokey make people go crazy.

At least, that's what everybody says. Our part of Wyoming is plagued by winds: hot winds, cold winds, dry winds, wildwinds. Wildwinds are the worst. Not only do they torment us from the outside, but they also seem to bluster inside us: battering around in our lungs, whistling through our capillaries.

I wouldn't be surprised if some of that wind blew into the passageways of our brains.

On the afternoon of my last beauty pageant, almost eight years ago, the wildwinds had already begun. That was what got into me, I like to think: I acted crazy that day because my head was filled with wind.

But that doesn't explain why that afternoon sticks in my memory like a tumbleweed blown against a barbed wire fence no matter how much I would like to forget it. It's because two of the biggest events in my history came gusting together at once: I saw Mandarin Ramey for the first time. And Momma gave up on me for good.

How I despised those beauty pageants. The judges with

white teeth and orange skin. The itchy dresses like bathtub poufs. The makeup lacquered on my face, and the shoes binding my feet like those of the Chinese concubines in my chapter book *Women of Faraway Lands*. The usual girls screeching the same three songs—"I Feel Pretty," the national anthem, and "Home on the Range."

Instead of singing, I recited historic speeches. When paired with my classic cuteness, it made me just unusual enough to stand out. I won plaques and trophies. A bowling ball airbrushed with wild mustangs. Gift certificates to restaurants with names like the L & L Hitchin' Post Inn and the Cow Town Café. Momma entered me in every pageant within two hundred miles, and some even farther away than that. We'd spent the majority of my early life on the road, zigzagging through the state in Momma's little pink hatchback, from Sundance to Saddlestring, Evanston to Medicine Bow.

The final act of my pageant career could have happened in any one of those places. But to Momma's everlasting humiliation, I screwed up in our own backyard.

The *Little Miss Washokey, Wyo., Pageant*—as the butcher paper banner affixed to the stage read—was held every spring on our school's great lawn. I'd turn seven later that month, which meant the stakes were high: Momma said the winner of the Little Miss Washokey pageant would be eligible for the tri-county pageant in Benton. After that came the state pageant in Cheyenne. And after that, the nationals, which just might make me world famous.

Our talents had been showcased, our speeches recited, our hypothetical questions answered, and the dozen or so of us were packed onstage for the grand finale, which consisted of us bopping in our clashing dresses to music rasping from a tape deck. The wildwinds plucked at the curls of our hair, tugged at our skirts. Momma had pinned a lilac bloom behind my ear, and the wind tore it away.

I remember watching it whirl across the stage like a paper boat caught in an eddy of rainwater, my mouth hanging open.

That was probably when the wind got in.

In the beginning, pageants had been fun for me. Well, maybe not the pageants themselves, but everything that went with them: our exciting road trips, shopping and prepping, all that special time with Momma. But as each pageant season came and went, Momma grew more serious. Or maybe she didn't—maybe she'd always been dead serious about the pageants, and at almost seven, I was finally old enough to realize it.

Either way, as I watched my purple flower gust over the edge of the stage and disappear, I knew I wanted the fun back.

Momma never forgave me for what I did next.

I gathered the front of my yellow dress with both hands and, to her absolute horror, flipped it over my head.

The audience—parents, schoolteachers, old folks with nothing better to do—gasped in unison. And maybe they sucked in too much wind themselves, because they all began to laugh. Their laughter encouraged me. Whoever was managing the tape deck cranked up the volume, and the other girls stopped dancing to watch as I bounced and skipped and twirled, waving my dress in the air. I kicked over the microphone stand with a bang. I even turned and shook my lacy white bottom.

Clutching at her lopsided french braid, Momma stumbled over the folding metal chairs and the people in them, her face puckered with fury. She marched onstage, shoved down my dress, and latched on to my arm. She didn't let go until she had dragged me around the corner of the old brick schoolhouse.

"What's gotten into you, Grace?" Her face was inches from mine. "Why'd you have to go and do that?"

I licked my lips and tasted Vaseline. "Spring fever," I suggested.

Momma usually chuckled at what she called my precocious remarks. But that time, she just mashed her lips together and shook her head.

"I've told you showing your panties in public is obscene. What were you thinking? You knew how important this pageant was! But you decided to make a fool of yourself in front of *everybody* and humiliate me, you, the entire family . . ."

Momma and I *were* the entire family. I stuck out my bottom lip and nodded at appropriate intervals, hoping she would hurry up and finish yelling so we could get home. Momma scolded me often, but we always hugged and made up.

It was then I noticed Mandarin Ramey.

Of course, I didn't know she was Mandarin, not yet. She was just a strange girl, standing a few yards away beneath a cottonwood tree, staring openly at us.

In one hand she held a lilac bloom. Her other hand was stuffed into the pocket of her jeans—boys' jeans, with patches on the knees. Dirt smudged her wind-chapped cheeks. Her skin was darkly tanned, but her eyes were pale hazel, the color of a glass of tea held up to the light. Her tangled black hair seemed to catch the wind, to ride it, like Pocahontas in the Disney movie. She looked like one of those feral children, raised by wolves or worse.

She was the most beautiful thing I had ever seen.

Momma's voice pierced through my trance. "Are you listening to me?" She gave me a shake. "Have you heard a single word I've said?"

Again I glanced at the strange girl, the girl who was Mandarin Ramey, searching her eyes for contempt. But her expression was unreadable. I wondered if she'd seen me flip up my dress. I hadn't felt embarrassed until then.

"Beauty pageants are stupid," I said to Momma. "What's the point?"

She yanked her hands from me as if my skin had turned scalding hot. It took her a second to regain composure. Then she seized my shoulder with crablike pincers and hustled me toward the car, her whole face crimson.

I felt sorry for a second. But then I risked one last awestruck glance back.

The girl twisted the lilac between two fingers, flicking the pale purple bloom back and forth. Her ink-flower hair shifted and danced in the wind. She stared steadily back at me, holding my eyes as if by an invisible length of chain—binding me to her, even then.

only weep when you win

My little sister, Taffeta, peered through a kaleidoscope as we walked to school, her face tipped back, her exposed eye squinched shut. She'd found it in the alley behind Arapahoe Court. Since she refused to give me her hand to hold, I led her by the mitten clipped to the sleeve of her red plaid jacket.

"Stop pulling, Grace," she complained. "My mitten's gonna get yanked off."

"Then pay attention to where you're going."

With her eye still pressed to the battered tube, Taffeta shook her head. She looked like a cat with its head stuck in a Pringles can.

"Fine," I said, releasing her mitten. "If you slip in a patch of slush and crack open your head, don't come bawling to me, all right?"

There wasn't any slush left, though. A few weeks earlier it had clogged the gutters like congealed fat, but by now the last of it had melted.

No matter the season, Taffeta always dragged her feet during our morning walk. She hated school with a passion I never could understand. Her kindergarten classmates adored her, just like the judges of every beauty pageant she entered. She had immense brown eyes and hair the color of baby-duck feathers. A legendary music in her voice. People approached us on Main Street all the time just to hear her speak—which my mother loved.

"Everybody just wishes they had a gift like hers," Momma often said.

As a child, I'd resembled Taffeta, even though we were just half sisters. But whatever in me had appealed to pageant judges had long since vanished. My childhood softness had become a skinny awkwardness, as if my fourteen-year-old self had been nailed together from colt legs and collarbones. My hair was the yellowy tan of oak furniture. I french-braided it every morning to ward off the wind, but pieces always broke free and whipped my face like Medusa coils.

"Taffeta?" I called, realizing she was no longer beside me.

I found her crouched beside a fire-ant pile, using her kaleidoscope to poke at the few creatures braving the early-spring air. Twin splotches of mud soiled the knees of her white tights. I sighed, knowing that Momma would find a way to blame the mess on me.

"Taffeta, get up," I ordered.

"Don't call me Taffeta. Call me Taffy and I'll come."

"Taffy's awful," I said, although I didn't think much of Taffeta, either.

"You're awful."

"If you don't get up, I'll freak out."

"You won't."

I started toward her. But my boot skidded in a slick spot, and I had to grab the chain-link fence so I wouldn't fall. I glanced around wildly and decided nobody saw.

"I need to tie my shoe," Taffeta said.

She refused to let me tie them for her, so I crossed my arms and waited. I could already see the school building all the kids in Washokey shared: a faded brick rectangle from the olden days, set against a panorama of dry hills and open range. Endless space. A dead planet.

The badlands.

I'd wandered through the Washokey Badlands Basin so many times I'd memorized the feeling. The forlorn boom of wind. A sky big enough to scare an atheist into prayer. No wonder cowboys sang about being lonesome. Yet somehow, I felt part of something significant out there, collecting mountains whittled into stones to carry with me, like pocket amulets.

I dug in my tote bag until I found that day's stone: a hunk of white quartz the size of a Ping-Pong ball. It wasn't anything special, but I liked the feel of it. Rounded on one side, rough on the other, small enough for me to close my fist around it.

"Done," Taffeta announced.

I grabbed her wrist, ignoring her protests as I towed her schoolward.

Like always, we paused at the edge of the great lawn, still glittering from that morning's watering. But my stomach knotted up even more than usual. The winners of the All-American Essay Contest would be announced in homeroom.

"Can't I go with you today?" Taffeta asked. "I'll be good, Grace, I promise. I hate school. Todd at my table looks up my dress."

"You know you can't come with me. Just keep your legs crossed like Momma told you."

Taffeta scowled at me. "School is horseshit."

My jaw dropped. Before I could demand where she'd heard that word, Taffeta scampered off toward the other kindergartners, brandishing her kaleidoscope. They swarmed around her like ants to a fallen bit of candy.

I remained awhile longer, squeezing my quartz stone and watching the high school students on the other side of the lawn. At the beginning of the year, administration had decided I belonged with the sophomores, a year ahead of my class, instead of with the kids my age. Like I could possibly fit in any less.

It was as if all the other students spoke some language no one had ever taught me. The pretty girls, who squealed with laughter. The monkey-armed guys in cowboy hats, who never looked my way. The wholesome farm kids, like glasses of milk, and the bored bad kids, who made their own fun. I didn't even fit in with the so-called brainy kids—the handful of them—because either they knew how to fake it, to stand out in a *good* way, or they were weird. Like Davey Miller, who thought wearing socks with sandals was the greatest idea since Velcro.

The bell rang, and the other kids headed for the double doors. I knew that Mandarin Ramey probably wasn't among them, but I searched for her anyway.

❁   ❁   ❁

My homeroom and history teacher, Ms. Ingle, was proud to be an American. She plastered proof on every available surface. Even the ceiling was a crazy quilt of glossy rectangles, blazing with stripes, spangles, pictures of presidents, and a massive map of Wyoming, emblazoned with *The Equality State* in four-inch fancy letters. Her boyfriend, Mr. Mason, ran the Washokey Historical Society, located in a trailer parked behind the gas station. I'd spent all ten hours of fall's community service project there, organizing sepia-colored photographs of covered wagons and surly pioneers.

Although I liked Ms. Ingle, sometimes I found myself sneering at our forefathers or extending my middle finger, unseen, in my lap.

Then I felt guilty, as if George Washington were hiding underneath my desk.

Davey Miller tapped my shoulder. He sat behind me and was always trying to make conversation. "What's up, Davey?" I asked.

"I forgot to give your pencil back yesterday," he said, blinking hard.

The blinking was a nervous tic. It made him appear

forever on the verge of tears. His little sister, Miriam, was the same age as Taffeta. When Davey dropped her off to play, he often lingered in my kitchen to talk until I fabricated some excuse to make him leave.

"Keep it, Davey," I told him. "I've got plenty."

Before he could say anything else, Alexis Bunker, who sat to my right, backhanded me across the shoulder. Washokey High mixed kids of all grades in homerooms, and just my luck, Alexis and I had been placed together.

"Grace, guess what!" she squealed. "Did you hear?"

Alexis had squinty blue eyes, freckle-prone skin, and blond hair she'd hot-curled so many times for the regional teen pageants it looked like frayed twine. The summer before, she'd sprouted an enormous chest, and it amused me to watch her attempt to navigate around it. Since our mothers had been best friends since their childhoods, Alexis and I had also considered ourselves best friends until we started high school and realized we had nothing in common. At lunch, I still sat with Alexis and her cronies—aka Alexis & Co.—only because I had no sophomore friends to sit with. Most friendships in Washokey were founded on circumstance, not connection.

"Did I hear what?" I asked, rubbing my shoulder.

"Mandarin Ramey got caught sneaking into the school pool last night with some older guy. Paige's sister Brandi's boyfriend was out taking his dog for a walk and he saw. He says the guy must've been like thirty. Ain't she a slut?"

I feigned disinterest as Alexis colored in the details. Nothing she said could shock me, of course. I knew more about Mandarin than anyone.

"Well, ain't she?" Alexis insisted.

I touched the rock in my jacket pocket. "She is," I agreed.

Because that was one of the two truths everybody knew about Mandarin Ramey:

1) *Mandarin was beautiful.*
2) *Mandarin was a slut.*

The loudspeaker beeped, and Alexis swung forward in her seat, clunking her beige cowboy boots in front of her. Washokey kids wore all kinds of cowboy boots: stiff and new, creased and battered, bright-colored and fashionable. Alexis's boots, though, were the only ones with spurs.

"May I have your attention, please. May I have your attention, please."

Mr. Beck, the principal, requested our attention twice during morning announcements. He wanted to take full advantage of his daily five minutes of fame. Usually, I ignored him with the rest of the class, but that day I stared straight at the speaker, a black circle like a pupil with no eye around it.

"Good morning, everyone, on this terrific Tuesday, April tenth, with the temperature in the low sixties. This is your principal, Mr. Beck."

"Beck's stuck in the sixties," a guy called from the back of the class.

"Ha, yeah, I bet he's taking a puff of the dooja right now," called another.

With perfect timing, Mr. Beck coughed. Everybody laughed except Ms. Ingle, who opened her mouth and then closed it.

"First news of the day," Mr. Beck continued. "I'm pleased to announce I have the winners of the All-American Essay Contest, kindly funded by the members of Washokey's 4-H and Kiwanis organizations, right here on this paper in front of me. Hold on to your seats!"

I curled my fingers around the bottom of my seat. My essay flashed before my eyes like a reel of microfilm, each paragraph flipping by with an imaginary tick. Certain sentences hopped out at me, the turns of phrase I'd wrangled like rodeo calves. I'd written exactly what I thought would win me the grand-prize trip.

"Third place and twenty-five dollars goes to Becky Pepper, junior."

Becky Pepper was a 4-H kid, bused in from one of the farms or ranches that made up Washokey's unincorporated south. I suspected she'd written about the history of beef breeding or dairy science, something the judges would love.

"Second place and fifty dollars goes to—"

Mr. Beck coughed again. I sat very still.

"Grace Carpenter, sophomore. And one hundred dollars and admission to the three-week All-American Leadership Conference in Washington, D.C., goes to our very own junior-class president, Peter Shaw! Congratulations, Peter."

My heart plummeted to the soles of my feet as I watched the other kids mob Peter. They mussed up his hair, snatched at his glasses. When Ms. Ingle went over to congratulate him, I couldn't stand it any longer. I snaked my arm through the strap of my tote bag. Unnoticed in the confusion, I rushed out of the classroom.

❋ ❋ ❋

I was going to end up just like Momma. It was my fate. Born in Washokey and stuck there forever, trying to make myself stand out among the same old people. No matter how hard I tried to steer my life in a different course, something would always knock me back.

These were the thoughts that packed my brain like grid-locked traffic as I crouched in the end bathroom stall, with one arm draped over the back of the toilet. Although no one was there to see me, I tried my hardest not to cry.

"Only cry when you're happy," Momma liked to say. "Only weep when you win."

But it was through eyes blurred by tears that I noticed the graffiti at the bottom edge of the stall door, scrawled in thick red marker:

School is Horseshit.

I mouthed the words over and over. Had Taffeta seen them here? She was an advanced reader for her age, like I'd been. But this bathroom was in the high school wing. The elementary school kids used another, unless it was a real emergency. And besides, a person could only read the phrase from ground level—sprawled out on the grimy tile floor, like me.

How pathetic.

I mashed the heels of my hands into my eyes. Admittedly, I had no desire to be a politician. Or a leader of any sort. But I longed for those three weeks outside of Washokey, longed to see a different part of the country, to sample parts of another life. Miles of green grass. The Smithsonian—especially the gem and mineral collection. People in business suits. Here I saw nothing but jeans.

The essay contest was supposed to tide me over until my real, final escape to college. And if I tapped into that deep-down part of myself I didn't like to face, I had to admit it—I also wanted to win for the sake of winning.

And to think that Peter Shaw—four-eyed shotgun shooter, demolisher of innocent anthills, a *football player*, for crying out loud—had written a better essay than I had!

Now I'd have to wait two more years to leave. An unfathomable length of time. Two more years of imprisonment in the sun-scorched badlands, surrounded by the same old scandals, the same dusty streets, the same products on the grocery store shelves. How could I possibly stand it? Without something to break up the monotony, I would fade into the hills like one of those solitary ghost-people, who spent their days listening to the wildwinds batter their corrugated shacks.

When I was younger, I used to beg Momma to move away from Washokey. She always shook her head and said the same thing: "I tasted it. That city freedom. But then I came to my senses."

As if Jackson Hole could compare to New York, or San Francisco. We wouldn't even have to leave Wyoming, I pleaded. We had passed many memorable places on our road trips between pageants. Why in the world were we stuck in the Washokey Badlands Basin?

"In a world that's so big and wide," Momma would reply, "you can't blame me if I prefer this knowable portion."

The more Momma told me she wanted to stay, the more I wanted to go. I used to suspect that the badlands were inhabited with malicious spirits who didn't want us to leave. Although now I knew better, I still didn't feel better. Because if it wasn't spirits keeping me in Washokey, then it must be something much stronger. I wondered if Washokey life had infected me—if it had altered some secret part of my brain or reprogrammed the amino acids in my DNA so if I ever got out, I would never be truly happy.

Like a conch shell singing for the ocean. Washokey would pull me back.

Sniffling loudly, I must have missed the creak of the door opening. I didn't know I had company until the faucet splashed on.

I froze midsniffle.

For a moment, I considered hiding out. But then I remembered how, back in fifth grade, Alexis & Co. used to wait outside a bathroom stall until the girl inside finished and then make fun of her for taking so long.

I scrambled to my feet, flushing the toilet on the way up, and pushed open the door.

Mandarin Ramey stood at the sink.

I saw her in fragments, like close-up snapshots. Her kohl-smudged hazel eyes. Her angular cheekbones—everybody said her mother had been part Shoshone. Her black hair, streaked with damp ridges and valleys from the comb of her wet fingers. The uneven hem of her white sweater. Jeans worn low on her hips. As she arched forward to shut off the faucet, the dip of her spine engraved in the apricot-colored skin of her back.

She wiped her hands on her jeans. Then she faced me.

"Grace Carpenter," she said.

My name sounded foreign on her tongue. How could she possibly have known it?

"So it was you bellyaching in that bathroom stall."

Mandarin Ramey knew I'd been crying. I felt like throwing up.

"It doesn't matter to me one way or another." She leaned against the dented metal sink. "I was only saying. It's no shame to cry—I heard the essay contest announcement on the loudspeaker. A rotten deal, if you ask me. Peter Shaw's got prairie oysters for brains."

She seemed to be waiting for me to speak, but my lips wouldn't work.

Mandarin Ramey had never stood so close to me. She had never spoken to me before. In fact, Mandarin rarely spoke to anybody at school. She preferred the men she served at her father's bar over boys her own age, and after her attempt at friendship with a girl named Sophie Brawls went sour a couple years back, she avoided girls altogether. It was amazing how much we all knew about Mandarin. How much, and how little.

"I won fifty dollars," I said at last.

Mandarin smirked. "Yeah, but it'll be a stupid savings bond, the kind you can't touch till you're of age. And you're how old, fourteen?"

"Almost fifteen."

She studied me, her expression blank. Without moving her torso, she dropped one hand to her hip and slipped a cigarette from her back pocket. Every move she made, from the cock of her head to the cross of her ankles, was graceful, yet calculated, as if she were posing for an unseen camera. She poked the cigarette between her lips and lit it, sucking in so hard her cheeks collapsed inward.

Then she offered it to me. "Want a drag?"

Even the idea—sharing a cigarette with Mandarin Ramey, putting my mouth where hers had been—made my face flush. I shook my head and turned to the door.

"Ain't you gonna wash your hands?"

I stared at her in horror. She smiled at me. A haze of smoke lingered around her head like a halo.

Which would be more embarrassing—escaping now with unwashed hands, or lingering to wash them? With every split second of internal debate, I died a little more. Finally I hurried to the sink beside hers, jabbed on the faucet, and scrubbed my hands as quickly as I could.

"I was just giving you trouble, y'know." She yanked a trail of brown paper towels from the dispenser and stuck them in front of my face. "I don't bite. Really."

I dried my hands without meeting her eyes.

"Aw, get your ass back to class. Me, I aim to finish this cigarette. I'll see you in math, all right?" She gave me a playful shove, herding me out.

As the bathroom door creaked shut behind me, I staggered down the empty hall of lockers and around the corner. There I backed into the wall, crackling a poster for the Future Farmers of America. My tote bag slid off my shoulder onto the ground. I could still feel the imprint of her hand on my shoulder, still smell the faintest trace of smoke on my clothes. Mandarin Ramey had spoken to me.

And not only that . . .

Mandarin Ramey *knew my name*.

I gazed out the window across the hall. Great sheets of earth swept into mesas furry with sage, then tumbled brokenly into valleys. The only color in the landscape was an early patch of Indian paintbrushes with blooms like ruby shards. As I watched, several red-winged blackbirds startled and took flight.

2

like mandarin

Depending on whom you asked, Washokey, Wyoming, had two or four claims to fame.

First, Washokey had the biggest jackalope statue in the western half of Wyoming. It sat in front of the grocery store on Main Street. Jackalopes were Wyoming's official mythological creature: jackrabbits with pronghorn antlers, the essence of Wyoming sense of humor. Nobody actually believed they existed, with the exception of armchair tourists on Wyoming message boards.

Second, and more notoriously, Washokey was the site of Wyoming's 1968 hippie massacre. It wasn't really a massacre. Only three people were killed, including the killer. But the headlines put Washokey on the map.

Washokey's other two claims to fame were subject to question.

The town had made headlines again the year I was born, when someone spied the likeness of the Virgin Mary in a cluster of boulders by the Bighorn River. But that was also the year of the great storm, when the wildwinds bellowed through town fiercer than ever, and the river brimmed over its banks and jumbled up all the boulders like a kid spoiling a marbles game. In all the years after, nobody could figure out which rocky cluster was the special one. Except for one person. And I wasn't telling.

Washokey's final claim to fame was Mandarin Ramey.

Mandarin appeared in the doorway of our geometry classroom. The noisy flux of students bottlenecked behind her. She paused a second, backlit, as if surveying her realm. Then she sauntered across the classroom and fell into her seat with a huffy exhale of breath, leaning back so the hem of her sweater lifted tantalizingly.

I kept one hand around the stone in my jacket pocket as I opened my notebook to last night's homework. Although math was one of my best subjects, I made an effort to remain unnoticed in a class of sophomores and dyslexic juniors.

Mandarin was the only senior.

"We're going to start our chapter on polygons today," Mrs. Cleary announced, "which I know you've all been waiting for!"

Hunching over my desk, I began to draw a border of circles along the bottom of my paper and added freckles, stems, and leaves. Mrs. Cleary, a Washokey native, made math hysterical. Not like funny-hysterical, but hysteria-hysterical. She hopped around in too-tight pants with her granny panty lines showing and waved her arms like a cheerleader. She chirped on and on, transforming the most interesting stuff into nonsense.

I should have enrolled in precalculus when they'd given me the chance.

But I'd known that Mandarin was in this class.

I knew what and when all her classes were. I'd memorized the paths she took through the halls.

I knew where she lived (in the blue house on Plains Street), when and where she worked (Thursdays, Fridays, and Saturdays at Solomon's, her father's bar), and which foods she preferred at lunchtime (fruit, and only fruit—the more unusual, the better).

It wasn't like I stalked her. I only observed, which was something else entirely. And everybody had *some* level of fascination with Mandarin Ramey.

Although I was pretty sure nobody else kept a mental tally of all the men she slept with. I could never be too sure, of course, because I based most everything I knew on rumor. And there were *always* rumors about Mandarin, though not all of them involved her men.

Like the one about her joyriding with a truck stop prostitute. And the one about her streaking through a baseball game during a breakout from the Wyoming Girls' School, which she'd attended for three months during her sophomore year. And the one about her running a road-enraged bonehead off the highway in her father's truck.

Mandarin denied or defended nothing. Which meant, according to the other students, that the rumors *had* to be true. Especially since she'd moved to town at age nine and had missed taking part in those formative childhood years when we'd memorized one another.

Mandarin's scandals gained the most attention. But that wasn't all I envied about her.

Her elegance. Her disdain. The subtext in every little thing she did. With Mandarin, the *tap-tap-tap* of a ballpoint pen against her desk was a come-on, a raised hand, a *fuck you*. Even her name was seductive: *Mandarin*, like the syrupy canned oranges I ate with my fingers. Because her mother was a mystery and her dad sure wasn't talking, nobody knew where she'd gotten it—whether it was Native American, maybe from the Mandan Indians we'd learned about during our Lewis and Clark unit, or whether it involved the Chinese language. Everybody agreed it was impossibly exotic, like her cheekbones, her long black hair, and her gravelly slow-tempo voice.

"Mandarin!"

My pencil lead snapped. I covered my drawings with both hands.

"Come up here and do number three from the homework on the board," Mrs. Cleary said. I noticed that her nails were painted pale yellow. It looked like she had some kind of disease.

Mandarin hesitated, eyebrows raised. Then, at her own

insolent pace, she got up and sauntered to the front of the classroom. She tugged once at her low-slung jeans before selecting a piece of chalk. Washokey High was so backward only half our classrooms had dry-erase boards.

What is it like? I wondered as Mandarin began to sketch. To be the one the entire school talked about, lusted after? To serve as everybody's favorite topic of conversation? To walk down the street and leave grown men gaping as you passed?

❋ ❋ ❋

Solomon's sat at the other end of Main Street, as far from the high school as possible. It wasn't the only bar in Washokey. In a town of just thirteen hundred people, there were four places for cowpokes to get shitfaced—not even counting Della Bader's seasonal Farm Bar in the unincorporated south.

But Solomon's was one of the most popular. Mandarin served cocktails there until two in the morning on weekends, though she wouldn't be eighteen until September.

On Saturdays, sometimes I hid in the doorway of the Sundrop Quik Stop across the street and watched Mandarin arrive at work. She had to pass the Methodist church, where a cluster of sunburned men often gathered out front, waiting for the afternoon service to begin so they could enjoy their evening festivities. I liked to imagine their conversations:

Would you look at that, the first man would say.

If only she wasn't just interested in them out-of-towners, the second would reply.

Hell, I'd risk a jail sentence to have that girlie squallin' in my bedsheets.

Shee-yit, I'd risk it all.

But if Mandarin heard whatever they said, she never reacted—even though she had an epic temper. Maybe she kept quiet because she knew she'd be slinging them beers that night.

She never paused to read the card-stock signs taped to the bar's foggy windows: *Happy Hour, Doller off Domestics,* and *Karyoke Singin Thursday Nites!* Stepping over the yellow chow dog that slept in the doorway, she disappeared through the swinging saloon doors into the murky, smoky gloom.

❀ ❀ ❀

So far, Mandarin had drawn a lopsided three-dimensional cylinder on the blackboard. She dragged the chalk beneath the shape with a deliberate screech, causing all the girls in the class to clap their hands to their ears.

The boys didn't even twitch. Like me, they were spellbound.

They knew they had no chance, though. Mandarin's men were usually five years, ten years older, and from other, larger places: Casper, Laramie, even Denver and Billings. Men with no reason to stick around, except for her.

At least, that was what everybody said.

Mandarin never broadcasted her flings the way other students did. She never parked at the A&W for floats and chicken fingers, or copped feels under blankets at autumn bonfires. All that was too time-consuming. Mandarin treated her men like the apples she bit the good parts from, then pitched; like the still-smoldering cigarettes she famously crushed beneath her bare feet.

I wondered how many of them she thought about afterward, and which ones, and why.

❀   ❀   ❀

I'd actually seen Mandarin with a man just once. It was early the past October, the limbo between scorch and freeze. I remembered pressing my braid into my nose and mouth as I walked down Plains Street, as if the scent of my shampoo would ward off the wind, the tang of impending snow.

Plains Street had no sidewalks, only pebbled borders where dry lawns crumbled into asphalt. Mandarin's house was small and shabby, like all the homes on her block. Some fortressed their yards with chain-link fences and padlocked gates. Others hid in thickets of cottonwoods or billowy lilac bushes. Mandarin's blue-gray house looked naked in contrast, without a single bush or tree to shade it from the sun and wind.

I took advantage of any excuse to pass by, though I rarely saw her. But just catching a glimpse of the place where she slept, ate, and got dressed—the place where she brought her conquests on nights her father worked late at the bar—gave me a thrill.

When I had approached Mandarin's house that day, I'd seen her standing outside, talking with some guy. Though I had no experience guessing the ages of men, I supposed he was in his midtwenties. As soon as I was within earshot, I stepped behind a tree.

"It's just that I'm real busy," Mandarin said.

"But I'm only gonna be in town till Tuesday."

"There ain't nothing I can do about that."

"I just can't stop thinking about you. And I can't stand it, the thoughta all them brainless bastards pawing all over you. It makes me sick to my stomach."

Mandarin plucked a cigarette from the pocket of the man's denim shirt and lit it. She sat on the top step, absently blowing smoke through pouted lips.

"What you should do is come with me," he said.

She took another drag.

"Can't you just picture it? We could get a little place by the mines, a double-wide if I get the raise they promised. I'd come home to you every night, and you'd always be there, taking care a me."

"You're not serious."

I heard a hazardous tone in Mandarin's voice, as if her consonants had edges. The man didn't seem to notice.

"Course I am," he said. "Don't it sound like heaven?"

She waved her hand holding the cigarette, brushing him away. "I'd rather be a lot lizard at a highway truck stop than any man's babysitter."

The man hesitated, as if searching for deeper meaning in her words. Then he yanked the cigarette out of her hand and tossed it onto the dry lawn. She jumped to her feet.

"What's the matter with you?"

"You're a slut and a bitch, you know that?"

I gasped into my braid as Mandarin leaped up and struck the man's chest, twice, three times. He caught her arms and pinned them behind her back. She struggled, but he was stronger. He pulled her against his chest and kissed her mouth.

Mandarin used to get into fights all the time, with girls, boys, anyone she thought deserved it. In the years after administration had sent her to the Wyoming Girls' School, she seemed so resigned in comparison, all that fire put away somewhere. I imagined it a sort of turmoil she kept inside, like a scarlet crayon scribble.

I wanted her to keep fighting. But instead, she let the man pick her up and carry her back inside the house.

I waited for the fallen cigarette to dim and die, wishing I'd had the courage to run across the street and save her. Then I turned and sprinted down the block, feeling like a child, my braid slapping against the hood of my parka.

❀ ❀ ❀

Washokey's women did not love Mandarin, especially her teachers. Outwardly, they mourned her wasted mind. "Miss Ramey," we heard them tell her, "your looks. Your adventuresome character. Such a sin to waste them, when you could be so much."

But in secret, they gossiped like the rest of us. I was sure of it. They expected Mandarin to fail, every last one of them. And because they expected it, they *wanted* her to. They didn't want to be proved wrong. Not by Mandarin Ramey.

I could see it in their faces—like now, as Mandarin finished the last calculations of a math problem gone horribly wrong. "Nice try," Mrs. Cleary said, the irony sopping from her voice as she wiped the problem off the board with one brutal stroke of an eraser.

"Anybody else?"

Nobody offered. So she zeroed in on the one person who couldn't refuse.

"Grace? What about you?"

I pressed my math book to my chest and hurried toward the front of the classroom. On my way, I happened to catch Mandarin's eye.

She winked.

Blushing uncontrollably, I began to resketch Mandarin's math problem. Behind me, I heard the other students scraping their chairs over the floor, exchanging notes and whispers.

All about her. Never about me.

Sure, maybe most of the attention Mandarin got was negative. But it wasn't the kind of disdainful *brainfreak* attention I got, when I got any at all. Hers was lustful. And jealous. Because even as they condemned her, every single girl wanted to *be* her.

But nobody more than me.

I want to be beautiful like you, I thought, as if Mandarin were listening.

I want apricot skin and Pocahontas hair and eyes the color of tea. I want to be confident and detached and effortlessly sensual, and if promiscuity is part of the package, I will gladly follow your lead. All I know is I'm so tired of being inside my body.

I would give *anything* to be like Mandarin.

3

small towns don't forget

I stood in front of my full-length mirror and brushed my damp hair over my shoulders until it hung straight. I wedged my hands into the pockets of my jeans and hiked them down until the angles of my hips stuck out over the waistband. Then, without taking my eyes off the mirror, I began to saunter.

By now, I had it down. I'd been practicing in secret all year.

But I could never pull it off in public. I could never saunter down the halls at school, for fear of someone pointing and laughing.

"Faker!" they would howl. "Wannabe!"

Like back in fourth grade, when all the popular girls had

glued glittery stickers to their temples. I'd talked Momma into buying me a set. Because the drugstore had sold out of the flowers and butterflies the other girls wore, I chose a sheet of lusterless tropical fish. They were still pretty: koi and Siamese fighting fish with trailing tails. But only minutes after I entered the classroom, I was dubbed Fishface, far worse than Faker or Wannabe. The next day, there wasn't a single sticker in sight.

I wasn't a trendsetter. I was a trendstopper.

Until then, I hadn't stood out. But nobody had, not really. In early elementary school, when there had been only twelve girls in each class, by decree we were all best friends. There was little competition. The only people who cared about the Little Miss Washokey pageant winners were the grown-ups—and Alexis Bunker. Eight years ago, after I'd disqualified myself, she'd won the crown, and she reminded us about it for years afterward.

The change came so swiftly I never saw it coming. All of a sudden, the other girls had discovered *Glamour* and *Cosmopolitan*, flatirons and eyeliner, and the ability to purchase clothes online instead of at the Walmart in Cody. Alexis's dedication to the regional pageants became admirable instead of uncool.

And everything that mattered to me—rocks and books and schoolwork—was deemed peculiar.

I didn't want to stand out in a bad way, like I had during the Fishface disaster. But as the years passed and the gap between me and everybody else widened, I couldn't make myself fit in either. So I did the next best thing: I quit trying.

I let myself fade into the collage of faces and hallways. And I pretended I didn't care.

Now I scowled at my reflection. Behind me, my bed bulged with a mountain of mismatched pillows. A row of swans Momma had cut from pink flowered contact paper trailed along the tops of my walls. My carpet did not quite make it from one side to the other, leaving a strip of floorboards exposed. My computer was a neighbor's hand-me-down. The stacks of novels on my shelves came from the junk shop and garage sales. Except for the plastic shoe boxes of rocks stacked beside my dresser, hardly anything about my room reflected me.

Not even my reflection.

The door banged open behind me. I whirled around, tugging up my jeans. Strands of opera music drifted in through the doorway.

"Dang it, Taffeta! Can't you knock?"

She flounced in anyway. "Why? What were you doing that's so secret?" She wore a blue jumper with white kittens prancing along the neckline. Momma always changed my sister's clothes after school. As if life itself were a beauty pageant. "Were you doing something *obscene?*"

"None of your business."

"Momma says come to dinner. It's Hawaiian salad."

Whatever that meant. Momma loved to concoct strange recipes from miscellaneous cooking magazines and use Taffeta and me as guinea pigs. When she stumbled upon a particularly impressive dish, she'd cook it for all her lady friends and claim it as her own invention.

"Fine," I said. "Now scram. I'll be right behind you."

As soon as I heard her thump down the stairs, I knelt beside my stack of shoe boxes. I removed the first two—the ones that contained shoes—opened the third, and swapped the quartz stone for a baby geode, the size of a half walnut. If dinner got too infuriating, I could poke my thumb inside the stone, feel the angles and rock candy ridges, and think about geology instead of my mother.

❋ ❋ ❋

My Little Miss Washokey fiasco launched our downward spiral, though it didn't become obvious until Taffeta was born. Now Momma and I moved through our house like strangers, each disapproving of the other.

Momma's disapproval of me seemed more like confusion, bewilderment. As if she could never understand how she had created a person so different from herself. A daughter who preferred books to beauty, who cared nothing about winning—until the All-American Essay Contest, and look how that had turned out.

What I felt about Momma was more of a sourness in my mouth than a feeling, a taste like rotten milk. I hated how everything Adrina Carpenter did was an obvious attempt to compensate for her own fall from grace fifteen years earlier, when she'd gotten pregnant with me. Although her schemes rarely worked the way she meant them to.

Exhibit A: Femme Fatale

Employed as a freelance saleslady for Femme Fatale Cosmetics, Inc., Momma took it upon herself to beautify the tri-county area. She found her best success with weathered old ranch wives yearning to make themselves lovely for their livestock and husbands. She knew just how to appeal to the itch she claimed every woman had, an itch that only amplified the farther a woman removed herself from civilization.

But no matter how successful a businesswoman Momma claimed to be, I knew we lived off the inheritance from my father and Taffeta's child support, not Femme Fatale profits.

Exhibit B: Our house

Because Momma had spent time in Jackson Hole as a teenager, she thought of herself as sophisticated, the most cultured of all her friends—although everybody knew she'd grown up in our house at 17 Pioneer Ridge. When her grandmother died twelve years earlier and left us the house (Momma's parents had died when she was a teenager), Momma pledged to make it the envy of Washokey.

The result was a museum of unfinished projects: partially papered hallways, mismatched pieces of secondhand furniture, half-hemmed curtains that hung in different lengths.

Exhibit C: Décor

One of the monthly magazines Momma subscribed to included foldout posters of famous paintings. She ironed each one and displayed them in fifty-cent frames from the junk shop, staggered diagonally down the stairway. I knew them like old friends: Van Gogh's *Wheatfield with Crows*, Degas's *Ballerinas in Blue*, Bruegel's *Landscape with the Fall of Icarus*.

Momma took pride in memorizing the accompanying articles and quoting art-related details to her girlfriends. She only occasionally made an ass of herself by jumbling up the facts. Nobody ever noticed, but it made me shake my head.

Exhibit D: Me

Momma's first hope. Her worst mistake. And her harshest critic.

When I was younger, Momma's affectations ranged from mildly annoying to utterly exasperating. But I thought she fooled everyone else—until the spring I turned eleven, when I came across Alexis's mother, Polly Bunker, talking with Mrs. Snelson in the gas station deli.

The gas station deli—aka the Sundrop Quik Stop—was the kind of place where men finished beers first and then paid for the empty bottles. It sold milk and sandwiches, fireworks alongside handles of Jim Beam, and novelty crap like rubber cow pies and lighters bejeweled with American flags. I was perusing the distressingly limited selection of paperbacks when I overheard the two women talking.

"She said it was Armani!" Polly Bunker exclaimed. "But Tracy Drummely told me she put it out four days ago at the Bargain Boutique. The tags said *Old Navy.*"

"Oh no." Mrs. Snelson chuckled. "Military surplus?"

"You think she'd bother to be more sneaky about it. But ever since she won that Femme Fatale sweepstakes a couple months back, she's gotten cocky."

"Like it'd have fooled anybody."

"What big-time designer'd ever pick orange and pink plaid, anyways?"

When I blinked, *I saw* plaid. Orange and pink plaid. The colors of Momma's new coat. Polly Bunker and Mrs. Snelson were making fun of my mother.

In a tiny town like Washokey, nothing's worse than being

made fun of behind your back—especially by somebody like Polly Bunker, Momma's so-called best friend and the worst gossip in town. I knew Momma was different than other Washokey mothers. She didn't drink. She didn't go to church. Sometimes she played poker, but she wasn't any good. She didn't date, claiming that women didn't need men to be happy; her marriage to Taffeta's father, an electrician from Idaho with a Mazda Miata so small he drove with his knees halfway to his chin, had lasted less than a year. I always assumed, as she must have, that all these distinctions made her somebody the other mothers admired. Not somebody they mocked.

The humiliation lingered long after I left the deli. It lasted for weeks, flooding back every time I saw Alexis or Mrs. Bunker, or even the Sundrop Quik Stop.

But worse than the humiliation was the pity. It felt like Christmas-flu vomit double-boiling in my gut. The worst feeling I had ever felt, compounded because I didn't *want* to feel it. Not for my mother.

As I neared the kitchen, the opera music grew louder and louder until I went around the corner and found its source: an old boom box at Momma's feet.

I hated opera music. The women sounded like hysterical monkeys. The men sounded like they were gargling. But Momma loved it—or at least, she pretended to.

She sat beside Taffeta at the glossy round table and had

pulled out a third chair in invitation. A blue pageant dress was draped over the fourth chair, like a guest. I seated myself and stared at the soggy glob of pink-tinged lettuce on the plate in front of me. I recognized chunks of canned pineapple, and what were possibly bits of ham.

"I found this recipe in *Cuisine at Home* magazine," Momma said. "Doesn't it look divine?"

She spoke with the bad British accent she'd been working on for a few weeks. Just the past month she'd been trying to talk like a Southern belle.

Momma was only thirty-three, but the Wyoming sun had aged her face prematurely. That day she'd wound her brown hair into a french twist, and like any respectable cosmetics saleslady, she wore plenty of makeup. Her lips appeared to be shellacked. Mascara clung so thickly to her lashes they looked like spiders. When she slipped one foot from its platform espadrille sandal and switched off the music with her toe, I could imagine her sitting at the table practicing that motion while we were upstairs.

"So, Grace," she began. "Polly Bunker called and said you lost the essay contest. Why didn't you tell me?"

"I didn't lose, exactly," I said. "I got second place. I won fifty dollars."

"She won fifty dollars," Taffeta repeated.

Momma smiled patronizingly. "You mean they gave you fifty dollars in consolation. That was awfully kind of them. They don't always give runners-up prizes."

I speared a pineapple fragment so brutally the tips of my fork clanked against my plate.

"Though speaking of winning," Momma continued, "Little Miss Washokey is coming up. And we all know what an important pageant this is. When Taffeta wins this year, she'll be eligible for the tri-county pageant, and after that, the state pageant, and after that—if the Lord wills it—the stars!"

I wondered what the Lord thought about her invoking his name. I glanced at Taffeta. She just sat there, sucking her fingers—a habit left over from toddlerhood. At least it wasn't her thumb.

I guessed you could call Taffeta Counterexhibit A: Momma's final hope. Taffeta's miraculous voice was proof things might be on the upswing. That year, Momma hadn't entered her in any pageants prior to Little Miss Washokey. Everybody in town knew about Taffeta's voice, but Momma didn't want to reveal her secret weapon prematurely.

"Grace, you remember competing in your Little Miss Washokey, don't you?"

She brought it up at the start of every pageant season. Like clockwork. I felt something gritty between my teeth. I stared at my mushy lettuce, trying to determine what variety of Hawaiian produce could account for a crunch. "Not really," I replied.

"Well, everyone else in this town does. Especially Polly Bunker. She'll never let me forget about Alexis's win. She wouldn't have won at all if it weren't for your debacle onstage. I know you remember."

"I remember too," Taffeta said.

"You weren't even born yet," I said. "Loser."

"Grace, enough!" Momma's accent had vanished.

Whenever she was angry, she talked just like every other grown-up in Washokey. "I want to have a pleasant dinner for once. Can't we ever conversate like a normal family?"

"We're not a normal family," I muttered.

Momma cleared her throat. "Grace, go to your room."

I wanted to roll my eyes. *Too little, too late,* I thought as I pushed my chair back and headed for the stairs. Why did she even try?

My fifteenth birthday was coming up in May, but I knew not to expect anything more from Momma than the cake and the box of last-season Femme Fatale makeup she gave me every year. She never asked about the books I read, or the rocks I lugged home. She only looked at my report cards so she could brag about my grades to her friends. She knew nothing about me.

But I knew all about her.

That was what happened when you stuck around in the town where you'd grown up—even your daughters learned your stories.

Like me, Momma had felt the pull of far-off places during her girlhood in Washokey. When her parents died in a highway accident, she saw a chance for escape. At eighteen, she left her grandmother's house and moved in with her uncle on the other side of the state.

I knew what had really happened during her three-month stay in Jackson. I knew all about the nights she'd spent in the brush beside the Snake River after her uncle had turned out to be some kind of pervert. The solace she'd found in crummy bars. And the nice police officer who'd rescued her at her lowest point and driven her home to Washokey.

He'd gotten her pregnant with me on the way, although she didn't know it until he was long gone.

Momma had spent fifteen years of both our lives trying to compensate for her disgrace. It didn't work, of course. Because small towns don't forget.

And neither do daughters.

4

her almost smile

After Ms. Ingle handed back my history exam on Wednesday, she lingered by my desk. "Would you mind staying after class for a few minutes?" she said in a low voice. "I'll write you a pass."

I nodded, watching as she continued up the aisle. Her brown dress drooped around her skinny frame like a burlap bag, and her nylons sagged in the knees. I knew she refused to buy Femme Fatale cosmetics from my mother, preferring the cheaper grocery store brands. She often kept me after class to discuss more challenging assignments, or simply to talk history. Sometimes she showed me historical postcards Mr. Mason had purchased online: pictures of women picnicking in stiff skirts, or frontiersmen crossing the bridge over the Bighorn River.

In spite of her fondness for Washokey history, Ms. Ingle was an out-of-towner, assigned to our school due to a lack of able teachers. No matter how long she lived in Washokey, she'd always be someone different, someone we pretended to scoff at but really envied because she'd had a whole other life outside of Washokey. Just like Mandarin Ramey.

Once the bell rang, I approached Ms. Ingle's desk.

"I thought I'd give you a couple days before I told you I'm sorry about the contest," she said. "I suppose you can't win them all."

Don't tell Momma that. My hand located the small piece of nephrite jade in my pocket. Jade was Wyoming's official mineral. The stone was the color of verdigris, like an ancient Greek coin gone turquoise with age.

"You know, I've been thinking about you, Grace."

"Okay . . . ," I said.

"I've always regretted that we haven't been able to challenge you the way you deserve to be challenged. Though I stand by the notion that advancing you another year isn't the best option."

I shook my head so hard my brain almost rattled.

Sure, skipping me again would get me into college—and out of Washokey—faster. But I already felt light-years behind the rest of my classmates in all the real-life things that mattered. If they made me a senior next year . . . I shuddered. Already, the only sophomore who talked to me was Davey Miller, and he talked to everybody, whether they listened or not.

Ms. Ingle knew how I felt. She'd pried it out of me the first week of school, after I'd overanalyzed a "What's *Your*

History?" essay and turned in a twelve-page manifesto. Our junior high teachers had spooked us into believing that high school would be tough.

"You've excelled in your alternative course work," she continued. "But I've noticed you haven't signed up for a community service project yet."

Washokey students had to take part in ten hours of community service in both fall and spring. Momma wanted me to help backstage at Little Miss Washokey—an appalling idea, but I hadn't come up with anything better.

"Unless you were planning on assisting Mr. Mason again . . ."

"I haven't decided." *No way.* Some of those ancient photos had sharp edges. I still had scars from the tintypes.

"Of course, cataloging our history for future generations is priceless. But I've been thinking. How would you like a project whose results are a little more . . . immediate? And that takes advantage of your extensive brainpower?"

"I don't know," I said. "I guess."

Ms. Ingle hesitated. When she spoke again, I could tell she was trying to sound nonchalant. "By any chance . . . do you happen to know Mandarin Ramey?"

My thoughts blanked out for a second. Then they returned as a series of exclamation points instead of words.

"Grace?"

"Well, no, not like *personally* . . . But I know who she is, yeah."

"Mandarin's predicament is the opposite of yours. We should have held her back years ago, but she swore she'd drop out if we did. We've lightened her load enough for her to scrape by. Yet anytime our help is obvious, she rebels. I've never met anyone so averse to a helping hand."

Ms. Ingle held out a glass candy dish filled with Reese's Pieces. Taffeta called them Reesey Peeseys. I took a single orange candy to be polite. It stuck in my throat.

"She needs help in all her classes," Ms. Ingle continued. "But geometry and history the most—which happen to be your two best subjects. Mandarin also hasn't chosen a community service project. She needs twenty hours to count for both semesters, since she didn't complete a project last fall. I was hoping you could help her choose one. You don't have to participate, but any sort of guidance—"

"I'll do it," I said.

As soon as I uttered the words, a bizarre image flashed behind my eyes: Mandarin and me sitting side by side in the library, leaning over a massive reference book as thick as an ancient Bible. For some reason, we both wore glasses.

I felt a tickle of laughter in my throat threatening to overflow. I coughed to keep it down. I didn't want to look crazy. But the absurdity of the two of us, paired up—hysterical. Not just Mrs. Cleary hysterical, but straitjacket-bound, funny farm–inmate hysterical.

We might as well frolic through a horse pasture, holding hands.

"You look apprehensive," Ms. Ingle said, misreading my face. "Maybe this isn't a good idea."

"No," I said. Or I thought I'd said it. It was as if I were outside myself, listening to me speak. "I can do it. But . . . I just want to get this straight. My service project is helping Mandarin find a service project?"

"With some tutoring on the side." Ms. Ingle smiled. "You're a good person, Grace. I knew you had a strong sense of self. With the wrong person, Mandarin could be a . . ." She paused. "I just trust you won't be influenced."

I felt the urge to laugh again, but this time at Ms. Ingle, for so thoroughly misreading not only my facial expression, but everything about me.

"There's just one problem," I said.

"What's that?"

"Why would Mandarin want my help? I'm just a sopho-more. The youngest sophomore in the school. It would be embarrassing for her. She'd never want to work with me— not in a billion years."

Ms. Ingle took a small handful of Reesey Peeseys and rat-tled them in her palm. "That's not a problem at all," she said. "Mandarin asked for you herself."

❉　❉　❉

No matter what Ms. Ingle said, I never believed the whole preposterous mentorship enterprise would happen. Be-cause that was the very definition of my rocks-and-books-and-badlands existence: in my life, *nothing* happened.

So when Mandarin approached me on Thursday, I was completely unprepared.

I was standing in the hallway between fifth and sixth pe-riods, trying to buy a drink, but the fickle soda machine re-fused to take my dollar. Every time I crammed the bill into the slot, the machine spit it back out, like a wagging tongue. I began to feel frantic with thirst. In a few minutes I'd be late for English. To make matters worse, the machine sat at a nucleus of student traffic, and people kept jostling me, swishing their elbows against my overstuffed tote bag and knocking me sideways.

At last, I crumpled the bill into an unreasonable wad and tried to stuff it into the slot.

"I'll trade you," a voice said.

I whirled around, backing into the machine.

Mandarin was posed before me in a lavender sweater, one hand balanced casually against her hip. With the other, she held out a fresh, unwrinkled dollar bill.

"Go on," she said.

I plucked it from her fingers and gave her mine. "Thanks," I mumbled. "I'm really thirsty."

"Sure seems like it."

The machine took Mandarin's dollar on my first try. I pressed the button for a bottled water, and it banged down into the catch.

"Just water?" Mandarin said. "There's a fountain right around the corner, y'know. Spouting out an unlimited supply. For free."

"I know. It's just . . . the tap water here's kind of disgusting."

"Yeah, I guess it does taste dirty. Moldy, even. They probably pipe it straight outta the irrigation canal."

Mandarin watched as I unscrewed the bottle and sipped at the water self-consciously.

"I thought you were thirsty." She reached out. "May I?"

I handed her the bottle. She tipped her head and drank, her throat rippling with each swallow, as if my water were ambrosia, nectar of the gods shipped down from Mount Olympus. A trickle escaped from the corner of her mouth and she caught it with her index finger. Then she handed the half-finished bottle back to me.

"So there's a reason I tracked you down," she began.

My heart began pounding like an Indian drum. I hoped she couldn't hear it.

"I ain't doing too good in history," Mandarin went on. "Actually I ain't doing too good in any of my classes. Like math, as I'm sure you've noticed. I never got two- and three-sided shapes, not to mention five- and six-sided ones."

There's no such thing as two-sided shapes.

"And history. I'm flunking history. Plus, I haven't even chosen a service project yet—and neither have you, I've heard."

Now my heart pounded like a whole symphony of Indian drums. An entire drum circle.

"So I thought, maybe there's a chance you could help me out. . . ."

"But *why?*" I blurted.

Mandarin studied me, her eyes narrowed slightly.

"Well," she said after a long pause, "you're, like, Washokey's resident genius, right?"

"I do fine, I guess."

"You don't have to be modest," she said. "Not around me. Like I said, I'm flunking, and graduation's getting close. And I sure as shit ain't going to stick around, not even for an extra day. So, what do you say? Is there any chance at all you're free to come to my place this afternoon?"

I replied in involuntary gulps, like hiccups: "I can come. I can help."

"Perfect." Her smile exposed a row of crooked bottom teeth. "Come around five-thirty, if possible. Wait—you need my address. You don't know where I live."

I shook my head.

"Here." Mandarin withdrew a fat red marker from the seat of her jeans and took my arm, extending it in front of her. I held my breath as she tattooed her address onto my flesh in bold red letters: *34 Plains Street*. She didn't release my arm right away. I felt the cool touch of each of her fingertips separately, like bits of ice.

"So five-thirty, yeah?"

"Five-thirty," I said.

"Bring your textbooks. I always forget mine."

Finally, Mandarin dropped my arm. She waved, her hand fluttering like a hummingbird's wing, and sauntered off down the hall.

My eyes traveled back to my arm, tracing the cherry-colored letters, and stopped at the water bottle in my hand. I glanced around to make sure I was alone. Then I tipped my head back and tried to swig like Mandarin had. But when the final bell rang, I choked.

❋   ❋   ❋

In less than two hours, I was supposed to knock on Mandarin Ramey's front door. So after dropping off Taffeta, I headed for the Tombs.

The Tombs was a granite jumble that looked like a grave-yard stirred and stacked by the wildwinds. It ran along the edge of the Bighorn River, about a quarter mile outside the city limits. All sorts of legends surrounded it—about Indian sacrifices, burials, lynchings—the sort of stories common in small western towns. Enough to keep people away. Out in the badlands, I came across beer cans in the strangest places, but I never found them at the Tombs.

I had discovered the Tombs the past August, during one of my rock-hunting quests. I'd made the mistake of setting out at noon. Only half an hour in, I felt charbroiled. I sought shade among the piles of tomb-shaped rocks cooled by the river trees and meandering water.

I found the Virgin Mary on my third visit.

Each story described her differently: a head sculpted from stone, or a profile, or the whole holy likeness, holding baby Jesus. So-and-so's cousin's grandpa-in-law claimed she cried tears of holy water, or cured plantar warts, or sipped wine from a straw—all that mumbo jumbo typically attributed to magical Madonnas.

They would have been disappointed by my find: way up high, where the geometry of stone formed a sort of cave, a woman painted in a black and greasy substance, like wet charcoal or tar.

And she was extremely basic—not much more than an outline, though more complex than the cave paintings we'd seen on a field trip to the Medicine Lodge Archaeological Site. She wore a hood, or maybe a blanket, draped over her head. Because she was so obviously Native American, I knew she couldn't be the Virgin Mary, unless she'd been painted after some Catholics had come and force-converted a local tribe.

But she was definitely a mother.

I liked to look at her. There was something comforting about her drowsy eyes, like those of a purring cat. Her almost smile. Her forearms, shaped like a cradle.

Now, as I sat in the cave, embracing my knees, pondering the unbelievable reality—that *I was going to Mandarin Ramey's house* in ninety minutes, seventy minutes, less than an hour—I could have sworn that the Virgin Mary gazed at me sympathetically.

Of course, it would have been better if I could have found that comfort in Momma. But even the idea of that weirded me out. And she was preoccupied, anyway.

I ran my finger along a cleft in the stone floor, trying to appease my anxiety.

I'd imagined countless times the ways Mandarin and I might meet. During earthquakes. Tornadoes. Other natural disasters, like the storm that had created the Tombs. I imagined us holed up here together, sharing our innermost secrets while rain hissed into the river and thunder boomed outside. It was always a large-scale event that brought us together.

Never anything as ordinary as a community service project.

And I had never imagined—not in my most outlandish, plains fire–fueled, tornado-twirled fantasies—that Mandarin would come to me *herself*.

All because she thought I was, like, Washokey's resident genius?

No girls ever went to Mandarin's house. Not since Sophie Brawls—the only real friend Mandarin had ever had,
or that anybody knew about.

Sophie was one of the ranch kids bused in from the
south, like Becky Pepper. She wore dresses all year long. Even
in the winter, with clunky snow boots, gravy-colored tights,
and a hooded parka. I only ever noticed Sophie in town because she had the largest eyes I'd ever seen. Like soap bub-
bles, set in a pearly round face with pink cheeks.

When Sophie started running around with Mandarin,
everybody noticed her. Their friendship was short and intense. Inseparable for two months and then came the fight.
A *real* fight. Alexis swore she'd seen Sophie in the office
afterward sobbing, with scratches like streaks of jelly on both
sides of her neck.

Someone in my grade called it a dyke fight. A few people laughed, but the label didn't stick. This was Mandarin
Ramey, after all.

The fight was the reason Mandarin had spent the last
three months of her sophomore year at the Wyoming Girls'
School. Sophie Brawls never came back. Since then, Mandarin had let no one into her life—well, other than her endless parade of men.

I listened to the wind whistling between the boulders,
reaching inside my hideaway like an invisible hand. When I
lifted my face, I smelled lilac blossoms. It really was spring.
As if life couldn't get any more stressful, pageant season was
beginning.

5

two of a kind

Mandarin's front door hurtled open before I had a chance to knock. I almost stumbled down the porch steps. Something about Mandarin made me back away each time we met, as if she were an explosion of heat or light. I felt like shielding my eyes.

"Hey," she said.

She wore a white men's undershirt over her low-slung jeans, and she'd tied her hair back with a scrap of thick yellow yarn. It made her look younger, her cheekbones more pronounced. We stood there for a second in uncomfortable silence. Maybe she was waiting for me to speak.

Finally, she held open the door. "Well, come on in."

Her carpet was the sickly brown color of an old man's den. A muted television made the dim room flicker and flash.

In the intermittent light, I saw coffee-colored stains on the ceiling in menacing shapes and olive green furniture grinning at the seams. An oak dining table had been crammed into a corner, with one of the chairs overturned.

Mandarin followed my gaze to the table. She went over and righted the chair without saying anything. Then she led me down the hall, flipping on every light switch we passed.

She paused in front of her bedroom door, her hand on the knob.

"Before we go in, I feel like I need to give some sort of disclaimer, or whatever. Like a surgeon general's warning. What you're about to see has got absolutely nothing to do with me. If that makes any sense."

"Okay . . . ," I said.

I wondered if her walls were quilted with pages torn from celebrity tabloids, like in Alexis's room, or childish relics, like mine.

But the small space beyond the door revealed none of those things—just more of the same shabby brown carpet, pouring into her room like sewage. The same weird stains on the ceiling. The only furnishings were her bed, a tall dresser that leaned to one side, and a bookshelf with no books. Scuff marks patterned the lower third of her walls. There were no posters, no drawings, no photographs. No personality. As if the girl living there considered it a temporary apartment.

"It's pretty shitty, yeah?" Mandarin asked, as if reading my mind. "Can't say I didn't warn you."

I shrugged.

"Well, I'm glad you made it over here."

"*Really?*" I said before I could stop myself. I hugged my textbooks more tightly.

"Sure." She grinned. "I mean, I thought you might not come. I'm not dumb, y'know. I get how weird this is."

"It's no big deal."

"I said I'm not dumb, all right? Course it's weird. I'm, what, three years older than you? And you're here to help *me*. How is that not weird?"

I shrugged again.

"It's bizarre," Mandarin said. "But here's the thing: I got no shame. I know you're, like, some kind of child genius, yeah? So I'd rather have you help me out than one of the kids who've been going to school with me since fifth grade. They're all assholes. Not even worth the butts in my ashtray. If I *used* an ashtray, that is."

I didn't know what to make of the cheerful tone of her voice, her grin. It was like she took pleasure in being a misfit. While I felt exactly the opposite.

"I really do need help, though," she went on. "I just slacked off and nothing makes sense to me anymore. And I promised I'd graduate. I promised my dad, I mean. He's a good guy, deep down. But I can't stand it when teachers try to jam their faces in my business. I'd have asked another student for help, but, like I said, so many of the smart kids are assholes, and the passably decent ones are, like, terrified of me. . . ."

She glanced at me. I probably looked terrified.

Her grin appeared to have frozen to her face. "Well. Want anything to drink? Or a snack?"

I shrugged for the third time.

"You don't say much, do you? It's all right. Just make yourself at home. I'll be right back. And don't worry, I won't bring you tap water." Mandarin pulled the door shut behind her, leaving me alone.

Alone in Mandarin Ramey's room.

I hugged my books so tightly the corners bit into my stomach. It was surreal. What every boy and man in town—and most of the girls and women—wouldn't give to take my place.

When I heard the phone ring on the other side of the house, and Mandarin answer, the temptation to explore became irresistible.

I didn't know how long I had. So I started at the closest point: Mandarin's dresser. Opening the drawers would be too invasive, so I settled for the Indian basket on top. I combed my fingers through the knickknacks inside: barrettes, bandages, tampons, a windup plastic puppy.

The top shelf of her bookcase held a dead cactus in a pot. It looked like old-man flesh, wrinkled and white-whiskered. A stereo stood on the shelf below. On the shelf below that, facedown, as if it had toppled forward, a picture frame.

I picked it up. It was a Polaroid of Mandarin as a little girl: scowling, the sun in her eyes, wearing jeans with an elastic waistband and a white T-shirt.

The photo reminded me of the way she'd looked the first time I'd seen her, eight years earlier. I wondered who had taken the picture. The person behind a camera told as much as who was in front of it. My pageant photos in Momma's album were proof.

I set it back facedown on the shelf.

When I turned around, the first thing I saw was Mandarin's bed. I stared at the balled-up comforter, the rumpled sheets, the pillow still indented from the curve of her head. And suddenly, I imagined her there: rolling across the mattress, her black hair sticking to her naked back, a male forearm curling around from underneath—

I blinked the image away as Mandarin burst through the door.

She thumped two glasses onto the dresser, shoving the Indian basket carelessly aside. "It's ginger ale," she said. "I considered lacing it with a shot or two of vodka, but then I thought, 'Nah, she ain't the vodka type. More of a Peach Schnapps kinda girl.' Am I right?"

"Well, no . . . I've never—"

She laughed. "Just yanking your chain. Course you don't drink. But seriously, what *do* you do?"

I hesitated. "What do you mean?"

"Like, what do you like to do? If we're going to be working together, we've got to be pals too, right? So tell me: how do you fill your time, Grace Carpenter?"

I fumbled through my brain. I hated questions like that. I never knew what to say, what was babyish, and what wasn't.

"I read a lot," I admitted to Mandarin's bare feet. Her toenails looked jagged, almost bitten. I wondered if the bottoms of her feet were scarred from all the stamped-out cigarettes. "And I spend a lot of time in the badlands. Looking for rocks and things."

"No kidding?"

She sounded genuinely surprised. I risked a glance up.

"Like what kind of things? Like, arrowheads?"

"Sure. Or like, fossils and . . ."

Mandarin was on her hands and knees, reaching under her bed. She pulled out a jar filled with what looked like broken wedges of peanut brittle.

They were arrowheads. Maybe fifty of them, all jumbled together. Did she have any idea how ancient they were? She should have wrapped them separately in soft cloth and tucked them carefully into a shoe box, like I did my rocks.

Mandarin motioned me over. "What do you think?"

She unscrewed the top of the jar and dumped the arrowheads onto her bed. Involuntarily, my hand shot out and grabbed one.

"It's perfect!" I exclaimed. "Look at it. Blue-white chalcedony, and not a single chip. Do you know how rare that is?"

"No clue."

"It's old, too. You can tell it's old. Like ten thousand years. These aren't even called arrowheads—they're projectile points. They're older than the bow and arrow."

I knew how much of a nerd I was being, but I couldn't help it. At least Mandarin seemed interested.

"Lemme see." She stuck out her hand.

I set the arrowhead on the cushion of her palm. She examined it thoughtfully. "Huh," she said. "What do y'know."

"And this one! It's tiger skin obsidian. My all-time favorite." I held the amber-colored stone up to the light. "See the glow?"

Mandarin tipped her head to the side. Her eyes were the same color as the arrowhead.

"Where did you *get* all these?" I asked. I'd been hunting

for years, and I'd only found seven. Only two unbroken, and even those were chipped.

"Oh," she said dismissively. "Around." She swept the arrowheads back into the jar. I hoped she'd offer me one, but she didn't. She set the jar on the floor and then flopped onto her bed. "Have a seat," she ordered.

"So, where do you want to start?" I asked, as if I hadn't heard her. "The Pony Express?"

"Start at the beginning. I've forgotten everything. How about cave people? Start with them." She smacked the bed beside her. "Sit!"

At last, like an obedient dog, I perched on the very edge of her bed. I thought I could feel the heat of her mattress through the fabric of my jeans. I shook my head and flipped open the history textbook in my lap.

"You know, I don't think cave people are in here," I said. "And we've got math to cover too. And I have to be home for dinner by seven. My mother takes it seriously."

"What, dinner?"

"Well, yeah . . . She likes to cook."

Mandarin sat up and peered at me, as if I were some strange specimen she'd collected in her arrowhead jar. "I bet you even sit around the table," she said. "Wow. I ain't had a family dinner like that—I don't think ever, to tell you the truth. Then again, a well-meaning but drunk-ass dad and a shameful daughter ain't much of a family. My mother killed herself before I moved to town."

"She did?"

I recalled what I'd heard about Mandarin's mother.

Supposedly, they'd spent the first half of Mandarin's life together, hopping from small town to small town in the southeastern corner of the state. Then, for reasons nobody knew, Mandarin moved in with her father in Washokey. About the mother herself, rumors were scarce.

I'd definitely never heard she was *dead*.

"Wanna know how she did it?" Mandarin asked.

"How she . . ."

"It was really gruesome—not for the faint of heart. You better sit down for this one." She paused, as if I weren't already sitting. "It happened in our old apartment. First, the cops found a noose made out of knotted-up dishrags, but my mother didn't own enough to make a proper one. Then, in the hallway, they found a whole bunch of sleeping pills, but just over-the-counter ones, lying all over the ground. And then, in the bedroom, know what they found? My mom, dead on the ground, with duct tape wrapped around her mouth like ninety times. She'd suffocated herself."

Suddenly, I found it hard to breathe. I wondered if Mandarin had been home when it happened. If she'd seen the body. "I—I'm so sorry."

Mandarin shrugged. "I'm over it."

I nodded. "Well, we don't have much time," I said. "Maybe we could come up with a list of community service ideas, and then we could—"

"Aw, screw community service."

I shielded my chest with my textbook as Mandarin rolled off the bed, stomped across the room, and kicked the wall. *So that's where the scuff marks came from.*

"But I thought you wanted—" I began.

"School is horseshit."

I mouthed the words I'd seen on the door of the bathroom stall as Mandarin flounced over to her stereo and
jammed it on to Prince's "Little Red Corvette." It was kind
of embarrassing, like a movie sound track that didn't fit.

"I love this song," Mandarin said, pacing around the
room. "Do you? Probably not. Everyone around here likes
that hokey country shit. Anyway, I know what I said. And I
meant it at the time. I always got good intentions. I just hate
it, all of it. I'm not stupid, even though people think I am. It's
just—there's *got* to be a better way, y'know?"

I tucked my feet under the bed so they wouldn't get tram-
pled, trying to make myself as small as possible. "A better
way to do what?"

"To get out."

"Out of where?"

"Of where?" Mandarin laughed contemptuously. "Of
Washokey! Of this little cow-shit town in the middle of
nowhere. There's nothing here! We're hundreds, thousands
of miles away from anything worthwhile. The whole town's
falling apart, the people are rotting, but for some fucking reason it's like nobody ever leaves!"

She stopped pacing.

"It's *suffocating.* And it ain't just suffocating me, but
everybody."

I thought of her mom and the duct tape.

"Everybody's dying a little more every second," she said.
"Like frogs stuck in a septic tank. But not a single person in
this shit town gets it. *Nobody gets it.*"

To my astonishment, she dropped to her knees. Right in

front of me, on the hideous old-man carpet. She grabbed my hands. I willed them not to shake.

"Except maybe you, Gracey."

Why do I get it?

"Did you know I read your essay?"

I swallowed hard. "You *did?*"

"They had 'em all hanging on the bulletin board outside Beck's office. I had a couple chances to flip through yours while I waited. I read it and I was like, *finally*, here's somebody who understands!"

I had trouble meeting her eyes. Because how could my essay have meant something to her when I'd written it for *them*—all the people she hated?

"It was just for the contest. . . . I don't even remember what I wrote, exactly."

"You're not like the rest of them. All everybody does here is bitch and moan about how they want to move to the big city, how there's never nothing to do here—but they don't mean it. Not truly. Otherwise, they'd *try*. But you . . ."

She squeezed my hands.

"You've got your shit together. You know how easy it is to get stuck in this place, and unlike the rest of them, you're actually trying to get unstuck. You see, Gracey? We're two of a kind. That's why I wanted you to come over. We'll die here if we don't get out."

She was so close to me I could see my reflection in her pupils.

"You've still got lots to learn. But we're two of a kind. I can *feel* it."

Two of a kind.

What if she's right? implored the hopeful girl inside me, pounding on the bars of my rib cage. *You have it in you.* What if I really could be like Mandarin?

"M-maybe I should go."

"Go? Why?"

Because I'm not you, I wanted to say. *You're wrong, and the girl inside me is wrong. I'm nothing like you at all.*

I couldn't look at her as I pulled my hands from hers, closed my textbook, and stood.

"It's not like I'm asking you to run away with me," Mandarin said. "I just wanted to talk. Even in your essay you said—"

"I've got to go," I said. "I'm so sorry." And then I fled.

6

let go

I listened to my sister sing while I did the dishes. Her voice was as warm and fluid as the sudsy water pouring over my hands. She was rehearsing Andrea Bocelli's "Con Te Partirò" for the upcoming pageant.

In *Italian*.

It had all started the afternoon when Momma put an Italian opera album on repeat. After just two loops, Taffeta was singing along. She couldn't understand Italian or read Italian words. But she could sing Italian perfectly.

That was my sister's secret weapon.

It was a mighty good one. So good it seemed almost blasphemous for something that transcendent to be unveiled in a small-town pageant. I'd been in dozens of child beauty pageants and attended dozens more. I'd never heard a contestant sing in another language. As a matter of fact, outside of our crappy high school language classes, I'd never heard anybody in Washokey speak another language, other than the handful of Mexican migrants who picked sugar beets in the fall.

I drizzled a trail of lime green soap over a pink plate and scrubbed. Although I never admitted it, I loved listening to Taffeta sing. As long as I stayed in the kitchen while she rehearsed, I could eavesdrop without Momma's knowing. But that night, Taffeta seemed tired. It was past her bedtime. Momma's off-key screeching kept interrupting the song. And worst, the memory of what had happened at Mandarin's house kept pushing against the backs of my eyeballs, threatening to flood.

Mandarin Ramey had invited me into her world. And I had *refused* her.

But her world isn't what I thought it would be, I thought, trying to console myself. Just like her crummy bedroom, or the inside of her house. The reality was entirely different from the fantasy. Like opening Pandora's box when I'd only considered the engravings on the outside. I thought she'd be her confident, carefree self.

I didn't know she'd be so *vulnerable.*

When I pulled my arm from the suds, I noticed Mandarin's address—*34 Plains Street*—still visible on my skin. I reached for the dish soap and squeezed a trail over the angular red letters. With the rough side of my sponge, I scrubbed until my skin felt raw.

"Grace?" Momma called. My sister stopped singing. "Could you come here a minute?"

In the living room, Taffeta stood on top of the coffee

table, wearing her new blue pageant dress. Her cheeks glowed pink with exertion. My mother, kneeling in a pool of sewing debris, squinted at the needle she was attempting to thread.

"You want me to do that?" I offered.

"No, I wanted you to . . ." She paused. "Just a second. One second. Almost got it. Oh, it slipped. These things are awful. There! It went in. Lovely!"

I glared at her. She was being Princess Adrina: teacup-toting British royalty out of a bad television miniseries. Her newest character to go with the phony accent. Even when we were her only audience, she felt it necessary to pretend. The real Adrina Carpenter emerged only when she yelled. Or on those mornings when she sat staring at the kitchen table, inexplicably depressed.

"I need you to hold the dress tightly around Taffeta's middle while I sew it together. This is real fine quality fabric, did I tell you?"

With both hands, I pulled the dress taut around Taffeta's middle. I leaned away from Momma as she leaned in to stitch. Even so, I was assaulted by the scent of the apple conditioner she used to glossify her brown hair, mulled with the smell of the spicy cinnamon gum she liked to chew. A pleasant fragrance to anyone else, but it made me gag. I breathed through my mouth.

Mandarin's mother is dead.

The thought set my insides reeling. Everybody knew that Mandarin lived alone with her father, Solomon Ramey, a man who seemed to exist only in and around his bar—except for the time I saw him at the Sundrop Quik Stop. He was tall and gaunt, his face dreadfully unique: a beaky nose, yellow skin, thin black hair, a crumpled brow. Like some kind of bogeyman. When I tried to imagine him at home with Mandarin—the two of them drinking coffee at the table or eating canned chili in front of the TV in that dark house— the scenario seemed outrageous. Almost as outrageous as my helping Mandarin with her schoolwork.

Mandarin's mother had always been this shadowy, mysterious figure the town knew little about. Some people supposed she was an alcoholic. Others claimed she had a pain disorder. Physical or mental, they never specified. Still others assumed she was simply too poor to take care of her daughter.

Nobody guessed Mandarin's mother was *dead*.

A dead father, like mine, was nothing shocking. In a town where every man owned at least two guns, hunting accidents happened frequently. Also mining accidents. And car wrecks, like the one Momma's parents had been in, even though the county highways were wide and lonely. Washokey men always found ways to get themselves killed. Often explosively.

Fathers, in a way, were expendable. Having a mother was the important thing, the thing that made you normal.

Well, except in my case.

Momma tapped Taffeta's stomach with the back of her hand. "Can't you suck in a bit more, baby?"

"But then I can't sing."

"At the pageant you'll have to suck in and sing at the same time. You might as well start now."

Taffeta glanced at me. Then she sucked in her belly as best she could and attempted to squeeze out the notes.

Without looking at me, Momma remarked, "So I heard you went to tutor the Ramey girl today."

I practically jumped. "From who?"

"I've got my sources."

Polly Bunker. Alexis's mom had spies everywhere, probably including Plains Street. Half the mothers in town were part of her coven of gossips.

"I don't like you going over there," Momma said quietly, as if Taffeta couldn't hear her. "That girl's a tramp."

"I *know* that," I said, hating the plaintive tone in my voice. "But she needs help in school. Ms. Ingle asked me to. It's for my service project."

"I thought we decided you'd work backstage at Little Miss Washokey!"

"*You* decided that."

She shook her head. "That girl's beyond help, Grace. The mother's who-knows-where, and the father's a drunkard. You *know* what they say about him. . . ." She lowered her voice even more and tipped her head toward mine. "About how when Mandarin was younger, he used to—"

"Momma, I don't want to hear it, all right! I know what they say!"

"I just don't want you getting mixed up with a girl like that. There's no future for her but trouble. Believe me, I know! I know better than anybody. And the last thing you need is for people to associate you with her. They'll look down on you, too."

She wound the thread into a knot and then snapped it off. "You can let go now."

In my bedroom, I slammed the door and fell face-first

onto my mountain of pillows. They had been my grand-mother's, and they reeked of musk and age. I smashed my face into them so deeply I could hardly breathe.

My mother was clueless. Didn't she see? She was only making Mandarin seem *better*.

❀ ❀ ❀

Late that night I lay awake with a single white sheet pulled over my ear. It was warm out, and I had left my window open. The darkness chimed with the midnight music of crickets.

Several minutes had gone by before the low hum rumbled into my consciousness. Distant at first, the sound grew louder and louder as it approached, until it came around the corner and surged into a roar. Smashing one hand over my nose, I kicked off my sheet, darted across the room, and slammed the window shut right as the mosquito truck lumbered down our alley. I could see it through the chinks in my backyard fence as it hunched along, saturating the air with poison.

I remained at the window until the truck rounded the corner. The roar faded into a dull rumble. Now the crickets were silent.

I'd forgotten that spring brought mosquitoes, followed by the pesticide trucks to destroy them. Spring also brought the cottonwood snow that stuck to the bottoms of my shoes. It brought the agony of fire-ant bites, the crash-shatter of thunderstorms, and the dread of another sunburned summer. Three endless months with nothing for me to do except reread old books and accompany Momma and Taffeta on pageant trips.

Even more than summer, I dreaded that first yellow cottonwood leaf in August, which meant autumn, and the start of school. At least school filled my time.

Most of all, I dreaded Washokey's winters. The chapped hands, the puddles in the hallways, the searing winds during our walk to school. The burny belch of radiators, making our classrooms reek like wet dog. And the two dreary weeks of holidays I spent cooped up with my mother. It took centuries for spring to arrive.

Spring—which I dreaded.

I dreaded *every* season. How tragically depressing. Like when I sat in class, staring at the clock, willing the second hand to move faster. Until I remembered I had no place to go. Not until college, at least.

As long as I lived in Washokey, would there be nothing for me to look forward to?

I stared out the window, both my hands gripping the sill. In our backyard, which we rarely used, I saw a plastic baby pool filled with stagnant brown rainwater. My rusty bicycle, half hidden by dry grass. A pair of Taffeta's old red pageant shoes.

I sighed, then crossed the room and fell back onto my bed.

I found myself thinking about an incident in seventh grade. A bird had somehow flown into the busy cafeteria during lunchtime. He darted from one side of the room to the other, flying faster and faster, until at last he slammed into one of the enormous windows. Then he picked himself up, dove across the room, and slammed into the opposite window. *Thunk.* He did it again, and again. The cafeteria was filled with hoots and laughter while the bird wrecked himself against the deceptive square of sky. I'd wanted to shout at everyone, to shut them up. But even if they'd heard me, no one would have listened.

Right now I felt like that bird.

Mandarin's words flared back to me all of a sudden, as if she were flitting back and forth across the dark room beside me, beseeching: *We're two of a kind. I can feel it.*

But how did she know?

And then I remembered: she had read my essay.

Sure, I'd written it for the judges. But there were some truths, too. Things I didn't quite believe but wanted to. About how we all had leaders inside us. And we couldn't let other people hold us back. Because that first step into the future had to be ours alone.

Before I fully realized I was moving, I'd jumped up, yanked open my dresser drawer, and thrown on my clothes over my pajamas. I shoved my desk chair over to the window. Heaving it open, I climbed from the chair onto the sill. I lowered myself until my feet were dangling in the open air, over the ground almost ten feet below.

I hung there for a moment, my heart thumping.

Then I let go.

7

a little piece of ocean

Although the county dump was only a couple of minutes out of town, the alley behind Main Street was littered with discarded couches, avocado-colored appliances, and Dumpsters overflowing with trash. Drops of sweat rolled down my back as I jogged down the alley, dodging the forsaken debris.

I passed behind the hospital where we'd all been born: a two-story house converted into a clinic. Next came the row of offices for mining companies and telecommunications, the gas station, and the Sundrop Quik Stop. The grocery store was on the other side of the street, along with the Buffalo Grill, the bank with an ATM no one trusted, and a solitary clothing shop that also sold souvenirs and fake turquoise jewelry. There wasn't much more to town than that. On side streets, the junk shop, the post office, and the

Washokey Gazette. Bars and churches—Baptist, Methodist, and Episcopal—all of which served as the social headquarters for Washokey grown-ups.

Solomon's was the only bar located next door to a church. As I approached it, I heard the twang of country music, along with male laughter slurred by booze. My jog slowed until I was trudging with my head down, as if there were a wind to lean into, though there was no wind, not that night.

I stopped when I saw the yellow chow dog sprawled in front of the bar's back doorway. Milky cataracts fogged his eyes. He panted at me, his purple tongue hanging out like a piece of Canadian bacon. Usually, he slept out front.

I stood on the other side of the alley, breathing in the lingering scent of mosquito poison, watching the dog's barrel chest rise and fall, and I thought, *I can't do this.*

Suddenly, the door swung open and Mandarin burst out, along with a blast of music. It seemed almost magical, as if I'd willed her appearance through telekinesis. She wore a black cocktail apron, spiked with pens and straws, and she'd tied back her hair in a proper ponytail, with elastic instead of yarn.

"Grace?" she said. "What the hell?"

I realized how creepy I must have looked, standing there in the shadowy alley. I took one step forward, then halted as a man came out of the doorway behind her. He was tall and thin with bug-out eyes and a dopey smile, like he couldn't believe his good fortune.

"Who're you?" he asked me.

Ignoring him, I took a deep breath. "I wanted to apologize for the way I acted earlier," I said. "It was stupid."

"Hey," Mandarin said. "No big deal."

"I'm really embarrassed."

"It's no big deal. Truly."

When I glanced up, she was smiling, but there was nothing mocking about it. "I really am sorry."

"All forgiven. Now cut it out, will you?"

The knots in my stomach finally began to unwind. "Whose dog is that?" I asked, pointing at the chow with the toe of my shoe.

Mandarin looked at him fondly. "He's kind of everybody's, but I guess he really belongs to my dad. Name's Remington, like the gun, but we call him Remy."

"Remy Ramey," I said.

"Sleeps most of the time. He's, like, sixteen. Even older than you."

"So . . ." I glanced at the door to the bar, still half open.

Mandarin laughed. "Don't even think about it. Hell, I'm too young to be here myself legally, but because of my dad, I get away with it. Anyways, I can get off early if I want."

"Right now?"

"Sure, right now. How 'bout we go for a walk?"

The dopey-faced man cleared his throat. We both looked at him. "Just you wait a minute," he began. "You said that—"

"Never mind what I said." Mandarin shouldered him aside. "Half the time what I say is full of shit."

His eyes grew even bulgier, like a disconcerted pug's— the complete opposite of scary, which I had assumed all

Mandarin's men were. Mandarin withdrew a wad of folded bills from her apron, unwound it from her hips, and tossed it into the weeds beside the back door. She shoved the bills in her pocket. Then she nodded at me, and we took off down the alley together.

❀ ❀ ❀

The irrigation canal ran along the southern edge of town, with narrow ditches branching in every direction. They gurgled beside the roads and along the edges of pastures, free water for people's sheep and horses. When I was eight, I'd leaned over a ditch to pat a neighbor's horse and had tumbled in. Because no one had seen me fall, I'd been forced to crawl out and slog home alone, leaving a snail trail of muddy footprints behind me.

Ever since, I'd avoided the canal and its treacherous ditches. But that night was different. The twitter of night birds tickled the air, and the only light came from the moon. Mandarin and I sat on a rocky bank, our feet in the water.

"And everybody starts looking around, all of us thinking the same thing: 'What's that god-awful stink?'" Mandarin brought her cigarette to her lips and took a quick pull before continuing her story.

"Then we notice the farmer. One of the hills variety. The type of guy who looks all blinky and weird when you see him in the grocery store, like the lights are too bright for him."

I nodded in recognition.

"He's wearing these big rubber farm boots, and they're completely *caked* with shit—so much his legs look like big hairy monster paws. Like, every possible kind of livestock manure. Cattle, sheep, chickens. Probably even elephant and brontosaurus. He sees everybody staring his way, and for a second it seems like he might take off. But instead, he comes over to me and he mumbles, 'Can I get a whiskey and water?'"

I giggled. "No explanation?"

"No! No apology or nothing." Mandarin kicked up one submerged ankle, sending water flickering across the surface. "And then I— Hey, look!"

At first I thought she was pointing at the rusted corpse of a car partially hidden in the reeds across the canal. Then I saw the bird with feathers like autumn leaves rummaging through the undergrowth.

"That's a pheasant," Mandarin told me.

"I know," I said.

Too late I wondered if I should have pretended not to know—the way I did in class so no one would think I was trying to show off.

"Once, I had to do an art project out of their feathers," I said quickly, "when I was a little kid. I hope they didn't have to kill one, you know, for the project. But I made a tiger, from all the striped feathers pasted on construction paper. Fangs from candy corn. My mother was angry when I brought it home. She thought I should have made a bunny, something cute."

I brought my fingers to my lips. The story had burst out on its own, as if it had been churning in my throat all this time. Maybe that was what happened when you had nobody to talk to. Thoughts and memories kept piling up, and when you finally had an outlet, they all came flooding out, like the river when they opened the sluice gates into the canal. *Whoosh.*

"It figures," Mandarin said. "Parents got nothing better to do in this town than interfere. Sometimes it's enough to make me glad my own mom's dead."

She pulled the rubber band from her hair and shot it into the water, splintering her reflection into a thousand tiny ripples. The pheasant screeched and bustled away.

"Scram, before the hunters get you," she said. "I love those stupid birds. They're one of the only good things about living in Washokey."

I mustered up my courage and asked, "Why do you hate it here so much?"

"Well, for one thing, the way the stupid macho assholes in this town take anything that's beautiful and free and then shoot it."

I felt a little stunned. Hunting was Washokey's favorite pastime, and belittling it was one of Washokey's greatest taboos. Almost everybody hunted. I'd even seen a photo of Momma in an orange hunting vest when she was about my age. Her father had been a hunter. And his father. Back forever. I hadn't thought about the act of hunting much. But I knew I hated the mounted animal heads decorating Washokey businesses.

"The trophies are the worst," I said.

"Right!" Mandarin nodded emphatically, as if our crossroads of opinions were a celestial coincidence. "Like a severed head's a thing to brag about. It's sick. Displayed right above the food in the grocery store, and over the tables at the Buffalo Grill—like they're supposed to make us hungry. And what's worst of all is when they play mad scientist and glue parts from different animals together. Like jackalopes. As if nature ain't creative enough herself."

"So why else?" I asked.

"Why else what?"

"Why else do you hate Washokey?"

Mandarin stood. For a moment, I thought that I'd asked the wrong question, that our night was over.

"If you don't know, one day I'll show you." She reached down to unroll the cuffs of her jeans. Her long hair shrouded her face. "When I think of a way. But I don't want to talk about it right now." She righted herself and tossed her hair back, and I saw she was grinning. "I feel too good tonight. Too high. What a fucking gorgeous night!"

She dropped her cigarette onto a boulder and stamped it out with her bare foot. I wanted to ask her how she did it, why it didn't hurt. "Mandarin—" I began, then stopped as she unfastened her jeans.

"I'm going in," she announced.

"In the canal? But . . . the water, it's polluted. It's runoff from all the farms. And it's got to be cold. . . ."

I scooted away from her as she stepped out of her jeans and pulled off her shirt. Her white bra was patterned with tiny daisies, her underwear lacy black.

"But what if . . ." I tried to object.

"If I drown? I guess you'll have to save me."

With that, she stepped off the bank into the canal. I crawled closer to the edge to watch as she reappeared, pushing her wet hair out of her face.

"Get in!" she shouted.

She plunged below the surface a second time. Then she burst out, flipping back her hair with a razor of water. Her skin gleamed like wet brass. I could see her nipples through the fabric of her bra before she sank back in.

"Is it freezing? Did it get in your mouth?"

"Who cares? It's only water. What's the good of being alive if you don't *do* anything?" She flicked a spout of water at me. "Other than surround yourself with lifeless things?"

Lifeless things? I wondered, uncomprehending. Like taxidermy?

Then I remembered our conversation in her room, when I'd told her I liked to wander the badlands, collect rocks and fossils. All lifeless things. Suddenly it seemed like such an empty, pathetic hobby. At the very least, I could spend my time collecting something alive.

Like . . . what? Beetles?

I knew that wasn't what Mandarin meant. She was talking about experiences, not objects. I should be collecting life experiences.

Which I had no experience in.

I hesitated only a moment more. Then I began to undress, awkwardly, one foot getting stuck in my jeans when I tried to tug them off. In my pajama shorts and top, I knelt at the very rim of the bank. The water looked like liquid asphalt, hot and bottomless. I touched the surface with my hands as Mandarin sank back underwater.

She burst out again—but this time, she grabbed my arm.

With a great splash of black water, I tumbled in. Mouth open, eyes open, stinging shock and cold. At last my floundering feet found the bottom. It felt like cake batter, clotted with river gunk and rotten plants and who knew what else. I wiped the scum from my eyes and opened them. Mandarin swirled around me, laughing.

"You didn't have to do that," I complained, the closest I could get to being angry. "I was coming in."

"It woulda taken hours! You got a tree branch up your ass, or what? Relax. Enjoy. It's a fucking gorgeous night!"

Without another word, she closed her eyes and fell into a back float.

I watched the drops of water roll off her cheeks. Then I imitated her, falling back until the surface caught me. The sky was blue-black, cloudless, like a baker's countertop smeared with sugary stars. I tried to relax, but every second I was aware of Mandarin's presence, as if the water had a slope to it, tilting me in her direction. I held my arms at my sides to prevent the awkwardness of our limbs knocking together.

"Want to hear something wild?"

Her voice startled me. I had to calm my body again and recapture my float.

"This water," she said slowly. "Sure it's dirty and cold and all that. But if you think about it, it's really a little piece of ocean."

I held my tongue, because I didn't want to be a know-it-all. But wasn't that obvious? We learned about evaporation and precipitation in elementary school. Didn't all water come from the ocean at some point?

"Let me explain. This canal goes into the Bighorn River, right?"

"Right."

"And then the Bighorn becomes the Green River. And somewhere the Green River becomes the Colorado River. And eventually, the Colorado River goes into the Pacific Ocean."

An unseen animal crashed away in the undergrowth. Maybe another pheasant. Or a jackalope. I held back a giggle.

"The Pacific Ocean," Mandarin repeated. "That's where I'm going when I leave town."

But I don't want you to leave. "When you turn eighteen?"

"Sooner. My birthday's not till fall. And I won't be any freer when I'm eighteen than I am now. I ain't getting into any colleges, that's for sure."

She was quiet after that. I thought about what she'd said. Though Momma hadn't gone to college herself, I'd grown up knowing that it was a certain part of my future.

What would I do if college wasn't an option?

I tipped my head toward Mandarin, studying her. Her hair drifted like seaweed, blacker than the water around it. She reminded me of Ophelia, floating down the river with the sky reflected in her eyes.

"You see," she said, "I've got a plan."

"You do?"

"I just need to get some pictures taken. There's lots of agents out there, in California—that's where I want to be, by the beach and everything—and so I was thinking I could get into modeling. The pay is real good."

Modeling. Mandarin a model. How come I'd never thought of it before? No future was worthy of Mandarin but one strobe-lit with camera flashes.

I realized I had grabbed her arm. Before she'd even righted herself, I yanked my hand away and hid it behind my back.

"You have to," I said. "It's perfect, Mandarin. It's the best idea I've ever heard."

"Do you really think so?" She sounded genuinely hopeful, like my opinion was of the utmost importance, maybe even decisive. "You think I could make it out there?"

I could picture it. On the covers of magazines, Mandarin's torso carving the space behind article titles. Her profile in ads for dangerous products—silver sports cars, cigarettes, liquor served in drawing rooms bloated with wine-colored tapestries. Her cheekbones slashed with bronze. Her bed hair perfected.

California was the farthest possible place from our Washokey life. But didn't small-town-girl success stories make the best headlines? What sweet revenge against everyone who called Mandarin worthless, a piece of trash. Not just a slap in the face, but a punch. A dropkick, an elbow to the gut. A stiletto between the legs.

Of course, I knew that the odds of making it big were slim. And I knew that Mandarin in California meant no Mandarin in Washokey. But I wanted so badly to please her.

"You'll be great!" I exclaimed. "They'll love you. You'll be on the cover of everything."

"Well, that's it, then! That's my plan."

Mandarin laughed and spun like a water sprite, hands slicing the water, splashing me in dark sheets. I giggled and splashed her back, savoring her joy like a glass of icy water after a long walk in the badlands.

❀ ❀ ❀

As I crept through the living room, I glanced at the clock above the mantel. It was twenty minutes after four—the latest I'd ever been awake. But I was the only one.

Nobody had noticed I'd been gone.

The day before, it might have bothered me. But now I didn't care. It didn't matter anymore what Momma thought, whether Momma cared. Everything seemed to make sense as I lay under my single sheet, screaming silently and pounding my feet on the mattress, my wet hair fanned out over my pillow, the gray light in my window growing brighter with the arrival of day.

Maybe I wasn't anything like Mandarin right now.

But I could be.

I forced myself to forget the things that didn't quite fit. Like the map of the Bighorn River I remembered from my Wyoming geography book. As far as I knew, it never led to the ocean. It went as far as the Rocky Mountains. And then it stopped.

8

that girl my mother had been

Alexis & Co. crammed themselves on the cafeteria bench across from me, watching me extract my sandwich from its petals of pink tissue paper. Ziploc bags were too pedestrian for Momma. Sometimes she used the funny pages from the *Washokey Gazette*, or holiday wrapping paper, even in the spring. I took a bite, chewed, and swallowed, as if there weren't a panel of judges scrutinizing my every bite.

"That sandwich looks real good," Paige Shelmerdine said.

I glanced at it. Tuna salad with diced green apples, slathered on a fat french roll. One of Momma's better creations.

I wasn't surprised Paige had broken the silence. She was the girl whose voice rose above any collective din. Even when no one else was speaking, she felt the need to shout.

Physically, Paige reminded me of a lima bean. She had wispy red hair and skin so pale it looked greenish, and she stood the way Taffeta did: swaybacked, with her stomach sticking out. Paige's older brothers were responsible for some of the most momentous keg parties in Washokey history. Her older sister, Brandi, was even louder than Paige, though she mainly used her voice to flirt.

"Grace's ma's a real good cook," Alexis said. Only because she loved to eat so much. When we were in elementary school, she insisted on coming to my house most of the time, because our cupboards were stocked with better snacks. "If you think her sandwich looks good, wait till you see one of her ma's big ol' fancy dinners."

"I'll bet," said Samantha Dent, baring a grin filled with rubber bands. She'd worn braces for the past four years. "Maybe she could give my mother some ideas."

The Dents owned the Buffalo Grill, where Samantha worked as a hostess. She looked like a scrawnier, washed-out version of Alexis and tended to weep over the most trivial things, from ant bites on her ankles to grades with minuses. She was definitely the least offensive member of Alexis & Co., though she went right along with the other two in anything controversial.

I took another bite of my sandwich, delaying the inevitable. Paige's face pinched and pulled, as if something crawly was trapped inside her cheeks. Samantha kept peering up at me from under her thick blond bangs and then looking away when I caught her eye.

"Aw hell, Grace," Alexis said at last, "I can't stand it

anymore. My mom told me her cousin's stepmother saw you at Mandarin Ramey's house last week. That's not true, is it?"

My insides became a clamor of fireworks.

Four days had passed since my afternoon at Mandarin's and our subsequent late-night swim. And in those four days, Mandarin and I hadn't spoken to each other once. Not the day after, when I'd staggered into math exhausted but ecstatic. My searching smile found her seat empty. By now, I'd lost my nerve even to look her way.

The one time I'd seen her outside class, we'd locked eyes. We stared for two, three seconds. Too late to look away. *Maybe she's been waiting for me to come to her first.* The thought tapped against my brain like a windblown pebble. Cautiously, I lifted my hand to waist level, wiggled my fingers. Mandarin nodded back. And that was it.

As if none of it had ever happened.

Now, it seemed like some fantasy I'd had. Like I'd dreamed it all up in bed, intoxicated by wildwinds and mosquito poison. I forced myself to take another bite of my sandwich, to chew and swallow before I answered Alexis's question.

"She needed help with her schoolwork," I said.

All three girls let out gusty sighs. "So that explains it," Paige said.

Samantha nodded. "Makes perfect sense."

"I should have known." Alexis leaned in my direction. "I mean, we're, like, real close, you and me, Grace. Of course you wouldn't be going over there of your own accord. It's not like the two of you could be friends."

"But we *are*."

I continued to eat, pretending to be unaware of the lengthy silence that followed.

It was a big gamble, making a statement like that. In Washokey, lies were like secrets—they didn't last, unless the town collectively overlooked them. Like Mandarin's serving cocktails while being underage.

"Well," Alexis said, "why aren't you eating lunch with her?"

"Yeah, Grace," Paige said tauntingly. "Why aren't you?"

I hadn't thought they'd call my bluff so soon. I tried to think of an excuse: *Mandarin has a cold, so she told me to stay away.* Or *I'd rather sit with you guys!* How lame.

"Thought so." Alexis squeezed open a bag of chips with a pop.

I tried to scowl. "I don't have to explain myself to you."

"What does that even *mean*?" Paige said.

Then Samantha gasped. "There she is!"

My eyes followed the direction of her index finger. Mandarin had just emerged from the kitchen, carrying an orange and two bananas. There was something provocative about the way she held them, with her wrists bent back.

Alexis smirked at me. "Why don't you go to her?"

"Fine," I said. "I will."

I tucked my half-eaten sandwich into my lunch bag and stood up, trying my best to look confident. But the knots in my stomach were back full strength: Palomar knots and Trilene knots and Triple Alpine Butterfly loops, like in the Eagle Scout guidebook I'd found at the junk shop. No one ever approached Mandarin. Not even the bolder kids.

And I was not, by anyone's yardstick, one of the bolder kids.

Besides, if Mandarin had wanted to eat lunch together, she would have sought me out.

I took two steps, then hesitated.

"See? She's not friends with her," I heard Paige whisper.

"What did I tell you?" Alexis whispered back.

I pretended I didn't hear them. One hand went to my pocket, my fingers folding around a tourmaline stone. I waited just long enough for Mandarin to disappear through the doors. Then I headed across the cafeteria.

As soon as I stepped into the hallway, I ran all the way to the girls' bathroom.

I finished my sandwich inside the end stall. For the remaining twenty minutes of lunch, I stared at the scribble of red words, reading them over and over: *School is horseshit. School is horseshit.* Whether Mandarin had memorized it or written it there herself, I had no doubt she believed it. And right now I believed it too.

※   ※   ※

When I went downstairs at dinnertime, Momma was sitting with her chin in her hands at the kitchen table, which was covered with pageant paraphernalia instead of food. Taffeta sat in the corner with her legs splayed out, coloring her thumbnail with a purple crayon.

I hovered in the doorway, wondering whether Momma was adrift in pageant-related contemplation or she had come down with one of her gloomy moods.

The moods were rare, but memorable. I could always tell when they were coming on. She'd stand at the sink and stare out the window, or sit silently in the wingback chair in the family room, the only significant item she had left of her mother's, for hours and hours. I never knew what triggered Momma's melancholy. Thoughts of her parents? Nostalgia for the days before Jackson Hole? The lonesomeness of bringing up two daughters on her own? Not that she'd go for a Washokey man, even if she desired a husband.

"You can't fall for someone when you know all their stories," she often said.

Many times when she came out of her moods, she would start to ramble, recounting old stories that left both of us spooked. She spoke of human pelvises dug up in the empty hills. Children who had disappeared. The ghastly way that drifter had killed those hippies in the 1968 "massacre"—with an old lasso, Momma said. All sorts of afflictions and insanities she blamed on the yearly wildwinds, blowing the ozone out of the air and driving everybody mad.

Including her.

"Momma?" I asked warily. "Do you need help fixing dinner?"

It seemed to take a moment for her eyes to focus. "Dinner. I forgot about dinner."

"It doesn't matter."

"I've just been so preoccupied with the pageant coming up. . . . How about we go to the Buffalo Grill? We haven't been there in a while." With each word, her faux British accent increased. "Let's all get changed, shall we? Taffeta . . ."

Taffeta sat on her hands.

"Wash off that crayon first."

Going out to dinner meant piling into Momma's pink hatchback and journeying four blocks to the Buffalo Grill. With Momma, walking was never an option. It also meant seeing Samantha Dent. Better Samantha than Alexis or Paige, though.

Besides more classic carrion, like beef and chicken, the Buffalo Grill really did grill buffalo. It also grilled emu, elk, and jackrabbit. For a while it had grilled rattlesnake, until the local serpentine population dwindled so much there weren't any snakes left to catch.

Prairie oysters, however—more commonly known as "bull balls"—were the kitchen's specialty. Even before I fully understood how boys and girls were different, the appetizer had disgusted me. Little brown spheres, deep-fried to a crisp. Served with three kinds of dipping sauce. And parsley.

The trophies were worse. The heads were displayed all across the restaurant: stuffed pronghorns with glass marbles instead of eyes, bobcats frozen in death yowls, a massive male elk with a film of dust on his antlers. Everyone stayed away from the table underneath the elk, so as to avoid the fleas that allegedly fell from his beard. There was even a black bear, not quite a cub, but small enough that his murder had probably erred on just the wrong side of legal. A stuffed ground squirrel rode on its forehead—another instance of a Wyoming sense of humor.

Most people frequented the Buffalo Grill *because* of the questionable appetizers and taxidermy. One night I'd even seen Mr. Beck at a back table, eating soup alone.

Samantha led us to a booth by the window. I watched

her warily as she handed us our menus, but she wouldn't meet my eye. Sometimes I got the impression that Samantha disagreed with Alexis & Co.'s antics, though I knew that—like me—she'd never be brave enough to speak out against them.

"Wanna hear about our specials?" she asked. "We've got—"

"Not really," I interrupted.

Samantha looked stricken.

"Grace!" Momma exclaimed. "Sure we do, honey. Go right ahead."

Samantha mumbled about beef stew and deep-fried onion blossoms and then scampered away.

Momma glared at me. "That wasn't like you, Grace."

"I've had a rough day."

The waiter appeared, and I ordered a fruit salad. As soon as he left, Momma turned back to us. "We need to talk hairstyles."

Of course she didn't ask about my day. I should have learned to stop hoping. Not that I would have told her anything—God, no. I crossed my arms and slouched in my seat.

Watching me, Taffeta slouched in her seat too.

"I read an article on extensions a couple mornings back," Momma said. "At first I just passed it off as nonsense talk, since Taffeta's got such lovely locks and we could hardly ask for anything better." She reached out and buried her fingers in Taffeta's hair. Taffeta made a face. "But then I began wondering if the other mothers are doing it, and if so, are we at a disadvantage?"

Momma paused a second, as if waiting for my opinion,
but I knew she wasn't, not really. She only prattled on like
that when she'd already made up her mind.

"Problem is, the only extensions Shirley Colby's got at
the salon are those awful clip-on kind, like Barbie-doll hair.
I'd never spend my hard-earned money on that garbage. But
then I gave a few Park County salons a call, and one of them
said . . ."

We'd just gotten our food when another family came in.
The man wore a black and white checkered shirt that ballooned around him, as if he'd lost weight since he'd bought it.
Or maybe he'd donated all the pounds to his wife, who was
twice his size. She balanced a toddler on one generous hip. I
didn't recognize them, which was pretty unusual around here.

"Those are the Franks," Momma told me. "Tom and
Winnie Frank. Moved back a few weeks ago. Winnie used to
be Winnie Hildebrandt. She was in my year at school. One
of the only ones to leave the state for college. She thought
she was so smart, and look! Now she's back."

We watched them strap their toddler to a high chair.
Right away, it began to bawl.

"What a hassle," Momma remarked. "But pregnancy's
even worse, you know. Especially my first time around. I
think I must have spent the first six months sobbing in the
bathroom with my arm wrapped around the toilet. . . ."

I picked at my fruit salad and tried not to listen.

Momma had told me about her pregnancy so many times
I knew the story backward and forward. At eighteen, she'd
been just a year older than Mandarin was.

Being pregnant was humiliating, she claimed—the

morning sickness, the medical examinations, the ugly pro-
truding belly no amount of padding would obscure. But worst
of all, Momma had told me so many times the phrase seemed
tattooed inside my skull, was the awareness that this *stranger*
was growing inside her.

I had to remember it was me inside, the baby Momma
hadn't wanted in the first place. Taffeta was a different
story. One hundred percent wanted, even if the marriage that
had created her had been a joke. With me, Momma still
claimed she'd never considered abortion or adoption—
though whether God or my grandma was her reason, I never
knew.

I was afraid to ask.

And yet I couldn't help feeling sorry for her, that girl my
mother had been. She'd tried to escape Washokey. Because
of me, she didn't make it.

9

will you go?

On Friday morning, the wildwinds thundered down from the Bighorn Mountains. Dust and grit swirled over the ground in currents, stinging our ankles as Taffeta and I stumbled toward school. The chain-link fence surrounding the school yard quaked and rattled. My sister hid her face in my side at every gust, which made it even more difficult to walk.

All the students crammed into the building instead of hanging out on the lawn before homeroom. From the hallway, I could still hear the wildwinds bellowing, a mournful whistle that stabbed through the edges of the double doors.

By the time the late bell rang, Ms. Ingle still hadn't arrived. Kids speculated that her car had been blown over or a cottonwood had fallen on top of her house. Tag Leeland, a senior, claimed school policy dictated that after fifteen

minutes we were free to go. Alexis and Paige leaned against
the wall, whispering, with their heads tipped together. I
stood a few yards away with one hand in the pocket of my
jacket, running my fingers over a translucent piece of agate.

After a while, Davey Miller approached me. He did it bit
by bit, like a ground squirrel advancing for a morsel of food.
Like if I made too sudden a movement, he'd bolt.

"Hello, Grace."

He stood there with a goofy grin on his face, blinking
hard, until I said hi back. I remembered the time a group of
boys had stolen his purple baseball cap when he'd first moved
to town. A farmer had discovered it masking-taped to the
head of a steer.

"What's up, Davey?"

"Oh, nothing much."

I tapped my foot through a moment of blink-filled
silence.

"Seriously, Davey. What's up?"

"Um," he began. "Well. I was wondering . . ."

Before Davey could reveal what he wondered, a sudden
commotion stole our attention. The double doors at the end
of the hall swung open with a violent crash. A blast of wind
whooshed in, and the unexpected dazzle of light made me
squint.

The voice came before I could see again: "Gracey! Grace!"

Then Mandarin appeared in the glow.

Even as my befuddled brain was still trying to make sense
of it—that in front of God and everybody, Mandarin Ramey
had *called my name*—she was charging up the hall toward
us and skidding to a stop, her elbows knocking aside my

astonished classmates. When she seized me by the shoulders, I felt like she'd reached into my chest and taken hold of my heart.

"Grace, you've got to come with me. It's worth it, I swear."

This time, I didn't think twice.

Turning my back on Davey, slack-jawed Alexis Bunker, my homeroom, the world, I fell in step beside Mandarin. We sprinted back down the hall, the clap of our shoes on the tile resounding off the walls, startling poor tardy Ms. Ingle as she rushed around the corner from the teachers' restroom. We flew through the double doors into the bright world outside.

On the top step, we stopped. The doors slammed behind us. Our hair exploded around our faces in the sudden wind.

I gasped.

The air in front of us stormed white. Not with snow, but with the early harvest from the grove of cottonwood trees. Like dandelion down, the cotton whirled and tumbled in the wildwinds, catching the sunlight.

Sure, the cotton fell every year. But I'd never seen so much at once. This was a blizzard, a snowstorm from another world, littering the lawn with clouds.

Mandarin grinned at me, her cheeks pink, and I could tell: she knew I got it. If we'd turned back right then and gone to class, that shared understanding would have been enough to make me happy forever.

But it wasn't over. "So?" she said.

"So what?"

"So . . . what are we waiting for?"

She winked at me. Then she charged down the steps.

I stood there, clutching my stone, while Mandarin spun with both arms out, like she had in the canal, her hair wild with wind, the cotton lighting on her upturned face before swirling away. A piece landed in her mouth, and she laughed and spit. She scooped up fistfuls of cotton and flung them over her head. Finally, she turned to me.

"You, now," she called. "Come on!"

I tossed my bag aside, dropped my stone onto the steps, and ran to join her.

The cotton flickered around me, dancing off my skin. I stomped on the grass, sending flurries back into the air. I spun with my arms out, my head back.

"Watch out for the trees!" she shouted. "A concussion would ruin our party."

Dizzily, I came to a stop and leaned against a cottonwood with one hand. When I glanced up, I noticed movement in the school windows.

Faces were pressed up against the glass. Dozens of students, opening and closing their mouths like aquarium fish, whispering to each other.

"They're watching us," I said.

Kids in Washokey had never learned to stare with subtlety. Like whenever the rare plane flew over town—usually a tiny charter carrying tourists to luxury ranches near Cody—they would all crane their necks to have a look at it.

I felt mortified. Appalled, thrilled, every kind of emotion. But Mandarin didn't even glance up.

"Do you honestly care what they think? They can all go to hell."

But I *did* care what they thought. I always had. And this

time, I knew exactly what they were thinking: that Mandarin
Ramey (town slut, scandal-plagued celebrity, Washokey's real
beauty queen) and I, Grace Carpenter (just five minutes earlier nobody at all), were *friends*.

In a decisive second, I tipped my face toward the students
in the window and stuck out my tongue.

Mandarin screamed with laughter. Unexpectedly, she
rushed toward me and threw her arms around me. Before I
could react, she pulled away. "Gracey, I have something to
ask you. And you have to say yes. If you don't, I swear to God
I'll die."

"What? What is it?"

She took both my hands in hers and looked carefully into
my eyes. Cotton shimmered in the air between us.

"Will you go with me?"

For a moment, I couldn't say anything. A million miles
away, a hall monitor called to us from the top of the steps.

"What? Do you mean—"

"Yes," she said. "That's exactly what I mean. I want you
to go with me. To California. I know it's crazy. But the more
I think about it, the more I think that together we can be
something better, Gracey, something big. Please, please say
yes. I *need* you."

And just like that, my world burst apart. I was careening
through the universe. Each bit of cotton was a speeding star.
My head was dizzy, my mouth was dry. *Stop*, I wanted to cry
out. *You're moving too fast for me. You've got to slow down. I'm
going to fall—*

"Yes," I said.

"Yes? You'll go with me?"

"Yes!" I laughed helplessly.

"You've got no idea how much this means! Now it doesn't matter that you didn't win that stupid trip. We'll be long gone by then. Right after graduation, we'll go. We'll have an unbelievable time, I promise. What a fucking gorgeous day!"

We spun like children in a school yard game, kicking up billows of glistening cotton, drinking in the crazy-making wildwinds with each gasp. They tore strands of hair from my braid, whipping my face. I found I was blinking back tears— from the winds or what, I didn't know. At that moment, I would have followed her anywhere.

confectionary kingdoms

That Sunday, Momma drove to Sheridan to peruse the shops for last-minute pageant supplies. I was stuck with Taffeta, playing Candy Land.

I didn't usually mind playing games with my sister. But that afternoon, I felt like every minute wasted could have been the best minute of my life if only I were with Mandarin.

All weekend, Friday morning kept coming back to me like a scene from a movie. The feel of the cotton, velvety and weightless and slightly sticky with sap. Mandarin spitting and laughing as a piece went into her mouth. Spinning with our eyes locked, her hands gripping mine. Ms. Ingle's face when I'd stolen back into the classroom, still flecked with white fuzz.

"I'm glad to see the two of you getting along," she'd said

when she kept me after class. "How's the tutoring going? Have you come up with any ideas for Mandarin's service project?"

I tried not to think about the reality of Mandarin's request. All that mattered, for the moment, was that she had asked.

Now I sat on Taffeta's pink shag carpet, navigating confectionary kingdoms like Gum Drop Mountain and the Candy Cane Forest. With my sister, Candy Land took ages. She counted her moves out loud, stubbing her index finger on each square. Every five minutes, she'd call a time-out for a bathroom break or a snack. Sometimes she would space out entirely, murmuring a song to herself in Italian, her eyes fixed on some glittering molecule only she could see.

It was like being hurled backward into my dismal pre-Mandarin past. No wonder I was feeling mutinous.

Once Taffeta finished her turn, I drew a card. "Uh-oh," I said, holding the card so she couldn't see it. "Bad luck for you. On your next turn, you've got to go backwards."

"No way," Taffeta protested. "There's no cards like that."

"Candy Land put out a mass email to all game owners. I guess you haven't heard. Now the cards have different meanings. When people whose ages are double digits get red cards, the next player has to move in reverse. Sorry about that."

"That's not fair!"

"It's the new rules. I can't help it if you didn't get the email."

"You're lying, Grace! There wasn't any email."

"How do you know? You can't even read yet."

"I can too!" Taffeta insisted. "Stop making fun of me, or I'll tell."

"Do you think Momma will care?"

Taffeta's chin puckered, and for a second I thought she was going to cry. But then she whacked the game board with her fist. It flipped into the air, scattering cards and pieces.

I sighed.

"Hey, Taffy, I'm sorry. I didn't mean to ruin the game."

She wouldn't look at me.

"Fine." I stood up. "Be right back."

I returned with one of those giant chewy SweeTarts, salvaged from my rock collection box. Momma used to use them as pacifiers on our road trips.

"Listen," I said, flipping the candy between my fingers like a magician's coin. "I was just trying to spice things up. I didn't mean what I said about Momma." I paused. "Anyway, Momma's pretty clear about what's important to her."

"I'm important," Taffeta said.

"Of course you are."

"I'm more important than you. She likes me better than you."

How did little kids know exactly what hurt the most? When I didn't reply, she crept over to me on all fours and took my face in her hands, swiveling it toward her. Her bottom lip stuck out like a pink piece of gum.

"Grace, I'm sorry. Don't be mad! Momma likes us the same."

I dislodged her hands, trying not to let the hurt show on my face. "No, you were right. I'll admit it."

Determinedly, Taffeta shook her head.

Sometimes I could hardly believe my sister was real. She looked more like a doll than a flesh-and-blood child, with skin that seemed to glow from the inside, tiny dimpled hands, eyes as flawless as the brown glass marbles used for trophy eyes. I had to remind myself there was a person inside, listening, observing.

"Taffeta," I said. "Don't you ever get bored?"

She shrugged. "When there's nothing on TV."

"No, I meant—don't you ever have the urge to do something crazy?"

"Crazy like how?"

"Like stick your tongue out at the pageant judges. Or sing a different song instead of the one you're supposed to. Maybe a dirty one. Or at home, put your pageant dress on, and . . . I don't know, maybe go and sit in the baby pool in our backyard."

My sister wrinkled her nose. "Why would I do *that*?"

I sighed. "No reason. It's just . . . There's so much more to life, you know? Than Momma's pageants. Than Washokey."

My excitement felt effervescent, bubbling up into my throat. After an entire weekend of waiting, I was dying to let someone in on my secret. Taffeta's wide eyes goaded me on.

"If I told you something," I began, "would you promise not to—"

"Can I have the candy?" Taffeta interrupted.

All I'd been about to say gridlocked in my chest. For a second, I could barely breathe.

She tried again. "Can I *please* have some candy, Grace?"

I had no idea what I'd been thinking. I gnawed off a chunk of SweeTart with my molars before tossing it to Taffeta. While she chewed and slurped, I settled back against the bed, disgusted with myself.

❀   ❀   ❀

The next morning, my alarm startled me from a dream of a deserted highway, with giant pink jackalopes hunched on both sides of the road. Every massive hop—*whump, whump*—made my teeth chatter. My jaw ached as I dragged myself out of bed and over to my mirror.

"Oh, crap," I said out loud.

I'd slept in my braid, and now it pouched in a lopsided bundle at the side of my head. In my boy shorts and pajama top, I saw only the skeletal gap between my thighs. Washboard ribs instead of a chest. My hands and feet and eyes looked too big for the rest of me. If someone had told me that the girl in the mirror was twelve years old instead of almost fifteen, I would have believed him.

How could I take the same old body to school and expect everybody to believe I was anything like Mandarin?

I'd thought of the onlookers in the windows countless times, but I'd never pictured their faces. Alexis would have been there, and Paige Shelmerdine, for sure. Davey Miller. The sophomores and the juniors, like Peter Shaw. And the seniors, like Tag Leeland and Ricky Fitch-Dixon. Maybe even people from other homerooms.

I tried to picture how my classmates had seen me before

the day in the cotton. What I came up with were three im-
ages, three incidents—all events Alexis Bunker had never
let me forget.

The Saga of Grace Carpenter

Our fourth-grade English teacher, Mr. Moulton,
had moonlighted as a reporter for the *Washokey
Gazette* and had been notorious for his emphatic ad-
verbs. He was always trying to show off his literary
genius by coming up with journalism-related assignments. One day, he asked us to pair off and write
reports about our partners. There'd been an odd
number of students, and I'd ended up the leftover.
Mr. Moulton suggested I write a report about myself. I still remembered how it began.

*Grace Carpenter was born at eleven p.m. on what
turned out to be a cold and blustery night. The nurses
said she was the most complicated baby they had ever
delivered. Her mother, Adrina Carpenter, said she
howled bloody murder, like a puppy with porcupine
quills stuck in its rear.*

I hadn't realized that Mr. Moulton meant for us to read
them in front of the class. He graciously allowed me to claim
my seat early when a bout of fake coughing overtook me.

Sixth-Grade Graduation

June was sweepstakes month for Femme Fatale Cosmetics, Inc., when all purchases allowed
the buyer to compete for a year's supply of Femme

Fatale products. Though it brought in good money, sweepstakes had made Momma so busy she forgot to finish my graduation dress. The morning of the ceremony, I'd found it draped over the sewing machine. I didn't have any other dresses that fit; at twelve, I was already a jeans type of girl.

"Momma!" I'd wailed. "Graduation's at ten!"

She had sewed as if her life depended on it, but the result was still a catastrophe: lopsided in the front, so short in the back it barely covered my underwear. My limbs poked out like winter branches. Crossing the cafeteria to get my diploma in front of all the other students and parents, I had shriveled with shame.

Little Miss Washokey, Wyo.
My onstage strip show at age six.
Enough said.

In front of the mirror, I tugged my jeans low on my hips, as I had done in private so many times. Instead of a T-shirt, I put on one of the camisoles I used as pajamas, tight and purple with skinny straps. I brushed my hair loose over my shoulders. I had enough sense not to attempt anything as complicated as eyeliner or mascara, but I liked the sparkle when I touched a dab of Femme Fatale Misty Frost lip gloss to my eyelids.

Deliberately avoiding eye contact with myself, I practiced my saunter in the remaining minutes before I swooped up Taffeta and left for school.

"Why are you dressed like that!" she demanded.

"Dressed like what?"

"In your pajamas."

"It's not pajamas. It's just a shirt. Isn't a person allowed a change once in a while?"

Taffeta mulled it over, her shoes scuffling madly in her effort to keep up with me. "I guess so," she said. "Your hair looks pretty. But not your belly stuck out like that. Momma would say that was obscene."

"Bellies aren't obscene."

"Then what is?" she wondered.

"It depends on who you're asking."

❀   ❀   ❀

Momma claimed that first impressions were the most critical part of every pageant: "Act like that first step you take onstage is the most important step of your life."

So after Taffeta scampered away, I didn't pause at the edge of the lawn, mustering up my nerve to cross it. Instead, I tucked my hands into the pockets of my jeans and sauntered forward, my chin tipped up, my line of sight just above the featureless smear of faces on either side of me.

I faltered just once: when I saw the agate stone I'd dropped on the steps Friday morning. It glittered like Cinderella's slipper, but nobody had taken it.

To everybody else, it was just a rock.

I scooped it up and dumped it into my tote before pushing through the double doors.

In homeroom, I tried to sit like Mandarin: leaning back in my seat with my legs stretched out in front of me. But then my shirt rode up a few inches. I felt the air hit my bare stomach.

Am I overdoing it?

That moment of doubt was all it took. As if someone had flipped a volume switch, I became acutely aware of the gaping stares, the not-so-hushed whispers, the laughter. Did they notice how nervous I was? I stole a quick glance at Davey Miller. He was engrossed in his English text, blinking harder than usual. I clasped my trembling hands under the table, crossed my ankles. The top of my jeans bit into the flesh of my hips. I wanted to tug them up, to put on the sweatshirt balled in my tote bag. I felt eyes creeping over my skin like spider legs.

How does Mandarin do this every single day?

Mercifully, the loudspeaker beeped. As the other students settled down, I felt charged with a sudden surge of affection toward Mr. Beck.

"May I have your attention, please. May I have your attention, please."

Several people groaned. Business as usual.

"Good morning, everyone, on this magnificent Monday, April sixteenth, with the temperature in the low seventies. This is your principal, Mr. Beck. First news of the day: we've come up with a theme for the big spring dance."

The whispers rose to a crescendo, then quieted completely. For once, everyone was interested in what Mr. Beck had to say.

At our high school, dances were *huge*. Mainly because

Washokey evenings were particularly bland. Kids attended keggers out in the sticks, shot pool at the Old Washokey Sip Spot (where minors were allowed until ten), or lounged around the A&W. That was just about it. Dances, however, were the epitome of the High School Experience. I'd always wanted to attend one. Alexis & Co. had gone to homecoming, but I had pretended to be sick that week to avoid the awkwardness of inviting myself along. I might have sat with them at lunch, but we hadn't hung out beyond the cafeteria since sixth or seventh grade.

"The theme's going to be . . ." Mr. Beck paused for dramatic effect. "Cowboy!"

The class immediately toppled into chaos, shouts, laughter, the screech of desks. And though the school's use of "Cowboy" as an allegedly original theme insulted my intelligence, I felt swept up in the excitement.

"Hey, Alexis," I called.

Alexis turned to Paige, ignoring me. "Hey, isn't Brandi on the dance committee?"

Paige nodded. "If we want, you and me and Samantha can come in and help decorate. It'll be so exciting!"

Alexis glanced at me before scooting her desk farther away.

It hurt. It really did, in the seconds before I remembered myself. Hurriedly, I readopted my insolent expression, my casual pose. Those girls didn't matter. I was nothing like them.

❄ ❄ ❄

When the bell rang, Ms. Ingle called to me as I hurried from the classroom. I pretended not to hear her. I wanted to get to math early, because I didn't want to run into Mandarin unprepared.

It didn't matter. Because she was standing right outside.

She wore her lavender sweater, the one from the day she'd confronted me at the soda machine. It occurred to me that I was wearing purple too, that we matched, although she wasn't showing nearly as much skin as me. Her thumbs were tucked into the back pockets of her jeans, her hair slung over one shoulder.

I took a deep breath and walked over to her.

"Morning," she said. She didn't mention my skimpy clothing, my loose, unbraided hair. "I missed you this weekend."

I beamed like crazy, even though it didn't make any sense. Mandarin had my phone number. We all had everybody's; the Washokey directory was more of a pamphlet than a book.

"Hey, what's her deal?" she asked suddenly.

I followed the tilt of her chin to Ms. Ingle, who was waving at us from the doorway. I looked away quickly. "Wants to talk about service project stuff, I guess."

Mandarin waved back at her, pretending to mistake her gesture for a hello. "Geez, lady," she muttered. "Drop it already. We're on it, y'know?"

She turned to me. "Ms. Ingle can be such a bitch. Don't you think?"

I hesitated. Ms. Ingle had never been anything but nice to me. She was nice to everybody, in that wishy-washy marshmallowy pushover way. Never in a million years would I ever consider her a bitch. But I wasn't about to contradict Mandarin. Not this early in the game. So I nodded. "Yeah, Ms. Ingle's a bitch."

To my surprise, Mandarin smiled condescendingly. "No she ain't. Not really. Although she is always up in everybody's business. But it's her job, I guess."

"Oh," I said. "Right."

"Ready to go?" She reached out and took my arm. Any bewilderment I felt sailed away as she led me down the hall toward math, through an ocean of staring students, all of them probably wondering where in the world I'd suddenly come from.

11

all the way out to the sea

For the fourth time that week, Mandarin and I bought plate-fuls of fruit at lunch and sat side by side on a cement planter overflowing with lilacs. I mimicked her as she dug her finger-nails into an orange, twisted the stem off a banana, bit the ripe parts out of a peach.

"It's getting warmer out," she remarked.

I nodded. "I guess they'll open the pool soon."

"Yeah, not really my thing." She flung her banana peel into the lilac planter. "I love the heat, though. Can't wait for summer."

I took a bite of my unripe peach, because I wasn't sure what to say next. Were we *really* discussing the weather?

Problem was, Mandarin and I didn't have much to talk

about. We'd spent four lunch periods together now, the majority of the time in silence.

I knew we should discuss the service project, not to mention California. But I avoided both topics. The first because I didn't want to piss off Mandarin. The second because it made me nervous—and for some reason, she didn't bring it up either. Which was just fine. Even if our conversations weren't particularly inspired, our friendship was enough.

And now everybody knew about it. At least, the kids who cared. I savored their reactions when we passed them in the halls. Sideways glances, sudden silences. Jealousy that crackled toward us like blue electric fire.

I loved it. I *loved* their jealousy.

Especially Alexis Bunker's. The day before, we'd been stuck as partners in PE. She was supposed to hold my feet while I did sit-ups. Instead, she rested two dainty fingers on each of my sneakers, as if I had scabies or leprosy or some other ruthlessly contagious disease.

"Alexis," I said when her fingers slipped off altogether.

"What?" she retorted.

Instead of snapping back, I felt sorry for her. My friendship with Alexis had been so lackluster; we'd spent it watching cartoons in her basement and painting Femme Fatale makeup on her decapitated doll heads. I didn't doubt she and the other two-thirds of Alexis & Co. still did the same things. Now the most exciting thing in Alexis's life was the Miss Teen Bighorn Pageant she kept squealing about in homeroom, just loudly enough for everyone to hear. All the other Washokey girls had given up pageants long before.

Meanwhile, my days were filled with excitement.

Or rather, they would be. Soon.

Because that entire week, my friendship with Mandarin had been confined inside the school grounds. Which wasn't much of a friendship at all.

I swallowed my crunchy bite of peach, mustering up all my nerve before I turned toward her. "So," I said. "Are you busy after school today?"

She paused. And paused some more.

My question hung in the air so long it began to wilt at the edges. I wanted to fling myself into the lilac planter, pull a banana peel over my head, and hide.

"It's okay if you're busy," I said quickly. "I understand. I've got plenty to do anyway. . . ."

"How's seven-thirty?"

"Oh—seven-thirty's fine." I stuffed another bite of peach into my mouth to prevent a wildwind-sized sigh of relief. It was like I'd endured some sort of covert friendship evaluation and, at long last, was cleared for advancement.

❀ ❀ ❀

The A&W Root Beer Stand was a relic from the 1950s. Momma and Taffeta and I sometimes went through the drive-through for ice cream, but we never parked or sat at the tables. It was a rowdy place, where decades of students staked out benches as soon as the final school bell rang. I thought of it as haunted by the teenage versions of our parents and grandparents. Just not the teenage version of myself—until that night.

By the time I arrived, the sun had set. Crickets hummed

in the vacant lot behind the brown building. Two of the six orange patio tables were occupied by kids from school, so I chose the table farthest away from them, arranging myself with my back against one of the cement pillars holding up the corrugated tin roof.

From time to time, I leaned forward to scan the dark street so everybody would know I was expecting someone.

I'd had to delay my meeting with Mandarin until eight to help Momma triple-check Taffeta's pageant gear. Clothes tape and tulle—*check*. Glitter spray and body polish—*check*. When I left the house, Taffeta was sitting on the stairs, caged by the vertical bars of the banister, trying desperately not to slurp her polished fingernails.

I had jogged all the way to the A&W. Forty minutes later, I was still sitting alone.

By then, I'd memorized the place, from the ink-blot blobs of chewing gum splattered all over the ground to the little gray spider doing push-ups on the tabletop, to the insightful philosophies of the kids sitting around me.

Flannel boy: *They're thinking of outlawing smoking in the restaurants.*

Girl with glasses: *No way. That's like outlawing drinking in bars!*

Boy returning from piss in vacant lot: *Hey, whose hands was on my burger?*

Football boy: *It was Ricky. You should cut his nuts off.*

Ricky Fitch-Dixon, from homeroom: *Innocent till proven guilty.*

Football boy: *It's proved, all right. I saw you do it.*

I also watched Sarah Cooper, the counter girl, as she

stared off into space. Momma claimed that the A&W wait-
resses used to deliver orders in roller skates until one girl
slipped on a puddle of milk shake melt and broke her tail-
bone. She had to wear a plaster cast over her butt like a dia-
per. After that, the owners adopted a new policy: Go up to the
window and get it yourself. Business never slowed, since the
A&W was the only fast-food place in Washokey—other
than the Sundrop Quik Stop, where the potato salad had a
purplish tinge.

I picked up a french fry, then set it back down. With the
money I'd begged from Momma, I'd ordered cheeseburgers,
fries, and strawberry milk shakes for Mandarin and me. By
now, everything was lukewarm. I felt like a new girlfriend
stood up on a date.

Maybe our friendship hadn't advanced after all.

Just as I was prepared to slink away, Mandarin plunked
herself down on the other side of the table with a world-
weary sigh. Instead of greeting me, she withdrew a cigarette,
lit it, and inhaled. I noticed a hickey the color of a squashed
raspberry on her neck before she flipped her hair over it.

"What?" she demanded.

I must have been glaring. I didn't know I had it in me—
the audacity to glare at Mandarin Ramey. "I don't know. It's
just . . . I was waiting a long time."

"Come on, Gracey. I was busy."

"I just thought we agreed on seven-thirty, is all."

"Don't give me the third degree, all right?" A puff of
smoke escaped from Mandarin's lips. I had the urge to pluck
at it. "I get enough of it at school. The last thing I need is to
get it from my best friend, too."

What!

I paused my brain, rewound. She had said it. I was sure. She'd called me her best friend.

I just couldn't believe it—that I could be the best at something, like friendship. To someone like Mandarin. And after such a short time.

"Well," I said, hiding my smile, "our food's all cold. I guess we can order more, if you like."

"No big deal. I don't eat burgers anyways, but thanks."

I should have known. I'd only ever seen her eat fruit. "Oh. Well, I got us both milk shakes. Strawberry."

"Perfect." She stubbed out her half-smoked cigarette on the tabletop. Then she took her milk shake and began to drink and drink, ravenous for that dairy protein missing from her diet. When she came up for air, the shake was half gone.

"So," she began. "Did you hear about the dance?"

I nodded vigorously.

I'd already imagined the entrance we would make. Just like in one of those teen movies. Everyone would be shimmying to the beat in their cowboy boots and hats, and then all of a sudden the music would stop—*screech*—because Mandarin and I had stepped through the door. In all my daydreams, I had long black hair, like hers. We would cross the gym, and everyone would part to let us through, their faces slack with admiration, as we made our way to the center of the dance floor. And then . . .

"My God," Mandarin said. "I wouldn't be seen at that thing if the devil jabbed his pitchfork in my back. What a nightmare."

I stopped grinning.

"Can you believe that idiotic theme?" She pilfered one of my french fries and held it between two fingers as if she were about to smoke it. "Cowboy. As if we aren't surrounded by cowboys every waking minute. And ranchers. And miners, all cruddy with bentonite dust. Dirty, worthless men."

It troubled me, the way she said it. I remembered meeting plenty of friendly, helpful cowboys and ranchers and miners during my pageant road trips with Momma. They gave us directions, pointed us to diners and motels. They patted me on the head and fished for mints in their dusty jeans pockets.

And anyway, Mandarin sure didn't act like she hated them.

Or so I'd heard, anyway. I was dying to know how she really spent her evenings and weekends. Was my tally correct? What exactly did she do once the door closed? How could I truly be like Mandarin if she never told me the details?

"Don't you go out with some of them?" I asked.

Mandarin took a long swallow of her milk shake. I suspected I'd asked the wrong question. I tried to clarify what I'd said, to make it sound innocuous, since I didn't want her to think I was accusing her of sleeping around. But all I could think of was "Like, your boyfriends?" which probably made it worse.

"I know what you're saying," she said.

"No," I interjected. "No, I'm not. Not saying what you think I'm saying, I mean."

"Don't lie. I can't stand liars."

"But I didn't—"

Deliberately, she set down her shake. "Listen, Grace.

Don't you go asking about things you don't understand. What I do in my own time is my business, and it ain't for anyone else to judge. Including you. All right?"

"Fine," I said in a small voice. "Sorry."

"I sound like a hypocrite. That's what you think, right? Hating on men, and then sleeping with them. Well, maybe I know a few more men than you do. So don't that give me a better perspective?" She picked up a clear plastic water cup and dumped the water on the ground. "Trust me. You sure as shit don't have to *like* somebody to take 'em to bed."

She overturned the cup on top of the little gray spider. Instead of squishing it, she slid the cup across the table and shifted the spider to her hand.

"Besides," she said as she released the spider in a patch of weeds, "I don't just hate men. I don't discriminate. I hate all people equally."

"Errybody freeze!" hollered a man. "I got a gun!"

Nobody froze. Because everybody recognized the wheezy, boozy voice of Earl Barnaby, the most notorious drunk in town.

Earl's everyday apparel included two dirty plaid shirts in contrasting colors, one unbuttoned over the other. His face was usually scorched pink, from the midday hours he spent passed out in parking lots. Momma said he'd been a year behind her at school, but he looked old enough to be her father.

He slapped his hand on the counter in front of Sarah Cooper. "Now, nice an' easy, empty that there register, or I'll blow this pop stand into the ground. I gotta catch a plane to the izzlands t'night."

Sarah rolled her eyes. "Aw, come on, Earl. Can't you just

leave us alone for one evening? I've been here almost since noon. I'm exhausted."

"But I gotta burgle. I'm a burglar, it's in my blood." He aimed his finger at her menacingly.

"The only thing in your blood is too much whiskey. Now fuck off, Earl, all right?"

The huddle of teenagers began to laugh. They weren't paying any attention to Earl, but he seemed to think their laughter was directed toward him. His shoulders sagged.

"Jess a little loan, darlin'," he pleaded. "My plane's taking off! I gotta get to the izzlands t'night, but I got nothing to get there with. Ain't there nothin' you can do?"

"I would, but it's not my money to give you," Sarah said.

When Mandarin turned back toward me, I saw that her whole face had changed. Like she was holding back tears. I'd never seen her look like that before.

"Are you all right?" I asked.

"At least Earl over there's dreaming of better places. But I swear, sometimes it seems like he and us are the only ones. It's like no one else is even aware that there's a whole world outside Washokey." She closed her eyes. "God, we need to get out of here!"

With her eyes still closed, she spoke again. "Did you know I've never even seen the ocean?"

I shook my head, then realized she couldn't see me. "No, I didn't know that."

"Have you?"

"Once," I said. "I had an aunt in Washington, and we flew there to see her before she died. I was seven or eight."

My memory of the ocean came crashing back. A gray sea.

Cliffs, tall trees. A plane journey to Seattle to meet my mom's dying sister. Momma rarely spoke about her, so the trip had been a surprise. It was during the pre-Taffeta, postpageant days of my childhood, when Momma didn't know what to do with herself, and I used books to hide. We slept on the pullout couch for three nights. Each morning, Momma rose before she thought I was awake, to sit on the porch and drink black coffee and stare out at the water.

"Tell me what it was like," Mandarin commanded.

"The ocean? It was big. And gray. And constantly moving. Like there was a storm inside it. It scared me, I think."

"I wouldn't be scared." She took a small, deliberate sip of her milk shake. "Y'know, there's strawberry fields in California. Stretching on for miles. All the way out to the sea. Rows and rows. You could run forever and never see them all. And the way they'd smell . . . Can you imagine?"

Though I should have known, the realization startled me: *for Mandarin, leaving is real.*

Because I didn't want to meet her eyes, I watched over her shoulder as Earl selected a half-eaten burger from the trash can and despondently shuffled away.

we're all a little bit crazy

I slumped in a metal folding chair at the edge of the Little Miss Washokey crowd. In the years since my last pageant, the school administration had built a cement stage outside the elementary wing. It gave the pageants and school performances a little more credibility, though the tape deck and the curtain strung up between two poles appeared to be the same.

I couldn't stop thinking about Mandarin. About how melancholy she'd sounded at the A&W when she'd talked about the ocean, the strawberry fields. I'd never met anybody with such changeable moods.

Except maybe for Momma, who was sitting beside me, her restless hands folded over the purse in her lap.

"I just don't think Lindsey's any good!" she hissed in a

voice that wasn't as quiet as she thought. "She's off tune. Though you can't say anything bad about that dress. Deborah's sewing is exquisite. Ooh! Now that was a sour note. What a way to end her act! That's all the judges will remember, the last impression, almost as important as the first. But she wasn't as bad as the Shaw girl, Petra? No, the brother's Peter, her name must be— Shhh!"

I wiped a fleck of spit from my cheek.

The MC, somebody's grandpa in a rumpled tuxedo, had stepped back onstage. He tapped the microphone, even though it was obviously working just fine. "Next is the lovely little Miss Taffeta Carpenter, singing Andrea Bocelli's 'Con Te Partirò' . . ."

He hunched over the microphone and added, "*In Italian.*"

That was exactly how Momma said that last part. Conspiratorially. Like if we spoke about my sister's talent in loud voices, it might disappear.

I hadn't been able to carry a tune as a child. So Momma had me recite things like Shakespearean sonnets, "Jabberwocky," and the Gettysburg Address. Once, I delivered that famous speech by Chief Joseph: *From where the sun now stands, I will fight no more forever.* I wore an Indian princess costume, with lipstick circles drawn on my cheeks. But that performance didn't go over well with the judges. Despite Chief Joseph's having been part of Oregon's Nez Perce tribe—not Wyoming's Arapahoe or Crow or Cheyenne or Shoshone—the chief's gloomy words probably reminded them of the parts of Native American history they'd rather forget. Like impoverished reservations, or the Trail of Tears. When it came to Indians, most white people in these parts believed that it was best to linger on the positives, like fry bread and dream catchers and turquoise jewelry.

Taffeta stepped out from the shadows backstage. Her blue dress looked ultramarine under the makeshift spotlight, one of those clamp lamps used for pet reptiles. Her cheeks glowed with a fever flush. The MC lowered the microphone to her level. She leaned in so close I heard her lips rustle against it.

Without any warning or any musical accompaniment, without so much as a drawing in of breath, my sister began to sing. Nonsense syllables, escalating into the first crescendo: "Con teee . . . partiró . . ."

Although most opera music made me want to retch—mostly on account of my mother's obsession with it—when Taffeta sang that song, it became my favorite song in the world.

I forgot about Mandarin as the power of Taffeta's voice coursed through the crowd. Taffeta felt it too. She tipped back her head and closed her eyes, like one of those child pop stars on the Disney Channel. She held out one hand plaintively while the other became a fist that pummeled the air. Her voice seemed to echo off the dim hills around us, transcending the whole town, all the people in it. For four minutes, we were cultured and worldly. Maybe even Italian.

She deserved a shower of roses, a standing ovation.

I wanted to climb onto my chair and call out, *That's my little sister!*

Then Momma whispered into my ear. "Oh, she's like an angel! This is all I ever wanted! All I ever wanted!"

And just like that, she ruined it.

I brought my knees up into my chest, aiming myself away from my mother. I couldn't even watch as my sister belted out the final piercing note to the song, holding it and holding it until I thought she would surely pass out or float away and vanish into the heavens, where we both agreed that she belonged.

❋   ❋   ❋

On our way home from the pageant, Momma drove with one hand on my sister's trophy—the first-prize kind, not the stuffed kind. Taffeta sat in back, wearing a rhinestone tiara, her feet tucked beneath her blue dress. I sat in the passenger seat with the window open, breathing in the wind.

It was during our epic pageant road trips that Momma used to tell me about the wildwinds.

"They push all the ozone out of the air," she would explain. "Ozone's the electricity that keeps us sane. That's why we're all a little bit crazy."

I never really understood what she was talking about, although when I read about the hole in the ozone layer in second grade, I feared an onset of global insanity even more than global warming.

"Did you see the looks on the judges' faces when Taffeta finished singing?" Momma asked now, as we rolled through town.

"Not really," I muttered.

"Like they were sucking for air? They'd all gone pale! I've never been so proud in my whole life." She tap-tapped her fingernails against the trophy. Its chrome plating was networked with a billion hairline cracks. "This is it, my darlings! The beginning."

I glanced back at Taffeta, who was sucking on her fingers.

"Next comes the tri-county pageant," Momma continued. "All the best and brightest little girls in the three counties. And after that comes the state pageant."

"The whole state?" Taffeta asked.

"The whole state! And I just know you'll win that one, too, hands down. Can you imagine their reaction when a six-year-old beats all those seven-, eight-, and nine-year-olds?"

This time, my sister didn't respond. Out of the corner of my eye, I saw Momma's joyful expression falter a bit.

"Don't you want to know what's after that, honey?"

"Okay."

"The *national* pageant! The whole entire United States of America. Fifty girls, one from every state. There'll be music scouts and TV producers. All the important people in the entertainment industry. And it'll be held in California."

I snapped my head around. *"California?"*

Momma glanced at me, like she'd forgotten I was there.

"Well, you can come too, Grace. But only if you'll be supportive."

I turned back toward the window. My eyes trailed along the barbed wire fence outlining somebody's front yard, as if it were a ranch or a pasture. *Trespassers beware.* Beyond the streets and houses, I could make out the dark haze of the horizon. As usual, it seemed unnervingly far away.

❀　❀　❀

When we arrived home, I shot up the stairs into my room and slammed the door. From the back of my closet, I withdrew my deepest, darkest secret.

My pageant album.

I'd stolen it from the junk drawer in Momma's room. She hadn't missed it. Taffeta's album, crammed full from cover to cover, sat on the coffee table in our living room. Mine was only half filled. The other half would have been reserved for future accomplishments, except I hadn't had any.

The first pictures in my album didn't bother me. It was the later ones, the ones I covered with scraps of notebook paper, that turned my stomach. Though sometimes I'd peel back the paper and peek at the tiny face underneath—pink cheeks, gleaming white baby teeth, a cloud of corkscrew curls.

Looking at my former self, I wasn't sure how much of the dread I felt was a real memory, and how much was a false one planted by the years between.

Because with the exception of the pageants themselves, all my memories of those days were good ones. The photos proved it: me standing in the crispy roadside weeds with Momma's hand on my head, the camera propped up on the car hood. I was three, and four, and five, and six. Momma was in her early twenties. Both of us grinning, always.

Momma entered me in every Wyoming pageant open to out-of-towners. There were plenty—especially in the towns too small to homegrow enough contestants. We visited the bigger towns too, except for Jackson Hole. *Bad energy there,* Momma said.

The year I was six I remembered the best. We had the most photos from that year, from the summer before first grade and the spring at the end of it.

I flipped through the pages, touching each picture. Rivers clogged with beaver dams. The sprawling flatness of Casper. The layered pink cliffs near Lander. Herds of bison at Yellowstone National Park and blurry pronghorn antelopes leaping through the Red Desert. A postcard from the art exhibit we'd seen of Bev Doolittle, a western artist who hid Indians and wildlife in her painted landscapes. I remembered pointing out pinto horses in the notches of aspen trees, the creased faces of Indian chiefs in boulders on the ride home.

We'd visited the Devil's Tower, like a wedding cake carved from ancient rock. The Tetons, jagged mountains whose name meant "breasts" in French. Hell's Half Acre, which made our badlands look not so bad at all.

No wonder I'd fallen in love with geology.

We'd gotten lost plenty of times, but it had always felt like an adventure. We had to coax directions from the owners of ranches and diners and trading posts, the kind of folks who thought long and hard before speaking. The farther out in the hinterlands, the more eccentric the directions. Stuff like:

When the dirt gets a sorta yellow color, you've gone too far.

Go on past the Lutheran church and then, at Edwin's house, make a right. (As if we had any idea who Edwin was.)

You'll see an old brown building that says Dairy Mart. Don't turn there!

In the following years, whenever Momma mentioned the things we'd seen—"Do you remember Indian Ridge?" or "Look, there's a picture of the Elkhorn Arch in Afton. We drove under it. Grace, do you remember?"—I claimed that it had been too long, that I remembered nothing.

But I did remember.

Maybe not all the places Momma and I had seen. But I remembered the way we'd been. Together.

I remembered how we'd always tried to stretch pageant season a little longer, to find just one more pageant for me to enter, to fill up the gas tank just one last time. Though like water swirling into a drain, everything eventually wound down to Washokey.

When Momma acted like my Little Miss Washokey screwup was such a fiasco, it brought to light a fundamental difference between us. I lived for our road trips. But for Momma, the pageants were the important thing. Our journeys had just been the means to an end.

There was only one photo of that last pageant. Momma must have taken others, but I didn't know what had happened to them.

This one showed all the girls dancing onstage, in the mayhem of our final act. I hadn't covered my face with paper on this one, since Paige Shelmerdine and her flamingo pink dress had done the job for me. Now I wondered if when that image was snapped, I'd already made the impulsive decision that would knock my universe sideways.

I tried to imagine Mandarin standing there, watching, somewhere just outside the frame. But through all my years of pondering, I never could guess what she'd been thinking when she saw Momma scold me backstage.

I still couldn't guess what Mandarin was thinking—like when she'd asked me to run away with her to California.

I chased that thought out of my mind and closed the book.

the fundamentals of leadership

On Monday morning, we arrived at school a few minutes early. Taffeta danced away into the throng of kindergartners. I stood in the cottonwood grove and scanned the lawn for Mandarin, although I knew I wouldn't find her. She usually arrived late in the mornings, since she considered attending homeroom a pointless waste of sleep.

I adopted an insolent expression as I leaned back against a tree. Or tried to, because the trunk was a little too far away. I ended up practically diagonal. When I adjusted my pose, the bark made a crumpling sound.

I turned and found a poster for the cowboy dance stapled to the tree trunk.

I stared at it. In tempera paint, a hokey country couple danced in a swarm of musical notes. Every phrase was framed with exclamation points: *Come one, come all!! Kick up your spurs at the cowboy dance!! The greatest event of the year!!*

The date: Saturday, May 19.

My birthday.

It was kind of like somebody sticking his fingers in his ears, wagging his tongue.

Despite myself, I sighed. Then I hiked my jeans down another centimeter or two, shouldered my tote bag, and sauntered toward the school building. But I got stuck halfway up the stairs, because Mr. Beck was standing on the top step.

Mr. Beck had a gray mustache and long ponytailed hair that was a timeline of his years: black at the tips, and fading to pure white at the roots. He wore jeans belted high on his gut, a suit jacket over a white shirt, and one of those wannabe cowboy bootlace ties, with plastic bear teeth instead of toggles at the ends. His high-heeled brown boots made him look forever on the verge of toppling forward.

I tried to go around him. But to my surprise, he stuck out his hand to stop me.

"Grace Carpenter?"

The loudspeaker voice sounded strange coming from a real person. Discreetly, I tried to hike up my jeans. "Sir?"

He grabbed both my hands. "I wanted to be the first to congratulate you!"

I glanced at the students around me. Staring, as usual—but now for the wrong reasons. Hanging out with the principal on the top step wasn't exactly enviable. Like when I got caught looking at pioneer postcards with Ms. Ingle. I wondered what would happen if I screamed at the top of my lungs. Then I realized what Mr. Beck had said.

"On what?" I asked warily.

"On your trip to Washington, D.C."

"Huh? Excuse me, sir, but I don't know what you're talking about."

I tugged one of my hands loose. But that was worse. Now it looked like the principal and I were holding hands.

"There were some unfortunate discoveries about Peter Shaw. Specifically, we found out his essay was plagiarized. That means copied, Grace. He cheated."

Thanks for the vocabulary lesson. "Okay, sure."

Peter Shaw's cheating wasn't any big surprise. People claimed he'd won the junior-class presidency via devious tactics.

"So in that case, first prize—the three-week All-American Leadership Conference in Washington, D.C., plus a one-hundred-dollar savings bond—goes to our runner-up."

I stood there for one silent moment before yanking my other hand out of his and slapping it over my mouth. "What do you mean?" I asked through the gaps of my fingers.

Mr. Beck withdrew a stack of pamphlets from his jacket pocket and offered them to me. "I've had a look at your itinerary. All kinds of field trips are included. The Pentagon. Arlington, and the cemetery. The monuments and museums. And of course, the White House. Maybe you'll be lucky enough to meet the president of the United States! Wouldn't that beat all?"

Alien places. Foreign words. Only a few of them made sense. I tried to wrap my brain around what he was saying.

"So I'm really going?"

"That's right." Mr. Beck beamed at me. One front tooth

was the same shade of gray as his mustache. "And don't forget the hundred-dollar savings bond. We'll swap it for your fifty. I'll call up 4-H and Kiwanis and let them know you're in. All you need to do is fill out the paperwork and mail it in with your mother's signature. Congratulations on your big win, Ms. Carpenter!"

The bell rang. Mr. Beck held open the double doors, and I stumbled into the hall. The white noise of the kids surging around me sounded like the roar of applause. In that instant, I forgot to saunter. I forgot everything.

I had won. For the first time in eight years, weeping was allowed.

❄   ❄   ❄

I studied the pamphlets in my classes. Pretty quickly, I discovered the problem with leadership conferences: they were all about leadership.

My courses included:

The Fundamentals of Leadership
This course examines the philosophy of leadership, the difference between leadership and management, and the leader-follower relationship.

Leadership in the Political Sector
This course explores the nature of leadership in both traditional and contemporary politics. Guest speakers will include assistants to members of Congress and an associate Webmaster from a government website.

Leadership: the Musical

Once you have mastered the essentials of leadership, it's time to perform! A requirement.

I wasn't sure how I felt about that last course. Actually, I
wasn't sure how I felt about any of the courses. For now, I
decided to concentrate on my victory. Everything that came
with it could be put off until later—including telling Momma.

Because although Momma loved a good win above anything else, I suspected her reaction might be a little under-
whelming, considering how busy she was preparing for the
tri-county pageant. An essay contest couldn't compare.
Momma didn't even read books for fun, let alone my school
papers.

My brain fog lasted until lunchtime, when I almost went
to sit by Alexis & Co. Fortunately, Mandarin intercepted me
just in time. She held a paper cup filled with grapes so purple they looked black. Only then did I remember she hadn't
been in geometry that morning. Mandarin's missing class
wasn't anything out of the ordinary, but I had the trouble-
some sensation I'd forgotten something.

"How's it going?" she asked.

"It's going great!"

Before I could elaborate, Mandarin pointed at my tote
bag. "What's all that?"

I glanced at my bag. The leadership pamphlets stuck out
like a peacock tail. "They're—"

Now it doesn't matter that you didn't win that stupid trip,
Mandarin had said in the cottonwood storm. *We'll be long
gone by then.*

And just like that, I realized what I had forgotten. But *how*? How could I have?

Because to me, it was never real.

I couldn't let Mandarin know about the conference. Not yet. I knew she hated liars, but I had no other choice. "Stuff for the service project," I said. "Just some ideas."

"Boooring," she drawled.

"Yeah. It is." I started to ramble. "But it could be fun, if we do it together. We don't have to whitewash walls or anything, like Tom Sawyer. I mean, really, the possibilities are endless. What about—"

Mandarin threw a grape at my forehead.

"I guess you're right, though." She bit another grape in half. "As much as I hate to admit it. I'd like to get the hell out of here respectably and all, so we should get that damn thing over with. How 'bout you come over after dinner?"

"Sure." I adjusted the pamphlets so they fell inside my bag, and followed Mandarin out to our usual place at the lilac planter, that morning's excitement already settling into something more like nausea.

❋ ❋ ❋

To make matters worse, Mrs. Mack had lab groups planned—and she'd stuck Davey and me with Paige Shelmerdine.

Mrs. Mack was a gnomish woman who hadn't even majored in science. She pulled all our experiments from an old textbook that varied wildly in its levels of difficulty, but she could never distinguish the basic from the impossible.

One week we might be mixing two simple chemicals and recording the shifting colors. The next week's experiment might require masses, microscopes, Avogadro's number, and calculations so nuanced even I had trouble figuring them out. Frequently, foul odors were involved.

I expected that day's lab to resemble the past week's Identification of an Unknown Substance. (The substance turned out to be grape Kool-Aid.) So when Mrs. Mack said, "Today we'll test properties of different rocks," it seemed like God was trying to cheer me up.

Or to compensate for Paige Shelmerdine.

Paige wasn't even supposed to be in our class, but her thrice-weekly remedial-reading appointments were scheduled for the same time as freshman science. Administration thought bumping her forward was preferable to holding her back. They didn't consider how she'd hold back the rest of us.

"There's so *many*," Paige complained as Davey spread our identification charts on the lab table. She had a stuffed nose, and she kept turning her head to the side and wiping it on the shoulder of her blouse.

Davey and I tried to ignore her. "'Igneous, sedimentary, and metamorphic,'" he read out loud. "'Split into hardness, composition, color, and grain size.'"

I pried open the yellow pencil box of rock samples. Most I could name right away. The local ones were all there: agate, quartzite, granite. Some, like obsidian and pumice, were obvious. Others could have been a couple of different things.

"You know what that one looks like?" Paige's hand darted in front of me to snatch a white stone. "A rock."

"Hilarious," Davey muttered.

"No, a rock. Not like a *rock* rock." Paige smirked. "Like a *crack* rock. You know, like crystal meth."

We stared at her like *she* was on crack.

"No way." Davey blink-blinked at the charts. "It's probably rock salt, or gypsum, or—"

"It's got to be gypsum," I said. "Scratch it with your thumbnail. If any comes away, it's gypsum." I reached out to take the stone from Paige, but she held it from me.

"I'll bet you want it," she said. "If it's really what I think it is. Some of the guys my brothers know, they're real meth-heads, the crazy sort. The kinda guys Mandarin Ramey runs around with. The kinda guys—" She snickered. "Well, y'all know what I'm talking about. Especially *you*, Grace."

I felt my face heat up. "Paige, don't be dumb."

Truth was, I'd never even considered whether Mandarin did drugs. That wasn't part of the rumors. I wondered frantically whether there might be a whole separate stratum of rumors passed around by the older kids, the kids who spent their nights partying instead of in their bedrooms, rereading paperbacks.

I glanced at Davey, but he was busying himself with his notebook, copying the parameters for gypsum off the charts. Unlike every other human being in the Washokey Badlands Basin, Davey didn't like gossip.

I reached across him to grab one of the charts and my loose hair swept over his arm. He yanked it away and blushed.

"You know, Grace," Paige continued, "everyone saw you acting all wild in the cotton that morning."

Will you go with me? Mandarin's voice, shouting in the wind. I hid my wince by pretending to examine a chart.

"Staggering all over the place," Paige continued. She leaned across the table and thumped the white rock on my chart. "Like you were on *drugs.*"

I glared at her. "Give me a break, Paige."

She held up her hands, the picture of innocence. "Don't be pissed off at *me.* It's only what everybody's saying."

"Well, everybody's full of shit."

"You're even starting to talk like her! Next you'll be wanting to look like her too. And after that, well . . ." She tried to wink suggestively, but her other eye closed too. "Who knows what you'll do next?"

"Let's just get to work," I said through gritted teeth.

"You look like you're doing just fine on your own," Paige said. "You and the school faggot."

Davey's cheeks turned magenta.

I squeezed the rock so hard my knucklebones showed through my skin. How good it would feel to fling it right into Paige's self-satisfied face. But then I'd get kicked out of class.

Instead, I did something I hadn't done for ages: I raised my hand.

"Mrs. Mack?" I said, loud enough for the entire class to hear. "Paige won't do any work. She's just sitting here, distracting us."

I knew my good grades would endorse my integrity. And at that moment, Paige was sitting with her feet up on another chair. Hurriedly, she dropped them to the floor.

Mrs. Mack glared at her. "Why don't you come up to my

desk, Miss Shelmerdine," she said, "and do the experiment with me?"

Paige, speechless for once, trudged to the front of the room and sat.

I glanced at Davey again. He kept blinking and blinking, filling the boxes on the identification chart with his tiny penmanship, avoiding my gaze. As if he didn't know what to make of this new Grace Carpenter. Well, neither did I.

14

nobody else in the world

As soon as Mandarin shut us inside her bedroom, I sensed something was wrong. The way she didn't quite look me in the eye. The way she fell backward onto her bed, as if she'd succumbed to a spell of overpowering fatigue. The possible layers in her opening lines: "Let's get this project over with," she said. "So we don't have it between us."

Feeling uncertain, I sat cross-legged on her ugly old-man carpet instead of joining her on the bed. I cleared my throat.

"Well, we did this experiment on the hardness of rocks in science today," I began. "I was thinking you could tie them into your service project somehow. Maybe we could contact some geologists, or something, and put together some sort of a display—"

"Rocks depress me."

I tried not to feel insulted. "We could find someone who studies paleontology. Or archaeology."

"Ology ology ology." Mandarin yawned and stretched, like a cat in a puddle of sun. "It's all about dead things. What's with you and the nonliving? What about the people?"

"I thought you hated people."

"Bullshit. I love people. What do you think I am, a sociopath? I'd never have said that."

I cleared my throat, deciding not to contradict her. I hadn't really liked the idea of using rocks, anyway—I wasn't about to show anybody my collection. That was my secret. "We could, like, paint something. Something that belongs to an old person. A fence."

"Like Tom Sawyer?" she mocked.

"We could clean out somebody's barn. . . ."

She rolled her eyes.

"Well, what service project did you do other years?"

"Nothing. Got my dad to sign the paper that said I did it. He'll sign anything, if he's drunk enough."

"Why didn't you do that this year?"

Mandarin shrugged. "They're on to me."

I was beginning to get the feeling she was playing with me, batting me around like a mouse between her paws. I tapped my pencil against my knee and let a bit of my frustration slip out. "Well, do you have any ideas?" I asked.

"I don't know. Whatever's easy."

"I thought you wanted to get this over with. You've got to help me think of something, just a little."

"I don't *got to* do anything."

"But you said you wanted to graduate. . . ."

Mandarin rolled onto her side, propping up her head with one arm. All of a sudden, her voice went arctic. "Know what, Grace? You're fortunate I'm helping you with this project anyways, after what you did."

"What I did?"

In reply, Mandarin whipped something from underneath her pillow and flung it at me. Dark and glossy, it sliced through the air and landed on the floor by my foot. "Want to explain what that was doing in your bag, Grace? Because it sure ain't 'stuff for the service project.'"

One of my pamphlets for the All-American Leadership Conference.

She must have stolen it when I wasn't paying attention. The winds picked up outside the window, and the air inside Mandarin's room seemed to shift. Ozone, or lack of it. For just a second, my mind seemed to vibrate. I couldn't pull my eyes from hers. "The conference is just for three weeks," I said in a small voice. "We can go after—"

"Three weeks," Mandarin repeated. "Only three weeks! Anything could happen in three weeks. In three weeks I could be dead."

"Don't say that."

"Well, it's true."

"We all could be dead in three weeks." I started to babble. "A meteor could fall down and smash us all to pieces. Like the dinosaurs. That's what happened to them. A stone from space thundered down and changed the weather, and *whoosh!* Wiped them all out."

Mandarin was still staring at me, but her expression had changed to one of contempt.

"I *swear* I was going to tell you, but I only just found out today! Turns out, Peter Shaw cheated. . . ."

"I just thought the same things were important to the both of us," she said. "Hell, I should've known better, right? I mean, nobody thinks like me. Nobody else in the world. And you? You were just pretending."

"I wasn't pretending, I only forgot—"

"You're right," she said loudly, cutting me off. "You should forget about it. We both should."

I rose to my knees. "Mandarin, *come on*. I don't even care about the conference. 'Leadership in the Political Sector'? That doesn't interest me. I couldn't care less about the political sector—"

Mandarin slammed her fist into the wall.

I heard the bang, saw the smear of blood where she'd gashed her knuckles. I stumbled away on my weakened knees. It was so sudden, so *violent*. I thought of the stories about Mandarin's fights. Sophie Brawls, and the scratches on her neck. I knew Mandarin scared people, but until then I'd never felt frightened.

And yet, I felt even more frightened I'd ruined everything between us.

"Mandarin . . ."

"Just go," she said quietly, cradling her injured hand. "And close the door behind you."

So that was it, then. It was over.

I grabbed my tote bag and left without another word,

shutting Mandarin's bedroom door as gently as I could. On my way out of her house, I cupped both my hands over my nose and mouth, as if less oxygen would reduce my chances of bursting into tears.

Then I saw the envelope.

Just part of it, sticking out of the mailbox. I would have overlooked it if I hadn't noticed the first few letters of Mandarin's name. Handwritten, in neat blue ink.

Although I was terrified Mandarin might come roaring out behind me, I pulled out the envelope. It felt lopsided, heavier than a letter should. I traced the outline of the triangular object inside, pinched it between my fingertips.

An arrowhead.

I remembered the jar of perfect arrowheads she'd pulled from under her bed. Blue-white chalcedony. Tiger skin obsidian.

Somebody was sending Mandarin arrowheads.

I looked at the return address. The strange name—Kimanah Paisley—meant nothing to me. Neither did the address: Riverton, WY 82501. Riverton was a few hours south. Home to the Wind River Reservation. More badlands.

And to whomever was sending Mandarin arrowheads.

My throat ached. What were a few weeks of friendship compared to what she'd apparently had with this mystery girl? Mandarin and I had spent barely any time together outside of school. She shot down every personal question I asked. Though I supposed she had good reason to—I'd betrayed her trust, all for three weeks at a stupid conference that was sounding worse by the minute. "Leadership: the Musical"? Really?

I considered taking the envelope. Mandarin had stolen my pamphlet, after all. But instead, I jammed it back in the mailbox and headed for the Tombs.

15

whoops

By Thursday, Momma's pageant fever was worse than ever, though the tri-county pageant wasn't until early June. She hadn't even bothered to get dressed. She bustled around in a baggy satin muumuu covered in a pandemonium of butterflies and flowers against a royal blue background. Her bosom jiggled underneath like smuggled water balloons. It was almost hypnotizing.

Each day, after school, she relegated hordes of menial tasks to me, like gluing rhinestones to Taffeta's flip-flops for the swimwear competition. I never protested, which Momma found extremely unusual. She must have thought I'd come down with wildwind psychosis, though she never asked what was wrong.

I still hadn't mentioned my contest win, the papers at the

bottom of my tote bag. I couldn't even think of the conference without my throat burning and my lungs going haywire.

On Tuesday, I'd approached Ms. Ingle after homeroom
to tell her I'd have to find another service project. "I'm really
sorry," I said, still feeling guilty about what I'd called her behind her back. "It's just not going to work out."

"Has something happened between you and Mandarin?"

I fumbled in my pocket for a stone and found it empty.
"Well . . ."

"Grace, has she done something to you?"

"Done something?"

"You can tell me anything, you know. If Mandarin's
been pressuring you to take part in activities you know you
shouldn't—"

"No!" I almost shouted. "Nothing like that. It's just that
I don't feel like I'm the best person to tutor Mandarin. I'm
just so young, you know? Maybe she'd be better off working
with an upperclassman, or at least a real sophomore. Someone like . . ." I thought quickly. "Like Davey Miller."

"*Davey?*" Ms. Ingle said incredulously.

"Okay, maybe not Davey."

"Grace, of course you're a real sophomore. You're at the
top of the class." She tapped her chin with two fingers. "I
think I know what the real problem is. I'm sensing a case of
low self-esteem. Is that correct?"

"I don't think . . ." I paused. If I denied it, I'd sound big-
headed. But I didn't want to agree, either.

"If so, it's entirely misplaced. In fact, you have more potential for success than any student I've ever taught. There's

plenty you can teach Mandarin. And she wants you to. Remember, she asked for you."

I didn't reply, but a sniffle escaped.

"Though if it's absolutely necessary, I can help you think up a different service project," Ms. Ingle continued. "Mr. Mason received a new shipment of historic bridge photographs he needs help filing. And I can speak to Mandarin about finding another tutor."

I thought I'd feel relieved. But once Ms. Ingle said it, I realized what it meant. If she didn't fight it—and I knew she might—Mandarin would be paired with somebody new.

Somebody older. More experienced.

Somebody unafraid to seize shimmery, windstruck, once-in-a-lifetime opportunities laid out before them.

Somebody who wasn't me.

"It's all right," I heard myself say. "I was just thinking out loud. I'll still work with her. No problem." Although I had no idea how, since Mandarin and I weren't speaking.

Then, as if I weren't upset enough, Ms. Ingle leaned in close and whispered, "I think your pants are a little too big. Would you like to borrow a belt?"

I'd eaten lunch in my bathroom stall all week.

Now I sat in the kitchen with Momma, hot-gluing tiny fabric flowers to a wooden hoop. I was making a mess of it—losing flowers, dropping flowers, gluing flowers to myself. Momma's anxiety didn't help matters. Every year, she seemed to enjoy pageant prep less and less, until the whole enterprise was more a colossal chore than an event she and Taffeta had enrolled in by choice. It was hard to believe her claims that she'd missed pageants terribly in the gap between my last and Taffeta's first.

I'd never have thought Momma would notice my distress, especially in the midst of her own. Until she placed her hand over mine.

"Grace, dear," she said, "is anything the matter? You're not in any . . . trouble with that Ramey girl, are you?"

"Momma, no!"

"I just meant, are you having a tiff, is all."

Only Momma would use a word like *tiff*. I balled up my fist underneath her hand. "Everything's fine," I lied.

"Okay," she said hesitantly. She glanced at the mess I was making of the wooden hoop. "Still . . . maybe you should take a break. Why don't you head to the store and pick up a gallon of milk?"

I was afraid of running into Mandarin on the street—it would be just my luck—but I couldn't tell Momma that. She handed me a five-dollar bill. I ripped a flower off my thumb and headed for the door.

❋ ❋ ❋

I pulled the hood of my sweater over my head and yanked on the strings, leaving myself a little circle to peer through. Then I gathered my tote bag in front of my chest like a padded shield. With my head down, I passed the back door to the grocery store and went around to the front. The ghosts of old-timey letters still decorated the gray brick building: *Drugs, Soda Fountain, Washokey Merchant*.

As I stepped inside, out came Becky Pepper, third-place winner in the All-American Essay Contest. I wondered whether she'd take my place at the leadership conference if I backed out.

I made my way to the dairy section and grabbed a gallon of milk. On my way back, I kept my eyes on the plank floor. If I glanced up, I'd see the trophies. Coyote heads preserved in full snarl, beady-eyed pronghorns, hawks with open beaks. The animals had decorated the grocery store my entire life. But now they made me think of Mandarin.

I'd almost reached the registers when I heard a high-pitched voice: "If it ain't Grace Carpenter!"

I tried not to cringe.

Polly Bunker had the shiny-pink skin of a pig, though the wiry, pale curls sticking to her skull reminded me of a shorn sheep. Her grin was that of a shark. She wore a frumpy floral dress with a black slip peeking from under the hem.

"Mrs. Bunker," I said. "You startled me."

"I startled you!" She inspected me with a frown. "Then you must be skittish, girl, 'cause I never startled anybody in my whole entire life."

I found that hard to believe. Back when Alexis and I had been friends, Polly Bunker was always materializing in the basement rec room with platters of Jell-O Jigglers and stainless steel bowls of Cheetos. She also used to come to our house unannounced, her chipmunk cheeks practically bursting with gossip.

She hadn't come over in quite a while, though. I suspected

that if Washokey weren't such a small town, Momma might have defriended her years ago. At least now, after Taffeta's pageant win, Polly Bunker couldn't retroactively gloat about Alexis's in quite the same way.

She latched on to my free arm and dragged me into the produce section. In May, grapefruits were the big sellers. Absentmindedly, I played with one while she tested the firmness of the green grapes. *Pinch, pinch.* I found it mildly depressing that the height of color in Washokey came from the seasonal produce shipped from other states.

"Alexis told me about your essay winning after all," she said. "I'm so proud of you! I always knew you were a good influence on my Alexis. You've got some rock-solid wits in that skull."

She squeezed a grape so hard it popped.

"So I been thinking to myself, I ain't seen my second-favorite girl in the world around the house lately. I miss you, Grace-face! Especially with your birthday coming up and all." Her gaze became one of exaggerated concern. "Tell me, dear . . . have you and Alexis been at odds?"

"We're okay."

"Well, that's not what I heard. And what I did hear has me worried. Is it true you've been running around with that slut Mandarin Ramey?"

The gallon of milk slipped from my hand and exploded. It splashed all over both of us, our clothes, our faces, spiking across the floor. Polly Bunker gaped at me, milk dripping from her hair.

"Whoops," I said.

I fled from the produce section, darting through the bread and cereal aisle to the front of the store. But when I reached the exit, I hesitated.

Momma was so pageant-brained, if I didn't bring home any milk, there'd be hell to pay.

I hurried to the dairy case at the other end of the store. I had to step aside as a stock boy came out of the back room, carrying a mop. When he kicked the door shut behind him, I locked eyes with the jackalope-head trophy affixed to the back of it.

He was a crappy jackalope, unlike the glossy mass-produced ones at the souvenir shop. His head was the size of a baseball. He seemed undignified, with his sparrow-colored fur all matted down, beads of glue showing around the base of his tiny transplanted antlers. And here he was, trapped forever, where nobody would ever see him. Not that they'd appreciate him, anyway. Such a tragic leap from the fields of his first life.

I found myself thinking of Mandarin again. Just like the jackalope, she was misunderstood. Stuck fast. Unable to free herself—at least without a little help.

All of a sudden, I had an idea. An idea so good it made me bounce.

I glanced around and found nobody nearby. They had probably rushed to the produce section to gawk at soggy old Polly Bunker.

Whoops.

I grinned and bounced again for good measure. Kimanah Paisley and Sophie Brawls didn't matter. They weren't here, but I was. And I'd figured out how to bring Mandarin and me back together. Something so grand, so dangerous, so *symbolic*, I could hardly believe I'd come up with it myself. I didn't know if I could pull it off. But it was worth the risk.

I just had to find the courage to take that first step.

16

weirdos on these premises

I crouched beside Remy Ramey, patting one stiff ear. He appeared not to notice. Somebody had given him a haircut to make him look like a lion, but they hadn't been particularly skilled at it. Probably drunk. I could hear country music coming through the closed door in front of me, and each twang of the acoustic guitar plucked at my anxious nerves.

I took a deep breath. *I just have to do it quick.* One big leap. Like bungee jumping off a bridge.

I pushed the door open and stepped inside.

Solomon's was so massive it seemed even darker than the night outside. My eyes strained. The air was hazy with smoke. I felt the urge to cough, but restrained the tickle in time, not wanting to draw attention to myself.

But when my eyes finally adjusted, I discovered they'd

already noticed me: the middle-aged men seated at the tall bar, nursing mugs of beer. Their red eyes gleamed through the smoke they exhaled. One of them leaned toward another and said something, and then they both glanced at me and laughed. I recognized the third man down as Earl Barnaby, the drunk from the A&W stand. He wore a straw cowboy hat, the five-dollar kind they sold at the Cody Walmart.

I was so far out of my element I felt like I'd left my body entirely. In that case, I decided, I had nothing to lose. I took another deep breath, tried not to choke, and approached the bar.

The bar top was made of glossy wood, sticky with spilled ale. I peeled my hands away and jammed them into my pockets, where I'd stashed my smallest red beryl stone for luck. The bartender's back was to me. I waited for him to turn, my heart racketing in my rib cage, as he cranked a beer tap over mug after mug until foam slopped over the sides.

Finally, I spoke. "Mr. Ramey?"

I'd never noticed how much Solomon Ramey resembled Mandarin. Beneath his tangled strings of dark hair, Mandarin's hazel eyes peered out. He had her height, her thinness. But his face was creased and aged, the folds of his cheeks so deep-set they could have been carved from clay.

"I ain't serving you." His voice seemed wet, as if he needed to hack something out. "How old're you, twelve?"

"I just . . . I wanted to know if Mandarin's here."

No emotions crossed his face at his daughter's name. "She's probably on an all-night break, knowin' her. Never up to no good. You're welcome to look around, but watch out. There's some weirdos on these premises."

A bald man seated closest to me raised his half-empty mug and hollered, "I'll drink to that!" The other drunks laughed.

"Thank you," I said to Mandarin's father. He winked at me. The corners of his eyes were crimson.

Like apparitions, people appeared and disappeared in the gloom as I crept through the bar. An older woman in a black beaded cowboy hat danced by herself, one hand atop her head. She pawed at me as I passed, trying to get me to join her. A trio of men stood around an old jukebox, sipping beer from longneck bottles. I passed the booths lining the side walls, peering into each one. Two old men playing cards. A collection of lipsticked girls in their twenties. A fat man sitting alone and smoking, the edge of the table wedged into his gut.

I found Mandarin in the very last booth. Or really, only part of her. The man she was making out with obscured the rest.

He had one hand nestled in her hair. I could hear them, the kissing noises. I felt like a pervert, but I was unable to take my eyes away. Finally, Mandarin pulled back to take a drag of her cigarette.

When she saw me, she just sat there, her cigarette jutting from her lips.

"Mandarin," I said. "I'm sorry for coming here, but . . . I have something to show you."

The man spit into a plastic cup of murky tobacco water. Had he been chewing tobacco and kissing her at the same time? Mandarin withdrew the cigarette from her mouth and tapped it on a blue ashtray. "I'm kind of busy right now."

"Don't be like that, Mandarin. Please." My voice wavered. "I'm really sorry, I swear. Please! I still want to go with you! I—"

"Shhh!" she hissed. "Quiet. Not now. I'll have a look at what you've got, all right? But real quick." She glanced at the man. "All right?" Resentfully, he slung the dead weight of his arm from her shoulders, releasing her to stand.

Mandarin put one hand on the small of my back and herded me toward the front door. "What're you doing in here, anyways? This isn't any place for a girl like you."

"But you're here all the time."

"I work here. And besides, I'm different."

Once the door shut behind us, Mandarin withdrew her arm and stepped back, as if remembering she was supposed to be angry with me. Her eyes flashed under the blinking bar lights. "So? What's going on?"

"Are you busy tonight?"

"Obviously. So can we just get on with it? What've you got?"

She was trying to act impatient, but I could tell she was curious. It gave me the upper hand. "Stay put for one sec," I ordered.

I went around the corner and retrieved my gift from where I'd hidden it—the thing I'd stolen from the grocery store door and stuffed into my tote bag that afternoon. When I handed it to Mandarin, she shrieked and almost dropped it. I snatched it back and held it by the antlers, with its little jackrabbit face aimed up at her.

"Are you *insane*?" Mandarin said. "I don't even want to *look* at it. The poor guy."

I'd suspected she would react like that. "Well, it—"

"Did you buy it from the souvenir shop? Because that's just, like, supporting the whole industry!"

"It's not from the souvenir shop. And I didn't buy it."

"Well, how'd you get it? The only other place I've seen one . . ." She paused. "Oh no you didn't. You stole it? Did you really? You *are* insane!"

"So are you busy later tonight?"

"Why? What did you have in mind?"

I brandished the jackalope head under the bar lights. "We're going to liberate the trophies."

liberation

The success of the liberation rested on two conditions.

The first was Mandarin's father's truck. Solomon Ramey owned a 1959 Studebaker Scotsman farm truck, pale green, with a wooden cage in back: the kind of contraption you saw stuffed with chickens or bawling baby goats on the highways. It had chubby bumpers, faded old tires, a front windshield dotted with chips. Maybe it would have been worth something fixed up—if it didn't look wind-blasted and drop-kicked and spit out. Even so, I expected that Solomon would be possessive about it. Washokey men loved their trucks.

Luckily, when I met Mandarin on her porch at two in the morning, she was twirling the keys on a silver ring. It looked like a jailer's key chain from an old western film.

"You got them?" I asked anyway.

In reply, Mandarin tossed the key ring at me. I held my hands over my face. The keys bounced painfully off my shoulder.

I leaned over to pick them up, wondering if she was still angry. But then she hopped from the steps and practically tackled me, hurling an arm around my waist. "This is going to be so much fun!" she exclaimed, towing me toward the driveway. "What a great fucking idea. You're a genius, Gracey."

I practically glowed.

"So what does your dad use his truck for?" I asked as we climbed in.

"Kegs," she replied, turning on the ignition. The engine came alive with an exasperated roar. I glanced at Mandarin, concerned.

"What if somebody hears us?"

"I can deal with them."

The second condition of a successful liberation might have been an even bigger gamble if I hadn't known Washokey so well.

Townspeople tended to trust one another. Not that crime didn't exist. While misdeeds behind closed doors generally went unreported, the weekly paper recounted occasional shenanigans: cars rammed into mailboxes, rocks through windows, fistfights in the parking lot of the Western Bar or the Old Washokey Sip Spot. But with the exception of the fights, there wasn't much person-against-person crime. No robberies, no burglaries, despite what Earl Barnaby claimed. The single break-in I could recall had been blamed on a drifter by the town's notoriously lazy police.

So I knew there were no alarm systems protecting Washokey's businesses.

I was counting on Mandarin's lock-picking skills.

Picking the lock had been Mandarin's idea. My grandiose plans hadn't taken locks into account. Fortunately, Mandarin's roommate at the Wyoming Girls' School had been an expert in forced entry, and eager to impress besides.

Mandarin went through a paper clip, a coat hanger, and three bobby pins before the padlock on the back door popped open. The whole while, I darted around anxiously, peering around corners, scanning the streets for nocturnal pedestrians, until Mandarin grabbed me by the back of my shirt and made me sit.

We slipped into the stockroom. Pallets were stacked to the ceiling, piled with shrink-wrapped cans of SpaghettiOs, green beans, Spam, neon boxes of macaroni. Mandarin used a case of Pabst Blue Ribbon to prop open the door into the store. I noticed four tiny nail holes—perfect for hanging a jackalope head.

Inside, we had a moment of silence, our eyes roaming from trophy to trophy. Their shadowy faces gazed sightlessly over the tops of the aisles. I hadn't cared much about them either way. But now they seemed somber and lonely, anchored in the dark.

Don't worry, I thought as I stared at the nearest one, a deer head. *We're going to free you.*

Just as I turned to Mandarin to utter something profound—I hadn't quite determined what—she whacked my shoulder.

"Tag! You're it," she shouted, and darted off into the canned-goods aisle like a kitten doped on catnip.

I had to keep calling her back as she skipped through the store, dancing, hiding, bursting out from behind displays of soda pop boxes. She devoured an apple and stuck the core among the lettuces. She drew angry faces on the eggs with her eyeliner.

"Who does this look like?" She held up a cantaloupe.

She'd drawn a face with a long droopy mustache. Mr. Beck, of course. "Ha," I said. "Great. Can we hurry?"

We lugged a stepladder from trophy to trophy. As Mandarin tossed me each animal head, she shouted, "Heads up!" Hilarious. I insisted on whispering in reply, as if my voice might tone down hers. This might have been my idea and all, but I was terrified of getting caught.

We stacked all the trophies in a shopping cart, bobcats and pronghorns and foxes together, an animal kingdom united in death. So morbid. But I still giggled at the absurdity of it. A cart full of heads. *Roadkill for dinner!*

In the parking lot, Mandarin hopped onto the back of the cart. "Push me."

I gave her a shove. Too late, I imagined the cart hitting a crack, and the trophies tumbling out all over the pavement. I hurried after her.

We loaded the trophies into the truck and tied a blue tarp over them so no one on the road would know what they were. "One sec," Mandarin said.

I watched her wheel the cart to the entrance and leave it neatly behind the others.

On her way back, she got out her eyeliner and drew a

mustache on the cement jackalope in front of the store. Then she drew eyelashes.

"I didn't want to sexually discriminate," she explained, slamming the door of the truck. "So how you feeling? Tired?"

I felt more wide-awake than I ever had. As if Mandarin's energy from the grocery store aisles had invaded my body. My instincts had been right. This night would define our friendship, cement it, render it unbreakable.

"Not tired at all," I replied.

"Good!" Mandarin said. "Then we can go get the others."

"What others?"

"The other trophies."

"What do you mean?" I squinted at her. "The ones in people's houses? In their barns? We can't, like, purge the town entirely."

"I *know* that," Mandarin said. "But it ain't worth it unless I get one in particular—that old wise one, from the Buffalo Grill. That elk."

"You want to break into the Buffalo Grill?"

"Why, you got a *thing* for the Dents?"

I thought about it. The thing was, the Buffalo Grill seemed more like someone's home. Like the hospital, it occupied an old house. People ate in former bedrooms or living rooms, with all the walls knocked down between. And while I didn't have a thing *for* Samantha Dent or her family, I didn't have anything against them. When Alexis and Paige weren't around, Samantha was actually kind of nice.

Then again, I knew Agatha and Dustin Wright, the owners of the grocery store. They weren't bad either. But that hadn't stopped me from pillaging their taxidermy.

"Let's go," I said.

As Mandarin drove, I kept catching whiffs of musk and old dead fur. I didn't see how that was possible, since the animals were way in the back. Then I sniffed my hands. Yep, it was us.

❋ ❋ ❋

"If Remy was an elk with its body chopped off, this is who he'd be," Mandarin whispered.

We gazed up at the massive head. I supposed it resembled Remy Ramey, if I squinted. It had the same tawny beard, the same glazed eyes. Probably even the same fleas. As long as you ignored the dusty antlers, like alien hands.

Mandarin pried the nails partway out of the wall with the back of a hammer. I dragged a chair out from the table below the head. "I'll hand it to you," I said.

"Don't be ridiculous! You can't handle it. I'm bigger than you."

"But I'm stronger."

Mandarin raised her eyebrows. "Says who?"

I didn't know why I'd said it—only that her limbs looked so frail. It had been years since she'd beaten up all those boys. And I'd never seen her eat anything more substantial than a milk shake and a handful of fries.

As if she'd read my thoughts, she challenged me. "You want to arm wrestle?"

I shook my head.

"It probably weighs more than a hundred pounds, y'know." She flexed her biceps. "We'll lug it down together."

We climbed up on chairs on opposite sides of the table and took hold of the elk's gritty antlers. I saw dead flies collected in the dip above its hairy neck. Mandarin said, "One, two, three!" and we tugged the thing from the wall.

She'd been right: it *was* heavy. And now that we were holding it, we didn't have anywhere to put it.

"Crap," I said. "Now what?"

"Unless we can jump together, we've just got to throw it."

My arms burned. "Let's put it back up for a second."

"No! No way. I'm going to throw it. Here goes. . . ."

The elk head crashed into the ground face-first. One antler knocked against a table. An empty water glass toppled over, rolled off the table, and shattered on the wood floor. We froze only a moment before we leaped down and grabbed hold of the elk's antlers.

Once we were safe in the truck, the elk head piled in with the others, Mandarin began to giggle. Her laughter slowly built until she was nearly hysterical.

"What?" I demanded.

"'What' is right." She was driving fast, too fast, but I didn't want to say anything. "As in, now what?"

I stared at her. Then I started to laugh too.

"You didn't plan any further than that, did you?"

I shook my head.

"What are we going to do?" she said. "Reattach them to their bodies?"

"And then sprinkle them with fairy dust, and charm them back to life." I paused. "Where are their bodies, do you think?"

"Skinned and eaten. If they were lucky. 'Cause at least they were useful that way. Died for a purpose, even a selfish one. But a lot of 'em probably were left to rot in some empty plain. Buried by the wind."

I imagined the elk's headless body lying out in the badlands, nothing left but old bleached bones, maybe scraps of fur, the dust blown up against it.

"How lonely," I said.

"Burial's always lonely." Mandarin looked troubled for a second, her thoughts moving through the dark.

"What about the people in Pompeii?"

"What's Pompeii?"

"That ancient city in Italy." I grabbed for my nonexistent seat belt as the truck sped faster. "A volcano erupted and buried the town and everybody in it in ash. Then the ash turned to stone. When their bodies decayed, it preserved the shapes. So archaeologists could see exactly how the people died. Some were embracing."

"Maybe they were angry old couples. Stuck together, with nowhere to go."

I shook my head. "You'd have to love someone a whole lot to die like that."

"Still, I wouldn't want to be buried." She kept accelerating, even though we were heading downhill. "Or burned."

"Then what? Be, like, frozen in one of those time capsule things?"

I tried not to shriek as Mandarin slammed on the brakes. We had reached the bridge. She sat silently for a moment, engine still sputtering, headlights fading into the darkness of the river below.

"I'd want to float away," she said.

✻ ✻ ✻

My back strained as we heaved our second-to-last trophy—the elk head—off the bridge. *Splash*. It dipped below the surface, then bobbed up again. Unlike the other trophies we'd hurled into the river, it floated.

We watched it drift into the middle of the water. The slow-moving current brought it against a clump of sticks, and it slowly swiveled around until it was looking back at us. Its milky glass eyes glowed in the moonlight. It reminded me of one of those fairy river horses, kelpies, the ones who dragged people underwater and ate them.

With a crack, the sticks shifted. The elk head floated into the tunnel of river trees, around the bend, and was gone.

The wind picked up, sending pebbles clattering across the bridge. I was starting to get this weird, haunted feeling, the same way I felt in the badlands when I lost track of time and it started to grow dark. Thoughts of ravenous kelpies and corpses turning to hill dust didn't help.

Mandarin must have felt the same way. She wrapped her arms around her body, hugging herself. From her fingers dangled the jackalope head, the only trophy she'd wanted to save. "Let's get out of here," she said.

"And go home?"

She shook her head. "Not yet. Let's go somewhere. Have you got anyplace to go?"

"What kind of place? Like the canal?"

"I don't know," she said. "Someplace magic."

Someplace magic? What did that mean? I considered the Tombs, and the Virgin Mary. The place closest to magic I knew. But for some reason, I didn't feel ready to bring Mandarin there. And what if the cave painting made her think of her dead mother?

"I can't think of anywhere," I said.

"Let's get in the truck, at least."

We crawled back into the cab. The wind whistled through the edges of the windows. Without warning, Mandarin lay down, resting her head on my thigh. She held the jackalope on her stomach.

"My birthday's coming up," I said.

I could have slapped my own face. What did I expect—a cupcake?

"Really," Mandarin said.

"It's not a big deal," I said hurriedly. "I mean, we never make a big deal out of it. My mother doesn't like birthdays."

"Why's that?"

"I think it's because she hates getting older herself. And she hates us getting older too. Especially my sister, Taffeta."

"The singing one?"

"Right," I replied, slightly amused. I'd never talked about Taffeta. "When it comes to beauty pageants, youth is important. Once Taffeta's nine or so, she won't have as many chances. It's the awkward stage. I screwed up my own chances when I was even younger than that, though. Taffeta's all she's got left."

"You used to be in beauty pageants?"

I was glad for the darkness, because I blushed furiously.

So Mandarin didn't remember the backstage scolding

eight years earlier, at my ill-fated Little Miss Washokey. It was a relief to be spared the shame of her memory, but it was also kind of disappointing. Because—well, I'd never forgotten. Obviously.

"Yeah," I replied. "Hard to believe that now, huh?"

And then, because I had to get it in, otherwise I would never have said it, I blurted, "So my mother wants you to come over for a birthday dinner. Next Saturday."

She'd mentioned it last night over supper.

"Oh, sure. Like I'd be allowed inside your house."

"Actually, I think my mother's kind of curious about you."

"Her and everybody!" In my lap, Mandarin twisted a piece of her hair around her index finger. "And I don't know why. When you meet me, I ain't all that interesting."

"It's really no big deal," I said again. Even if she wanted to come, it would be too weird. Though of course she didn't want to, anyway. Like the dance, that was just the way it was when you had friends like Mandarin instead of normal people. "I'll just tell her you can't come."

After another silence, I wondered out loud, "Do you think the trophies are all going to wash up somewhere random? Like Montana? Or in a beaver dam? It'd be funny if—"

"Are you really gonna leave town with me?"

I stared down at Mandarin. She was smiling. But her eyes weren't.

That night, we had entered the second stage of our friendship. The weeks before barely counted compared to what we'd just shared. It would take much more than a misunderstanding to break us now. But what she was asking . . .

I tried to picture the two of us strolling down some ritzy,

palm-lined West Coast avenue in high heels and enormous sunglasses. Paparazzi. Producers. Crowds of would-be actresses with crunchy hair and dogs in plaid suitcases. Men with chest hair and bracelets.

It would never happen.

So I felt safe making the promise a second time: "Of course."

Mandarin closed her eyes. I lifted my hand to touch her face, but I couldn't bring myself to do it, so my hand just hovered there.

"You must have seen my father," she said. I remembered when she'd called him well-meaning, a good guy deep down. But this time, she didn't say anything to defend him.

"I did."

"I have to get out of here."

I allowed my hand to drop to Mandarin's forehead. It felt cool, as if the night had sucked out all the warmth. I thought about how happy she'd been earlier that night, scampering through the grocery store aisles, drawing faces on the eggs. I could make her that happy. The tricky part was keeping her there.

"I know," I replied.

We could liberate a million trophies. We could fill every river to the brim. But it would never fully substitute for liberating ourselves.

18

like fairy glamour

The liberation had lasted until five-thirty in the morning. As a result, on Friday I was having trouble keeping my eyes open in homeroom. For once, I could sympathize with the boys who fell asleep with their faces in their lettermen's jackets. I wished I had a jacket for smothering snores.

I wasn't the only one out of sorts. Samantha Dent scurried into the classroom after morning announcements, her cheeks ablaze.

"Samantha?" Ms. Ingle inquired.

Like me, Samantha was never late. Before she could explain, Alexis stood up.

"Ms. Ingle, Samantha was *robbed* last night!"

"Not me," she protested softly as she sank into her seat. "The restaurant."

The restaurant? Bleary-eyed, I stared at her as if she were a character from some dream I'd had. And then it struck me: the trophies.

The robbers were us.

For a moment, I had the awful suspicion Mandarin had taken more than the trophies—that maybe she'd slipped some money from the cash register when I wasn't paying attention. I felt relieved when Alexis explained, "Somebody stole a hunting trophy off the walls of the Buffalo Grill. And all the ones from the grocery store."

But then she added, "They're worth, like, thousands and thousands of dollars, aren't they, Samantha?"

Thousands and thousands of dollars?

I had never considered that the trophies might be *worth* something. I'd thought of them more as old belongings, like the flea market rubbish at the junk shop, or my great-grandmother's old dresses and hope chests stashed in the attic of our house. Never as valuable property.

"The cops say it had to be a drifter of some sort," Alexis continued. "Because if it was somebody in town, where'd they put all the heads?"

My relief came back so intensely I felt dizzy. A drifter. They blamed it on a drifter, just like I had hoped.

I glanced at Samantha again, trying my best to keep my face expressionless. Her cheeks were more fiery than before. But then, they turned red whenever a teacher called on her.

"I'm sorry about that, Samantha," Ms. Ingle said. "I know how much your family values those hunting trophies."

Samantha shrugged. "I never liked them anyway."

❋ ❋ ❋

The article didn't come out in the *Washokey Gazette* until the following Monday. Mandarin pounced on me as soon as I set foot on the great lawn.

"I have something to show you. But . . ." She glanced at Taffeta, who was gazing up at her with eyes like crystal balls.

"Taffeta, get out of here," I said.

My sister scowled. "Make me."

"If you don't go stand with the other kids, I swear I'll—"

Mandarin caught my wrist. "Grace, what's your deal?" She squatted in front of Taffeta. "Listen, girly. I'm gonna tell you how to play the best game ever. It's called Red Rover. . . . Do you know it?"

Taffeta shook her head.

"I swear, it'll make you the most popular kid in school."

I waited as Mandarin explained the rules of the game with more patience than I'd ever shown my sister. When she finished, Taffeta went skipping off to the other kids. I watched her go, feeling vaguely mystified.

"Remember to use your elbows," Mandarin called.

Then she tugged me behind a cottonwood tree. From her pocket, she withdrew a crumpled piece of newsprint. "Look," she said, jabbing with her finger.

Hunting Trophies Stolen from Local Businesses
by Bill S. Moulton, Staff Writer
On Thursday night, all the hunting trophies were deviously stolen from the Buffalo Grill and the

Washokey Supermarket, both located on Main
Street. No other belongings were taken from either
business. The shockingly deplorable crime, un-
precedented in town, has been attributed to a
drifter, probably somebody who swiftly left the
state. . . .

"They called it 'shockingly deplorable,'" Mandarin said
with a grin. "Those idiot cops haven't got a clue. It's probably the most action they've gotten in years. Maybe they'll
pay a little more attention now. Hey! Looks like we've done
our service to the community!"

I handed the article back to Mandarin, smiling weakly.
"I'm sure they're overjoyed," I said. "But . . . seriously, have
you thought of a service project yet?"

Laughing, Mandarin threw her arm around me and
hauled me toward school.

❋   ❋   ❋

On Saturday, the administration opened the school pool
to the public for the first time since September.

The pool was just three years old, still exciting to our
town. The school had built it in hopes of training a
Washokey High swim team. Because no one wanted the
swimmers to tunnel through ice floes in the winter, the
school began construction of a gym around the pool. They
built the skeleton of one side before they determined they
didn't have enough money to complete it. So instead of

putting the remaining money toward something useful, they finished the solitary wall.

It was a nice wall, as far as walls go, made of textured gray cement with a big window. In the afternoon it cast a shadow, where people crammed their towels.

That day everybody crowded outside the chain-link fence, waiting for the pool to open at ten. It seemed like half the town had turned up. As usual, my family was kind of weird-looking. Momma wore a flowered poncho over her yellow one-piece. It made her look like a lamp shade with legs. Taffeta's arm floaties were so big she had to hold her arms out almost horizontally. I wore one of Momma's straw hats and sunglasses, as if that would disguise the dread I felt.

The pool was such a comedown. A crash landing. But compared to the past week, anything would have been.

In geometry, Mandarin passed me notes, tantalizing with curse words and caricatures of other students. When I opened them under my desk, I always made sure somebody was watching—other than Mrs. Cleary, who was too frazzled to notice anyway.

Mandarin waited for me after my English class, and we left for the cafeteria together. The days had grown warmer, and I'd traded my hooded sweaters and tees for men's undershirts like the ones Mandarin wore. Much better than my strappy pajama top. For the first time, I felt almost *sexy* as I navigated the halls at her side. But in a careless way, the best way, unlike the other girls, with their short skirts and wedge heels. When I caught them watching us, I felt intoxicated by their envy.

Navigating the pool crowd was the complete opposite, especially with Mandarin replaced by Momma and Taffeta in their goofy apparel. Worse, we hadn't been standing there long when Davey Miller came up and stood beside me.

"Hello, Grace," he said. He wore too-short blue swim trunks and had about twelve curly hairs in the center of his pale chest. I recalled how strange he'd acted during our science project. Maybe I was less intimidating standing beside my family.

"Hey. Sorry, I'm kind of busy." I scanned the crowd, as if searching for somebody. "What is it, Davey?"

"Um. Well. I was wondering . . ." His Adam's apple wobbled like a horsefly caught in his neck. "The cowboy dance. What do you . . . Do you think—"

I cut him off before he could say anything more. "It's such an idiotic theme, isn't it? I'm not going, that's for sure."

"Oh," he said.

"As if our town isn't one gigantic cowboy dance already."

He cleared his throat, and the horsefly jumped. "Yeah. I guess it *is* kind of dumb."

"Right," I said. "It is."

Davey finally got the hint. He rejoined his family as Kate Cunningham and Tyler Worley swung open the gate. Kate and Tyler were this year's lifeguards, along with Joshua Mickelson. Each year, Mr. Beck hired three seniors for the job, which was coveted by anybody with a passable physique. Lifeguards possessed a kind of seductive authority; we tended to forget they had to do things like clean the pool before they filled it with water. The snowmelt always uncovered a constellation of beer cans. And dead ground squirrels.

Everybody filed in like orderly first graders. As soon as Momma and I set down our stuff in an empty spot, Taffeta bounced up again, tugging at my hands.

"Can we go in the water now?" she begged. "Please oh please?"

I shook my head. "I'm not going in."

"I won't splash your face this time. I promise."

There was absolutely no way I was going to wedge myself into the mass of townspeople crowding the pool. "Momma will take you."

We both glanced at Momma. She was having trouble un-buttoning her poncho. She'd scrunched it up over her shoulders, like one of those ruffled collars from the nineteenth century.

Taffeta looked back at me, her eyes wide.

"I thought I saw Polly Bunker over there," Momma said, emerging at last. "Can't you take her in the water while I go say hello?"

"I'm feeling a little crampy," I lied, clutching my middle. She sighed. "Watch our stuff, then."

Alone at last, I leaned back on my elbows, the way I thought Mandarin might in a bathing suit—not that I'd ever seen her in a bathing suit. She wasn't exactly the type to bob in the water alongside the grandmothers. Posing like her was getting easier, though. As long as I refrained from looking down at my body, because then I'd blush and want to sit up and the whole impression would be spoiled.

In the pool, kids screeched and splashed among old ladies with baked-potato skin. Kate Cunningham sat in the lifeguard tower with her arms crossed strategically under her chest, trying to manufacture cleavage in her one-piece life-guard suit. Tyler Worley was perched at the deep end, ignoring Brandi Shelmerdine and her friends, who were obviously cavorting for his benefit.

Nobody even glanced at me. As if without Mandarin, they found me uninteresting.

I should work on being interesting on my own.

After half an hour or so, Momma returned without Taffeta. Her suit was wet up to her belly button. She sat beside me with her legs bent off to the side, like an old-fashioned pinup model. Thank goodness she didn't try to put on her poncho.

"Where's Taffeta?" I asked.

"With Miriam. Her brother said he'd look after them for a bit."

"He did?" I rose to my knees and peered through the masses of winter-bleached limbs. There in the pool bobbed Davey Miller with one arm around Taffeta and the other around Miriam. He caught my eye. "Grace!" he called.

I sat back down.

"Did someone just call your name?" Momma asked.

I shook my head, willing Davey to stay in the pool.

Momma opened a Ziploc bag of oatmeal cookies and handed me one. I concentrated on plucking out the raisins, collecting them in a little pile on my stomach.

"So how's school?"

I glanced up at Momma, startled. It was as if she'd spoken Japanese. "What do you mean?" I asked warily.

"What do you mean, what do I mean? It's a simple question."

"I don't know. . . . It's fine, I guess."

"Anything new at all? With you and your friend?"

Like I'd ever tell you. "Not really."

"Well, I've got some news for you."

I braced myself for pageant gossip.

"So Polly Bunker was talking to Della Bader's niece, Sheryl—you know, the one who dropped out of school in the eighth grade—and you'll never guess who she ran into at the Fremont County flea market."

"I have no idea."

"You'll *never* guess. She was looking in the old clocks section, searching for one of those vintage ones, the hickory-dickory-dock ones. Anyway . . . She found one she liked, and she went up to the lady running the booth. You'll never guess who it was."

"I give up, Momma. Who was it already?"

She paused for emphasis. "Mandarin Ramey's mother!"

I sat upright, spilling my raisins. "That's impossible."

"It was her, all right. Sheryl went to school with her down in Cheyenne before she came to Washokey. Kim Ramey. Or actually, I don't know if she ever married Mandarin's dad. I heard Kim was short for another name, maybe an Indian name. She's fifty percent Shoshone, did you know?"

I began to have cramps for real. "She's dead, Momma."

"Dead? No, of course she's not, Grace. Sheryl even spoke to her—"

"She's dead!" I exclaimed. "She killed herself, and Mandarin told me how. All right? It must have been some other woman. Someone who looked like her. But Mandarin's mother's dead. That's what Mandarin said, and she wouldn't lie to me."

Even as I said it, I didn't believe it. I wasn't sure what my expression looked like, but Momma must have assumed it was still directed at her. She dropped her gaze and began to rifle through her beach bag.

"It must have been a mistake," she said. She pulled a crumpled dollar out of her bag. "How 'bout you run along and locate that Mexican who sells ice cream?"

I snatched the bill and stumbled away. Just outside the gate, the ice cream man stood behind a freezer cart with sponge paintings of triple cones on the side. Numbly, I picked out a mixed-berry Popsicle.

When I turned, I was face to face with Alexis & Co.

Alexis was flanked by Samantha and Paige. They all wore bikinis. Alexis's breasts poured over a too-small top. She didn't have to cross her arms to boost them. Paige's lima bean tummy stuck out over her bathing suit bottoms. Samantha held a can of diet soda pop. All four of us recoiled, startled speechless.

Alexis was the first to recover. "Slut," she hissed.

The three of them veered around me in a flood of giggles, leaving me like a drowned ground squirrel in their wake.

The edge of the desk bit into my shins. The light of the computer monitor burned my eyes in the dark room. But even though I'd memorized it by now, even though I'd

known already and refused to believe, I couldn't stop squinting at the map proving Riverton was in Fremont County.

Riverton, WY 82501.

Proving Mandarin's mother was alive.

She worked at the Riverton flea market. She'd married
somebody named Paisley. Or maybe she'd been a Paisley all
along. She was sending Mandarin arrowheads. All the gruesome details of her suicide—the dishrags, the pills, the duct
tape . . . Mandarin had made them up.

And she didn't want me to know.

Finally, I switched off my computer and crawled into bed,
pulling the sheet over my ear. I felt more baffled than anything. Because *why lie? Why?* I couldn't begin to fathom
Mandarin's reasons. But I knew better than to ask. I wasn't
willing to risk another fight. Our friendship had barely sur-
vived the last.

Although, I couldn't help wondering: if Mandarin had
lied about something so momentous, what else might she lie
to me about?

In the days that passed, I didn't tell Mandarin what
Alexis had called me. I didn't know how to feel about it. It
made me wonder whether everybody thought of me as
Mandarin's protégé—her fuckup-in-training; a project, like
the community service she kept putting off along with any
conversation about our so-called escape—or whether they
believed I was actually like Mandarin.

I kept hoping some of her had rubbed off on me, literally. Maybe some cells from her fingertips when they grazed my arm, or from the neckline of the sweaters she let me borrow on windy evenings. Or after she borrowed my hairbrush, maybe her stray hairs interlaced with mine. I wanted to ask her to be my blood sister, like back in elementary school, and sense the exact moment when her blood began to flow into my veins.

I knew she'd think I was crazy if I asked. Though some days I almost convinced myself that it was happening on its own—Mandarin's spirit draping over me, like fairy glamour.

But all too soon, I remembered that appearances were one thing. I might walk the walk, but when it came down to what I believed made Mandarin *Mandarin*, I hadn't even begun to catch up.

Mercifully, she never called me out. We never talked about sex at all. It was as if Mandarin believed it irrelevant to our friendship.

And maybe it was. But as long as it was one of the factors that defined her, I knew I had to have it.

I just had no idea where to begin. When I thought back, I realized I'd never had much of a crush on anybody. Objectively, sometimes I saw what the other girls squealed about. Tag Leeland had nice arms, but his neck seemed too big, like a boa constrictor swallowing his head. I liked Mitchell Warren's melty brown eyes, but his skin disgusted me—at sixteen, he had the sun-worn, freckled hide of a fifty-year-old rancher. Not to mention the way he acted in the cafeteria, flinging Cool Ranch Doritos at people like ninja stars.

Even if I'd found somebody to fall for, it wouldn't have

mattered. None of the guys paid any attention to me. Except for Davey Miller, and he didn't really count. As far as I could tell, I possessed none of Mandarin's power—whatever it was that drew guys to her, made their eyes unpeel, their mouths hang open in that particular way.

Until one day at lunch, when I did.

19

stones in my pocket

I stood in the cafeteria line, waiting for the girl in front of me to select a cube of sponge cake. I'd informed Momma that I wanted to buy my lunch from now on. She was so harried with pageant prep, I thought she'd be relieved, but instead she seemed offended. I didn't get it. It wasn't like I'd directly insulted the lunches she packed.

By the time I got to the fruit basket, there were no bananas left, just green and red apples. As I reached out to grab one, my shirt crept up. It was shorter than usual; maybe it had shrunk in the wash. I instantly became aware of the two senior boys beside me, their attention angled in my direction like a sunbeam through a magnifying glass.

I almost jerked my arm back. But that wasn't what Mandarin would have done. It was about being conscious without being *self*-conscious. So I let my hem slide up just a little farther before I grabbed the apple and thumped it onto my tray.

One of the boys cleared his throat. I allowed myself a quick glance over. He closed the gap between us and stuck out his hand.

"I'm Joshua," he said.

Of course I recognized him: Joshua Mickelson, the lifeguard. He was compact, with curly blond hair and a nose that looked broken in sixteen places. Beside him stood Tyler Worley, the brown-haired lifeguard beloved by Brandi Shelmerdine and her friends. He leaned across Joshua and jutted his own hand in front of Joshua's.

"And I'm Tyler."

I tucked my bangs behind my ears and smiled slightly, then slid my tray down the line without shaking either hand.

"Yeah, it's nice to meet you, too," Joshua said.

"Are you new?" Tyler asked. "From another town, maybe?"

"A far-off place? A better planet?"

"I've been around," I said.

I paid the cashier and turned to face the cafeteria crowd. The boys kept close behind me. Their attention seemed competitive, almost aggressive. Or maybe I'd just never been hit on.

"I find that hard to believe," Tyler said.

"Yeah, we've been living in this stinkhole all our lives," Joshua added. "We'd know if a girl like you popped up. You must be lying."

"You must be new."

"Or," I said smugly, spotting Mandarin a few yards away, "you must not be looking in the right places."

Then I sauntered off, leaving the boys to witness our re-union. I still felt the heat of their stares, all that searing male attention focused on me and Mandarin as she put her arm around my waist and led me from the cafeteria.

The constant surveillance still excited me, but it seemed to exhaust Mandarin. To combat it, we located places all over town to hide from prying eyes.

We scaled the pipes behind Solomon's and reigned over Washokey's streets and alleyways from the rooftop. We climbed chain-link fences and the cottonwood trees that dropped over the canal. We found a sheep farm a quarter mile out of town, and we snuck into the stables when no one was around and cuddled the spring lambs. We even peed to-gether at the side of the road with cars going by, laughing so hard we both got hiccups.

We never went to our houses. I didn't want to deal with Momma, and ever since the fight Mandarin and I'd had at her house, we didn't go there, either.

But it didn't matter. We had our best conversations strolling through town, exchanging questions we both had to answer.

What would you be if you could be anything at all?

I wanted to be an explorer in the name of science, like Charles Darwin, while she wanted to be an actress in a Broadway show, even though she couldn't sing.

What's the most embarrassing thing that has ever happened to you?

I told her about my lopsided graduation dress, while she swore she'd never been embarrassed in her entire life.

Now and then when we played our games, I suspected that Mandarin was testing me.

"If you could go anywhere in the world, where would it be?" she asked one evening as we lay on our backs on the school lawn. The sprinklers arched over us perfectly, so we stayed dry.

I thought about it. "That's tough."

"Not California?"

"Oh, definitely!" I said. "I was thinking of islands and, like, ultra-exotic places—Antarctica, Brazil. But in reality, it'd have to be California."

"I hope so."

"Besides, the Amazon rain forest is in Brazil, and it's got spiders as big as dinner plates. And I read Antarctica is colder than anywhere on earth—the lowest temperature ever recorded there was negative one twenty-nine."

"I call bullshit," Mandarin said. "Coldest temperature ever's got to be Washokey Januarys."

Another time, as we sat side by side on plastic chairs outside the Sundrop Quik Stop, Mandarin asked, "So where do you want to go to college, Gracey?"

That time, my answer seemed to please her: "Out west. Doesn't matter where."

We both had cups of strawberry ice cream from the deli, and as I watched her eat, I wondered. If we left Washokey, what did she expect me to do—sign up for eleventh grade in some unfamiliar city? Had she even considered it? I didn't want to ask her, though. Like everything else, it could be put off until later.

But time was running out. That was what Mr. Beck had said when he'd called our house to remind me to send in my conference paperwork. Thank goodness I caught the phone before Momma answered. I still hadn't told her about my win.

With Mandarin, our question games worked because I knew when to keep quiet. I didn't bring up her father, or her schoolwork, or her men—though I was *dying* to find out more.

I also knew what not to tell her.

I never told her about Sheryl Bader's alleged sighting of her mother at the Fremont County flea market, or the envelope I'd found with the telling blue letters of its return address, the angular object inside. I didn't know how she'd react. So I kept my secrets bundled up like stones in my pocket, ones I still needed to decipher.

The day before my fifteenth birthday, Momma caught me as I was leaving for the Tombs. Mandarin was working that afternoon, and I feared being forced into child care while Momma shopped for pageant provisions at the junk shop. Unexpectedly, she wanted to bring me with her.

"I'd like your opinion," she said.

I must have looked baffled. Momma rarely admitted I had something she wanted, particularly an opinion. I suspected it had to do with my birthday. Most years she offered me swatches to flip through, corresponding to Femme Fatale makeup colors.

"I need to pick out some fabric for a new dress for Taffeta," she explained.

"What's the matter with the one you just made?"

"Nothing's the matter. I'd like to have a spare on hand, is all. Just in case. White's a popular shade. Plus, you never know if one of the other girls'll show up in a similar style."

"Why don't you go with Polly Bunker? She always has an opinion."

Momma was silent a moment.

"Polly Bunker talks too much," she said.

I stared at her. What did she mean? Did Polly Bunker talk to her about Mandarin and me? Was Momma *defending* me? I wanted to ask. But then I imagined the direction that conversation might head—especially if I was wrong—so I kept my mouth shut.

We dropped Taffeta off at the Millers', a two-story yellow house with a wraparound balcony that overlooked nothing inspiring. Miriam Miller was one of the few little kids in town who didn't participate in the Little Miss Washokey pageants. Sometimes I wondered if that was why Taffeta liked her so much.

The junk shop wasn't really called the Junk Shop. Its official name was Nelly's Bargain Boutique, even though Nelly Drummely had been dead ten years. It was now managed by Nelly's daughter Tracy, the person responsible for the store's current state of disarray. Tracy's sole marketing effort was her rotation of unique items in the windows: a Lite-Brite set, a bearded African mask, a wedding dress with a nine-foot lace train. The interior of the store was a hoarder's paradise. Momma was an expert at navigating the chaos. She had engineered most of Taffeta's pageant dresses from junk shop fabric, chopping and stitching together scarves and 1980s prom dresses with embellishments ordered online.

While Momma pondered the racks of clothing, I headed for the plastic bins. They overflowed with rubbish. Old stuffed animals—the plush kind, fortunately. Western novels with laminated covers. Superfluous kitchen gadgets, like bagel slicers and lime squeezers and plastic molds to squish butter into the shapes of pigs and turkeys. I never reached too deep, in fear of discovering a dead cockroach—or worse, a live one.

I found the rock tumbler in bin number two. The front of the box featured a pair of grinning children cupping handfuls of artificially glossy examples.

I had mixed feelings about rock tumblers. They smoothed out all the character of rocks, all the history, the genuine erosion. Still, I liked the idea of uncovering the potential of the stones in my collection—all their inner beauty revealed.

It didn't matter, because I had no money other than the hundred-dollar savings bond from my essay contest win. Another thing shoved into the bottom of my tote bag.

"Grace, could you come here?" Momma called.

I set down the box and followed her voice around the corner. Momma held up a lilac prom dress so narrow it resembled a single leg of tights. It had puffy sleeves like baby tutus, and a hem so short I couldn't imagine anyone wearing it without all her improper places exposed.

"What do you think of this?"

I hesitated. I didn't see how she could be serious; yet Momma seldom joked with me. "It's . . ." I paused. "I dare you to try it on."

Momma blinked at me for a second. Then, slowly, she began to smile.

"Not on your life, missus." She held it out at arm's length. "But don't you have a dance coming up? There's always a dance in the spring, isn't there? Maybe you want to try it on."

I giggled. "No way."

The jingle bell on the front door rang. We both turned to look.

Mandarin stood in the doorway, wearing a men's white undershirt and a cocktail apron over her lowest-slung jeans. "Well, hey there," she said. "I noticed the two of you in the window."

Momma raised her eyebrows at me. I glanced from face to face, knowing I had to make the introduction I'd dreaded.

"Momma, this is . . . Mandarin Ramey."

"Oh, yes," Momma said. "Of course."

"Nice to meet you finally!" Mandarin turned to me. "I'm on break. An extended break. How about we grab dinner? There ain't enough pervy drunks yet for my dad to need me, not until dark."

Pervy drunks? Was she *trying* to get me in trouble? "One second," I told Momma. Then I walked into Mandarin, pushing against her, forcing her to back up around the corner.

"What are you *doing?*" I whispered once we were out of sight. "You can't talk about drunks in front of my mother. She'll forbid us from hanging out, ever. She'll—"

Laughing, Mandarin shook me by the shoulders. "Snap out of it! I can deal with adults. Just you watch."

To my horror, she shoved past me and called, "Ms. Carpenter?"

"Yes?" Momma said.

"That's a lovely color dress you got there."

Momma glanced down at the lilac monstrosity still draped over her arm.

"Grace told me about her birthday supper tomorrow," Mandarin went on. "And I thought I'd be working, but I was fortunate enough to get my shift covered. I'd love to join you, if the invitation still stands."

I gripped the edge of a plastic bin to keep from visibly cringing.

Because the thing was, Momma hadn't specifically invited *Mandarin* to dinner. She'd said I could invite my friends—which undoubtedly meant Alexis. But to my surprise, she appeared interested. I could see menus, outfits, decorations flickering before her eyes. A guest was a guest, I supposed. Even a girl with no future but trouble, in Momma's own words.

"Why not?" she replied. I wanted to groan: the British accent was back. "We live at 17 Pioneer Ridge, up on the hill. How does six o'clock sound?"

Mandarin nodded, half smiling.

"So dinner tomorrow," I said, my skin still crawling. "All

of us together. Great. But I'm going off now with Mandarin, all right? Don't save dinner. We'll get something at the A&W, or whatever."

Momma shrugged. "That's fine."

She busied herself hanging up the purple dress, smoothing it out, puffing the outrageous sleeves, as if anybody cared.

20

the biggest event of the year

"I'll get it!" I screamed, but Momma reached the front door ahead of me. All day she'd been on edge, zipping around like a crazed hornet, perching on chairs and popping up as if they were strewn with nails. Only the concept of a brand-new audience for her affectations could override pageant prep.

She flung open the door, her ankles crossed as if she were about to curtsy. "Welcome!" she exclaimed before both our mouths fell open.

Mandarin wore a white blouse with ruffled sleeves, tucked into a pleated khaki skirt. Neither fit quite right on her angular frame. A white gash of scalp showed through the part of her hair, which she'd tethered in matching pageant-perfect braids. Her black shoes had two-inch heels. She wore *nylons*.

Since the previous afternoon at the junk shop, I had come to accept the freakish clashing of personalities my birthday dinner would bring. I'd even started to anticipate it. Finally, a chance to spite Momma, or at least to get her attention.

But this wasn't the Mandarin I'd meant to bring home.

Just when I was about to do something rash—laugh or shout, I didn't know what—Mandarin stole a glance my way.

This is just a game I'm playing, her expression read. *It's still me in here.*

Still, I felt only slightly placated as she turned to Momma and smiled demurely. "It's so nice to finally have a proper meeting with you, Adrina."

"Of course," Momma said after faltering for a moment at her first name. "I've been wanting to meet you, too."

"Is that right?"

Momma cupped a hand around her mouth and lowered her voice conspiratorially. "You're famous round these parts!"

I swallowed hard, attempting to keep my soul from fleeing out my throat in humiliation.

"Only joking!" Momma said, her British accent stronger by the second. "I've made us a delightful supper. Alaskan salmon, shipped all the way from the North Pacific. Baked in wasabi cream sauce. Bet you've never had authentic Alaskan salmon before."

"You bet right."

"The trick with salmon is baking it as little as possible," Momma said, winding her arm through Mandarin's. "Chewy salmon is the worst. But if you don't cook it enough, you might possibly give everybody parasites. . . ."

She led Mandarin around the corner toward the kitchen, leaving me alone in the entryway. I stood there a second, feeling as if I had missed something. Then I shut the door. On second thought, I twisted the dead bolt, to keep out any other disturbing imposters.

But apparently I'd trapped another one inside, as I discovered when Taffeta came sashaying down the stairs in jeans and one of her little-girl undershirts.

"Taffeta! Why in the world are you walking like that?"

She stopped in the middle of the stairs with one hand on her hip. "It's my new pageant walk."

"You look ridiculous. And if you don't change out of those jeans, Momma'll kick your butt halfway to Nebraska."

"But you've got jeans on too!"

"Taffeta," I said warningly.

She stuck out her tongue and charged back up the stairs.

In the kitchen, Mandarin and my mother were engaged in intense conversation.

"I mean, Alaska, Paris, Rome . . . ," Momma said. "All those places, I know I'll get there someday. But I haven't been in any sort of a hurry."

Mandarin seemed to be avoiding my eyes. In fact, she appeared fascinated with Momma's words, flicking the end of one braid like a paintbrush.

"And Washokey's such a magnificent place to raise the children, after all," Momma said. "Such a fabulous school. No robberies or muggings. That's why I settled here in the first place. I spent some time in Jackson Hole when I was your age, but it only took a few months away before I realized I had to come back."

"Washokey doesn't bore you?" Mandarin asked.

Momma answered a little too quickly. "No! Of course not." She shrugged. "Everything I need is right here. I grew up in these hills, and they've got meaning for me, they really do. A little vacation every once in a while would be nice, but . . ."

"Aren't you going to Washington, D.C., with Grace this summer?"

I stared at Mandarin in horror.

"Washington, D.C.?" Momma said. "What's that got to do with anything?"

"You mean Grace hasn't told you about the leadership conference?" Mandarin said before I could speak. "They found out that idiot kid Peter copied his essay, and Gracey here's the real winner."

Momma placed a hand on my shoulder. "Is this the truth, Grace? Why didn't you tell me you won?"

I shook my head. "I don't know. I just—"

"Grace was just telling me how lonely she thought she'd be, traveling by herself," Mandarin interrupted. "Wouldn't it be better if all of you went together?"

What was she *doing*?

I knew Washington wasn't part of Mandarin's plans for us. But just the thought of my mother and sister tagging along—Taffeta's brattiness, Momma's incessant prattling, like mistuned radios spoiling all the sounds and sights—was too much for me to handle. I wanted to double over. "But it's a conference, Momma," I protested. "I'll be in classes. I'll hardly have any free time. I don't think—"

"Grace doesn't tell me anything," Momma said to Mandarin, as if I weren't even there. "She'd have had a terrible time and I'd never have known. Washington, D.C., with my girls! It'll be perfect. And a perfect dress rehearsal to get us ready for our trip to California."

I saw Mandarin's grin freeze on her face. "California?"

"If Taffeta wins the state pageant in a month—or rather, *when* she wins—after she wins the tri-county, that's where the nationals are held."

"The beauty pageant nationals," Mandarin clarified.

Momma nodded. "I've forever wanted to go there. Some people call Jackson Hole—that's where I used to live—they call it California East, did you know that?"

I was still stuck on the nightmarish notion of Momma and Taffeta joining me in Washington. "Momma, you know the conference is three whole weeks long," I said. "What about work?"

"Are you kidding?" Momma turned from me to Mandarin. "The nice thing about my line of work—selling makeup products for Femme Fatale Cosmetics, Inc.—is that I get to make my own hours. I'm my own boss. So I get lots of free time. Usually June is my busiest month because of sweepstakes, but now they're doing it twice per year, and so it's no problem if I take some time off, especially for my brilliant daughters."

Momma reached out for my shoulder again, but I leaned down just in time, pretending to adjust my shoe.

"You know what, Mandarin?" she said. "Maybe you should look into cosmetics sales yourself. You've certainly got

the looks it requires. Beauty is everything, I'm telling you.
No one wants to buy lipsticks from a wrinkled old lady. Now,
I'll be right back. I have to use the powder room."

As Momma danced out of the kitchen, I turned to glare
at Mandarin.

"It ain't my fault you didn't tell your mom you won," she
whispered. "And anyways, can't you take a joke? Stop looking at me like that."

❋   ❋   ❋

An hour later, we sat around the dinner table, which was
cluttered with the remains of our feast: plates mucky with
pink slivers of salmon flesh and silvery skin, balled-up nap-
kins, empty glasses stained with cranberry juice. Taffeta
hadn't taken her eyes off Mandarin throughout the entire
meal. Mandarin sat across from me, leaning back in her chair
while Momma lit the candles on my cake. As with everything she cooked or baked, the cake was elaborate—three
layers, the top one leaning slightly to the left.

"Shall we sing 'Happy Birthday'?" she asked.

After a short pause, all three began to sing. Mandarin
sang low and deadpan, while Momma sang high-pitched and
off key. Taffeta's miraculous voice was buried by the incom-
patible tones of the other two.

"Now!" Momma exclaimed when they'd finished. "How
about a solo from Taffeta?"

When my sister finished her encore, there was a long
silence. I tapped Mandarin's toe with mine. She should have
known to compliment Taffeta's voice. Wasn't it obvious?

But she didn't, and the silence stretched on until Momma broke it.

"So, Mandarin," she said. "What did your own mother do for your birthdays?"

I wanted to kick Momma under the table. It was as if dinner had been going too well, and she thought the universe needed upsetting. Taffeta, a veteran of dinnertime tension, slipped halfway below the table so only her big eyes rolled about.

Mandarin stared at my mother straight on. "Nothing much at all," she said. "We hardly had the chance."

"Oh no," Momma said, feigning sudden enlightenment. "Oh dear! That's so unforgivably clumsy of me. I entirely forgot. It's rotten when a mother stays away like that, a dreadful shame . . ."

"It doesn't matter," Mandarin said. "She's dead."

"Is that so? Because—"

"Just stop it, Momma!" I cried. "It isn't any different than my dad, okay?" I looked at Mandarin. "I never even *met* my dad."

As if I had started it all, Momma thrust her chair away from the table and stood. "Grace! You will not talk about that man under this roof, in this kitchen, over this supper I laid out with love on your birthday. Understood?"

I glared at her.

"Now, how about some ice cream?" She twirled toward the freezer like a ballerina, her too-short cocktail dress flipping out around her thighs.

I glanced back at Mandarin. *I'm sorry. I'm so sorry,* I mouthed.

She shrugged.

As soon as we'd finished our excruciatingly silent dessert, I pushed back my chair and stood. "Where are you running off to so fast?" Momma asked.

I looked at Mandarin for help.

"Didn't you know?" she asked, beaming grotesquely. "Tonight's the cowboy dance. It's the biggest event of the year!"

An attack of laughter threatened to overcome me. I didn't trust my voice, so I nodded.

"The dance is tonight? Grace, honey, you can't wear those awful jeans. If you like, you can pick an outfit from my closet. How about that spotted teal dress with the belt?"

"Um, we're stopping by Mandarin's first. I'll just borrow a dress from her."

"Wait! You can't leave without your gift."

Momma pulled a box from under her chair. It was wrapped in pink tissue paper, the same kind she used to wrap my sandwiches. "I found it at Nelly's Bargain Boutique after you left," she said, sliding the package to me. "I couldn't believe I found it. It's *perfect* for you."

It had to be the rock tumbler. What else could it be?

I felt a sweeping rush of affection for Momma, a sensation so new it was almost debilitating. I used a bread knife to split the Scotch tape, aware of Momma's affinity for reusing wrapping paper. When I uncovered a shoe box instead of the rock tumbler package, my heart sank.

I lifted the lid and found a camera. Not a digital camera or a video camera. But the decades-old, film-only kind, as big as a brick and half as heavy. She'd also included a few rolls of film in black canisters.

"What do you think?" Momma asked. "I used a film camera for all your old pageant photos, you know."

I picked up the camera and touched the lens, the shutter release, the focusing rings, notched with tiny numbers. The attached leather strap smelled faintly of sun-warmed bomber jackets, of cowboy boots and rodeos. I unsnapped the lens cover and peered the wrong way, as if the camera were a gun aimed at my head. My reflection, tiny and distorted, peered back.

21

empty space

As Mandarin and I snuck onto the football field, nearly two hundred teenagers climbed the stairs of our school on their way to the cowboy dance.

They wore their cowboy best, or so I imagined: Stetson hats and pointy boots with heels, fringe and chaps, denim and leather, accessorized with spurs and lassos. The girls curled their hair in beauty pageant ringlets or bound them in double cowgirl braids, like Mandarin's. The boys sprayed themselves with their fathers' Cattleman Cologne—*a real scorpion in every bottle!* They passed through the double doors adorned with balloons and barbed wire, and filtered into the cafeteria decorated with bales of hay and cardboard steers.

That was how I pictured it, at least.

Mandarin and I could hear the wind-strewn music as we

squeezed through a gap in the chain-link fence. We clanged up the empty metal bleachers and chose seats at the top. Mandarin was barefoot and bare-legged, having left her nylons in a ball on my bedroom floor. She'd traded her skirt for a pair of my gym shorts, with her frilly blouse half buttoned. The sky was streaked with clouds that glowed around the edges, as if somebody held a flashlight behind them. I could barely make out the visitors' bleachers on the other side.

"I've never been here when there wasn't a game going on," I said.

My words reverberated off the bleachers, distorted and metallic-sounding. I shivered and lowered my voice before continuing.

"I think it's crazy how involved everybody gets. Especially since we play the same two teams over and over, and the winners and losers never change. I'll bet the wild animals within a twenty-mile radius bolt as soon as the floodlights come on."

I waited for Mandarin to smile, but she didn't seem to be listening.

"It's not like I've been to many games, anyway," I continued. *Three.* I'd been to three football games in my entire life. "My mother hates the noise. And . . . I never liked going with my old friends."

"I love it when no one's here," Mandarin said.

I glanced at her, but she wasn't looking at me.

"When everything's quiet," she continued. "Heavy and still. It feels like . . . like I'm disconnected. Like I'm suspended underwater. Nothing there but me."

She extended her arms, palms down, and closed her eyes, like when she'd floated on her back in the canal.

"Sometimes I feel that way even when there's lots of people around. In the halls at school. Or at the bar, real late. Like I'm just an empty space moving through the crowds. Like I'm not really there at all."

When she opened her eyes, they had a faraway cast, as if they'd lost the ability to focus. They made me think of the eyes of the elk head trophy, drifting through the tunnel of river trees. My breath caught in my throat. Before I knew it, I'd reached over and placed my hand over hers.

Mandarin glanced at my hand as if she'd forgotten I was there.

"Y'know, your mom's a riot," she said. I drew back my hand and tucked it between my knees. "Does she really make her money selling that fatal female crap?"

"Not all of it. There's an inheritance from my grandparents. And my father."

"Your *father*," she repeated, drawing out the word. "Who was he?"

"Some cop. When she was eighteen, she ran off to Jackson Hole after her parents died. She stayed with her father's brother."

Mandarin pulled the rubber bands from her pigtails and shot them into the dark, then began unwinding her braids.

"I guess he, like, felt her up a couple times," I went on. "I don't know the details. But after that, she moved back home to Washokey. A cop drove her most of the way in a police car. Did more than drove, apparently. Their fling didn't last much longer than the car ride, though. My mother didn't know she was pregnant until he was long gone."

Talking to Mandarin came easy now. It was hard to

believe I'd ever been too intimidated to do anything more than observe from afar.

"So did your mom track him down?"

I shrugged. "I think she was embarrassed. She didn't want to make a bigger deal out of it than it already was. He never wrote or called. But I guess he knew about me, because years later, she got this letter from a lawyer with a check from his insurance. He got shot. Not while on the job. While hunting." I paused. "Taffeta's dad only lived with us for a year before he split. Fathers are unnecessary anyway, my mother says."

"Damn straight." Mandarin withdrew a cigarette from the pocket of her blouse and lit it. "The biggest mistake women make is falling for men. They're worthless. They're worse than worthless."

"Then why do you . . ." I stopped.

Mandarin raised her eyebrows. I was afraid she was going to get angry, like she had when I'd broached the same topic at the A&W. But our friendship was a million times stronger now. And I was *dying* to know.

To my relief, one corner of her mouth turned up in a half smile.

"Go on. You can ask me anything, y'know. I just don't guarantee an answer."

"Why do you . . ." I paused again, trying to think of the best way to say it. "Why do you have . . . Why do you sleep with so many of them?"

"Come on, Gracey. Isn't it obvious? Or maybe you're just too young to understand."

I wanted to object, but I thought it might make me seem even younger.

Mandarin took a long drag on her cigarette. "There's just something so . . . ," she said, "I don't know . . . so *exhilarating* about making another person's whole body respond. All their attention's focused on you. Like in that moment, you are the most important person in the world."

"The most important person in the world," I repeated slowly.

Mandarin glanced at me. "To that one guy, at least. But I do it for me. Not for them. I hate how people insist a girl's giving part of herself away when she sleeps with somebody. While men are gaining something. Why can't it be the other way around?"

"What about what everybody says about you?"

"Who's everybody? All the stupid hicks in Washokey?"

I shrugged.

"Look—it doesn't matter to me what everybody thinks. You know that. But if I quit sleeping around, everybody'd think it *did* matter. See?"

"Kind of."

"But it doesn't," Mandarin said, as if she still felt the need to convince me. Or maybe even herself.

"So it's not because of . . ."

"Just say it."

Far off, a balloon cracked against the barbed wire decorations. "Not because of . . . what your father did to you?" I asked.

"That's what they all think, ain't it? Nobody'd ever

believe it, but my dad never laid a hand on me. I mean, he hit me and all, but no more than normal. He's been useless as a father, maybe. Even useless as a human being. But he never did anything like . . . y'know. Nothing like that."

We sat there in silence for a while, listening to what sounded like cheers coming from the direction of the cafeteria. Mandarin drummed her fingers on the bleacher seat. Then, suddenly, she grinned.

"Hey! Know what? I still haven't given you your birthday present."

She stood. A wind shuddered the bleachers, as if Mandarin's body had been the only thing keeping them still. She dropped the end of her cigarette and mashed it out with her bare foot. Then she reached into her cigarette pack and withdrew a small package of folded newspaper, taped many times.

"I didn't wrap it all pretty, like your mom did. And don't expect much. It ain't big. Or expensive. But—here." She handed it to me.

I pried open the wad of newspaper. An arrowhead fell into my hand. Not just any arrowhead, but the one I'd admired the most from her collection. Tiger skin obsidian. The moonlight gave it an unearthly glow. Before I could get a good look, Mandarin wrapped her hand around mine, folding my fingers over it.

"I thought you should have it," she said. "You'll appreciate it more than I do."

I held my breath, but she didn't explain any further. I felt her fingers tighten almost imperceptibly around mine. The edges of the arrowhead bit into my palm.

"So about our escape . . . ," Mandarin began.

"To California?"

"I know we ain't talked about it as much as we should have, but that doesn't mean I ain't been thinking about it. I got money saved up from cocktailing, way more than enough to start us out. I figure we can stay at a motel till we get an apartment. In the meantime I'll be looking for an agent. So I can model.

"But I don't have any pictures to show them," she finished.

It took a few seconds for me to understand what she meant.

"My new camera," I said. "I can take pictures of you!"

"You'd do that?"

"They might not turn out too well, but they'd be something to show people, at least. If you want, I could get a book from the library, maybe—"

"Gracey," she said, releasing my hand. "Did I ever tell you how much I love you?" And swiftly and deliberately, without any warning at all, she took my face in her hands and kissed me on the mouth. Then she jumped to her feet, her hair swirling around her face like a tangled black witch's wig. The bleachers boomed in the wind.

"I've got to go," she shouted. "Find me tomorrow! And happy birthday!"

She banged down the metal steps and leaped into the empty football field, rapturous, her arms outstretched as if she were about to take off. I remained where I sat, until the wind quieted and my stomach relaxed enough for me to stand.

22

a two-way mirror

As May came to a close, the final drumroll to the tri-county pageant began. Momma insisted I stay home every day after school to help prepare. Though all Taffeta's dresses and accessories had long been completed, Momma couldn't sit still. The afternoons were a frenzy of adjustment, reconsideration, taking apart, and putting back together. I spent my free time studying the photography books I'd checked out from the school library.

I saw Mandarin after school just once that week, when we met for milk shakes at the A&W so I could fix the mistakes on her math homework. I'd slipped out while Momma had been painting my sister's face in makeup with names like Frisky Flamingo and What in Carnation. Mandarin had ways to keep herself busy, she assured me, though I sensed that my unavailability annoyed her.

At long last, I convinced her to consider helping the kindergartners as her community service project. She could serve ten hours in as little as two days. And after the way she'd talked to Taffeta, I knew she got along with kids. But getting her to approach the kindergarten teacher was another story. "That bitch'll think I'm gonna corrupt 'em all," she said.

Taffeta seemed overwhelmed by Momma's pre-pageant storm. She was the eye of the hurricane, but in a way, she was overlooked. As soon as Momma stepped out the door to run an errand, she came after me for attention—bringing along a game of Candy Land, a page to color, an opera song she adored.

One time, she dragged the stereo to the kitchen and plunked it onto my lap.

"Listen! This is my favorite part."

She turned up the volume. I listened for a second to the high-pitched garble of Italian. "Taffeta," I said, "how is this your favorite part? You don't even know what the words mean."

"I do too," she insisted.

"No you don't—they're in another language."

"Yes I do, Grace." She swiveled the volume knob. *"Listen."*

Because graduation was drawing near, teachers ambushed seniors daily with pop quizzes to implicate the slackers. I still found it hard to believe that Mandarin planned to graduate, but that week, she ditched school only once: with me.

Although she claimed she never got in trouble for it, I suspected that the regulations of the ditching universe would be different for me. Like if I crossed the threshold of the school lawn and stepped onto the sidewalk, I'd be accosted by the whirl and whoop of an alarm, or a barricade of parents and teachers blocking my escape.

"Chill out," Mandarin told me after geometry on Thursday, the last day of May. "We'll be fine. Just don't run until we're outta sight."

When the bell rang after lunch, we headed the wrong way down the hall from the cafeteria. We strolled through the double doors, over the lawn, and past the cottonwood trees, and if anybody saw us leave, they decided to forever hold their peace.

Mandarin had chosen the perfect setting for our photo shoot: an old horse pasture where the canal joined the Bighorn River. It ran up against a barn, more cottonwood trees, and a row of abandoned stables. The whole lot of it was owned by Gary Householder, a sleazy old guy Momma said used to hit on her when she was a teenager. He worked as a supervisor in the bentonite mines, so we felt certain he wouldn't be home until late.

I'd been nervous about taking Mandarin's pictures, but as it turned out, shooting came naturally to us both: her posing, me observing, with the camera lens like a two-way mirror between us, deflecting all discomfort.

Each snap embedded another part of her in my brain. The way her lips, when relaxed, never fully closed. The jut of her cheekbones when she pouted. The deep depression in the center of her clavicle. There was no denying Mandarin's beauty, and yet so much of what was beautiful about her was in the way she moved, the contrast of her radiance against the dry sea of badlands. It would take a far better photographer than I was to capture that magic. But for some reason, Mandarin seemed to trust my judgment.

"Okay," I said, "now flip your head back and close your eyes. No, keep them closed."

"Like this?"

"Good, but don't talk."

I tried to shoot from different angles, like the photography books recommended: on my stomach in front of her, kneeling at eye level, standing over her torso with my legs on either side. "Now we need another background," I said.

Mandarin opened her eyes, and I stepped back. "Like where?"

I scanned our surroundings. "There's a wood fence over there. Maybe you could, like, hang on it, or sit on it—"

"Perfect! Let's go."

Mandarin leaped up, grabbed my hand, and pulled me after her, bouncing down the slope of the horse pasture like a new foal. She hoisted herself atop the splintery fence. Then she leaned forward with her elbows on her thighs, her hair swinging.

"How's this?"

In reply, I snapped two pictures. When I tried to snap a third, the camera clicked.

"Hey, I'm out of film," I said, feeling professional. "I need to reload."

Mandarin slid from the fence. While I tinkered with the camera, she wandered off, searching for a fresh background, I assumed. But when I glanced up few minutes later, I didn't see her.

"Mandarin?"

I spun around, scanning the field. Where could she have disappeared to so quickly? I noticed a knot of ash trees near the canal and was about to head to them when I heard her shout from the barn: "Hey, Grace! Over here!"

I approached the gaping doorway nervously, thinking of Momma's stories about Mr. Householder patting her butt or using a broom to lift her skirt when she entered the grocery store. Extra-gross, because he was twelve years older than her.

"Maybe we shouldn't be in there," I called. "Momma says Gary Householder's a jerk."

"Why can't you just say *asshole* like everybody else? You're such a fairy princess. Do you shit rainbows or what? Say 'Gary Householder's an asshole.'"

"Gary Householder's an asshole," I repeated, stepping inside the barn.

My eyes strained in the dark. I wove through a maze of debris: ancient rabbit hutches, bales of hay, sacks of animal feed coated in hill dust. Sinister-looking farming contraptions poked out of the mess, with rusted cogs, wheels, metal appendages like insect arms. Dust motes drifted in the light streaming through gaps in the twenty-foot ceiling.

"Seriously, Mandarin . . . This place gives me the creeps."

"Just get over here. It's worth it, I swear."

"What's worth—" I stubbed my toes on the rusty skeleton

of a bedspring. A cloud of dust billowed into my face, making me cough.

At last I found Mandarin in the farthest corner, unfolding a stepladder. "Check it out," she said, motioning with her chin. I glanced up and saw a meat hook jutting from the planks, draped with an old leather cowboy vest and hat.

"That old crap?" I scrunched up my face. "But they're filthy, Mandarin. They're disgusting."

"You won't be the one wearing them, you pansy." She tottered up the stepladder and lugged them down.

"You're actually going to put them on?"

Clutching the hat between her thighs, Mandarin shook out the vest—"for vermin," she explained—and held it out before her. The stiff fringe sprouted from the hems like thorns. The leather was marbled and stained, probably with nasty old Householder sweat.

"It'll be hot," Mandarin said. "Like sexy cowgirl pictures. *Playboy* style. But I won't be naked. See, I can take off my shirt, and the vest'll cover my tits." She slid the straps of her tank top from her shoulders.

I turned away to give her privacy. "But doesn't it bother you? It's a dead animal. What's the difference between a leather vest and a trophy?"

"Photography is art," she replied, like she hadn't heard my question correctly. "And art's all about taking chances. Taking risks. Otherwise you blend right in with the rest. No one will ever notice you. And look, I told you so! Sexy."

I turned around.

She'd left the vest open in the middle. I could see the ridges of her ribs smoothing into her flat belly, the hem of her jeans. Under the dim light from the rafters, the hat shaded her eyes in a pool of darkness. She struck a pose, her hands on her hips.

"So would you buy my magazine?"

I nodded.

"Hey! For my community service project, how about we send these photos to Mr. Beck? Maybe it'd spice up the morning announcements."

"Really, you should talk to the kindergarten teacher. She's not that—"

"Let's just get these shot," Mandarin said. "This thing's scratching my skin, and it reeks like a steer corpse. Hurry up."

I aimed the camera at her and peered through the viewfinder. It was hard to see, but I snapped a photo anyway.

"There's not enough light in here. Maybe we should go outside—"

A sudden clatter interrupted me. We jerked around in surprise. A deformed monster eclipsed the light from the open barn door: Mr. Householder, his arms piled with farm equipment.

"Who's there?"

Mandarin and I glanced at each other. There was nowhere to hide.

"Hey! What the hell're you kids doin' in my barn?"

Mr. Householder's angry face hit a shaft of light from the rafters, and he dropped the equipment he'd been carrying. He was short, with a pregnant-looking gut and eyes like pink candies set in pockets of dough.

I backed into Mandarin. She grabbed my shoulders and

repositioned me out of her way. "Nothing much, sir," she said. "We were just admiring your taste in fashion."

"Why the hell you got my things on? Those're my rodeo clothes! They're special." He took a step forward. "Take 'em off!"

Mandarin didn't budge. "They can't be *too* special, seeing as how they were stuffed way in the back of this dirty-assed barn."

"Take 'em off this minute, or I'll call the cops!"

"Oh gosh—you'll call the cops? What'll you say? 'Help, police! A teenage girl's stole my crusty old vest and hat!' What's your problem, anyhow? Who died and made you king asshole?"

He took another step, and his eyes focused on Mandarin's face.

"You've got to be shittin' me. If it ain't Mandy Ramey! I shoulda known by that filthy trashy mouth a'yours."

My jaw dropped. But Mandarin wasn't fazed. "I might talk trash, but at least I don't stink like I rolled in a dump."

"You got no right to talk back to me! I know all about you, Mandy Ramey." Mr. Householder smiled darkly. "And I know *what* you are, too—nothing but a tramp, a cheap baby whore. Ain't that right? Easy as pie! Everybody's had a piece. You even came on to my boy."

His boy? Dale Householder worked for the sanitation department, and his belly was even bigger than his father's.

"In his wet dreams," Mandarin said through clenched teeth.

"And he turned you down flat. He knowed where you been. Wanna hear a little secret?"

"*Fuck you.*"

"I used t'be friends with your daddy," he went on. "We was great friends back in the day, before he went and screwed up with that hoity-toity pretendian from elsewheres. I was there for him when she reappeared out of nowhere and left her big mistake behind. Guess she thought she was too good for him—and for you."

"Fuck you!" Mandarin screamed. "My mother's *dead.*"

She yanked off the hat and vest and flew at him like a furious harpy, hurling the vest at his gut and knocking him backward into a pile of scrapped wood. Mandarin scooped up her shirt and stood over him, making no effort to cover her naked breasts. "Go to hell and die, you sorry bastard."

She spit in his face.

Then she ran for the door. I glanced at Mr. Householder, who flopped around on the barn floor like a half-crushed bug, swiping the saliva from his eyes.

"Who you callin' a bastard, huh?" I heard him holler as I sprinted after Mandarin. "Huh? I ain't the one whose mom's a whore!"

When I burst into the light, Mandarin was already halfway down the grassy slope, heading for the thicket of ash trees by the river. So much for her tar-caked lungs. I finally caught up with her at the edge of the irrigation canal, not far from the rusty old car carcass. Her naked back was to me, and her shoulders were shaking. I'd never seen her so angry. I was afraid to touch her, to speak.

But I knew it was time. Time to tell her that I knew the truth, about the envelope and arrowheads, and that her lie didn't matter to me—because after all, when it came to bastard parentage, I wasn't any better.

I cleared my throat. "Mandarin . . ."

When she didn't answer, I squatted beside her and took a deep breath. "Mandarin, I know about your mother. I know she's sending you arrowheads."

Her shoulders stilled. Slowly, she lifted her face. *"What?"*

"I saw an envelope."

"Why the fuck didn't you say so?"

"I don't know." I rushed to explain. "It was after our fight. And . . . I guess I figured you had your reasons for keeping it a secret."

Mandarin stared at me a moment longer, her frightening eyes spearing mine.

Then she unclenched the tank top from her first. It was so crumpled it looked like crushed velvet. "She claimed she didn't have the money to take care of me proper," she said, yanking on her shirt. "And she wasn't in the right mental state. I didn't give a damn about that as a kid or now, but she insisted. I haven't seen her since."

"But the letters . . ."

"I don't even read her damn letters. They just remind me how much I hate her for leaving me here in this horseshit town."

She didn't even *read* them?

It seemed so immature. Like Taffeta's plugging her ears when I ordered her from my bedroom. It was as if Mandarin felt validated by their rift. As long as she ignored her mother's efforts, Mandarin could continue believing *she* was the one who'd been wronged.

Just when I was about to voice my frustration, she pressed her face into her arms and began to sob.

"Why do I let them get to me? Why do I let them? I just can't understand how anybody could hate me so much without even knowing me."

My heart felt stuck in my throat. "Gary Householder's an asshole." Tentatively, I touched her shoulder. "Remember? What he says means nothing, okay? He's just a stupid asshole hick with sheep shit for brains, who gets off on making people feel as small as he is."

Mandarin looked up at me again. Eyeliner streamed from her red eyes. She was an entirely different creature, spoiled by tears. "Get a clue, Grace. They're all like that."

"Who are all like that?"

"People," she said. "People in Washokey. They take, take, take, with no mind for anybody else. If you get in the way of their fun, they'll run you down and squash you."

"Come on. No they're not! That's impossible. They can't all be."

"You have *no fucking idea.*"

The words came out in a snarl. I jerked my hand away as she turned and stared across the water, her mouth a tense gash. And then she turned to me, suddenly inspired. "I know," she said.

"What?"

"I know what to do."

"To do? What do you mean, Mandarin?"

"I've figured it out. How to show you. To prove to you how they really are. All of them, in this town. To show you why we've got to escape before we're eaten alive."

I fought to breathe normally.

"I keep forgetting how young you are, and how much you haven't seen. No wonder you act like leaving's a joke. You got no idea about the real Washokey. About what places like this turn people into. If I don't prepare you, when it finally hits you, you won't be getting back up."

"Mandarin, you don't need to prove anything to me. . . . I already believe you!"

"No you don't," she said. "But trust me. You will."

23

with you i will leave

My dress was an old white one of Momma's, with spaghetti straps that tied over the shoulders and a sash abuzz with embroidered bees. The cups were so thickly padded it looked like I'd stuffed two rolled-up socks into my top. I complained until Momma let me wear a white cardigan to hide them. She'd somehow found the time to french-braid my hair, same as hers.

We had to look immaculate, like a family unit. When Taffeta won first place in the tri-county pageant, Momma said, we'd all be invited onstage.

I sat in the backseat of the car with a pair of secondhand high heels on my lap. My sister's feathery pageant dress—white, with familiar-looking puffy lilac sleeves—dangled from a hanger beside me.

Taffeta sat in the passenger's seat, dressed in a terry cloth tracksuit. Momma had spun her hair into Shirley Temple corkscrew curls, with a white orchid pinned above her ear. Her makeup looked airbrushed on. Momma had ordered her to keep her face as expressionless as possible so she wouldn't crack her artificial splendor.

Momma wore the shimmery gold junk shop gown she'd saved for years. She drove with white-knuckled tension. All day she'd been in her worst form, rocketing around the house, hollering at my sister and me, drinking mug after mug of burnt-smelling black coffee. The caffeine only fueled her nervous prattling, which increased until her brain seemed to rupture and she could hardly articulate a complete sentence.

"Road's shit," she said at one point. "Taxes wasted."

And later, "What to do about butt glue?"

Butt glue? Clearly, she'd gone insane.

We arrived in Benton, the county seat, a little after six. Benton—named for the mines, of course—wasn't much larger than Washokey, but it had the courthouse and a tiny Wild West museum. Momma swung Taffeta out of the car and set her down. She opened my door and leaned over me.

"Dress," she ordered. "Duffel."

After a short pause, I handed her Taffeta's dress and the wheelie duffel bag overstuffed with pageant gear. Before I could climb out myself, Momma slammed the door. I watched her speed off with the dress slung over her shoulder, her bag bumbling over the asphalt, and Taffeta hurrying to catch up.

I buckled my feet into the stupid strappy heels and slid

out of the car. My dress was too short. Paired with my skinny legs, it made me feel like a stork. Plus the heels chafed me in sixteen places. They made a clopping sound as I crossed the parking lot.

I stared at the piece of paper taped to the back door of the Benton High School cafeteria: *Authorized Personnel Only.* Then I pushed inside.

Backstage, dozens of little girls and their mothers churned through a fun house of mirrors and lights. Dressing tables were littered with makeup, blow dryers, spangled fragments of costumes. Mothers screeched to be heard over the commotion. Several little girls were wailing, their mouths shaped like figure eights. The space stank like a putrid fruit salad, coconut-pineapple mousse and strawberry-champagne lotion. I almost preferred the smoky beery reek of Solomon's. All the sights and sounds and smells whooshed to the bottom of my stomach, giving me an ominous sense of déjà vu.

It couldn't have been this bad. I would have remembered.

I risked a few steps into the hot-packed space. Immediately, a red-haired woman towing a little girl shoved past me. Her doughy breasts blobbed from her emerald dress. She held them in with one red-taloned hand as she stopped and leaned over the little girl.

"Hold still," she ordered.

The girl stuck out her lips in an exaggerated pout and the woman smeared them with scarlet. When I blinked, the color seemed to linger behind my closed eyelids.

As I searched for my mother and sister, I overheard snatches of conversation:

"Mommy, it's too tight! It squeezes my ribs."

"I wanted to put Vaseline on her teeth, but it makes her sick to her stomach. Or at least, that's what she says. Some kids'll say anything. I read on the net . . ."

"Lovely, Erica, lovely! Just like that!"

"Remember to smile like you adore them—even if you have to pretend."

I passed a tiny blond girl kneeling on a chair, in a dress so puffy and stiff with netting it seemed to exhale around her. With her elbows on a dressing table, she made faces in the mirror, batting her eyelashes, while one woman teased her hair and another sprayed it with a purple can of hair spray.

I passed a girl a few years younger than me balancing a baby on her hip while her mother practiced dance moves with small identical-twin brunettes.

I nearly crashed into a woman scolding a sobbing little girl, who kept pleading, "No, Mommy. Please, Mommy, not that song," while her mother repeated, "It's been printed in the program, DeeDee! We can't change it now."

As I navigated the confusion, I tried to shake each spectacle out of my brain. Mothers and daughters. Daughters and mothers.

Mandarin and her mother had no relationship, other than the mysterious letters and a jar of arrowheads. Momma and I didn't have much more than that. Or so I told myself. Ever since I'd screwed up Little Miss Washokey and Momma and I had grown apart, I'd felt cheated. But what was worse—our distance or the syrupy overflow of mothering slathered on these tiny girls?

And who was it really all about, anyway—the children or their mothers?

At last I spied my sister. Dressed in nothing but pink lace underwear, she was practicing her wave. Momma stood behind her, fastening her corkscrew curls into a Marie Antoinette updo. Bobby pins protruded from her lips like fangs.

I cleared my throat. "Momma?"

"That wasn't bad!" she said to Taffeta, spraying pins from her mouth. "Not bad at all. But you're not sucking in your stomach, baby doll. I can tell."

"Yes I *am*." Taffeta glanced at me.

"Potbellies are for four-year-olds. Did you see the figure on that redhead? You've got to remember: suck in, suck in, suck in. Think it in your head at all times. Like a drumbeat, playing behind your song."

"Momma, she—"

"We don't have much time left," she said, ignoring me. She slid the pageant dress from its hanger. "Ups-a-daisy."

Obediently, Taffeta raised her arms. The dress settled around her like a fallen flower. Momma knelt to tuck her feet into tiny gold pumps. Then she stood and surveyed Taffeta appreciatively.

"I've done the best I can. The rest is up to you. All you've got to do is remember to suck in. And don't stumble on your Italian accent, not even for a second. Give me a note."

Taffeta glanced at me again.

"Momma, lay off," I said. "There are too many people around."

"I need to check her pitch," Momma said. "Sing, Taffeta. Sing."

Taffeta blinked hard, like Davey Miller. I imagined her bawling, mashing her fists into her eyes, all her perfect makeup gushing black and wet down her rouge-tinted cheeks. There wouldn't be enough time to repair the mess she'd make. Mentally, I cheered her on: Cry, *Taffeta! Cry your eyes out.*

As if she could read my mind, she shook her head. She lifted her chest, sucked in her tummy, and belted out a tune.

❀ ❀ ❀

The cafeteria sweltered with other people's breath. I longed to remove my cardigan, but I didn't want anyone to stare at my unnaturally inflated chest.

We stood elbow to elbow in the front row of cafeteria benches, listening to the pageant contestants shout the national anthem. My hand drooped from its position over my heart. Momma mouthed the words along with the girls, her cheeks flushed with patriotic passion. Thank goodness she didn't try to sing. I tried and failed to find my sister's voice in the dissonance.

The song ended, and the crowd rustled into their seats. All the people in our row sat with their backs to the cafeteria tables, facing forward. I sat backward with my elbows on the table. I would be a silent protestor, I decided, like Gandhi.

Momma jabbed me in the side. "Turn around! Don't you want to support your sister?"

Grudgingly, I turned.

Onstage, the little girls had lined up against a blue velvet curtain. Taffeta was third from the end. So these were all the small-town pageant winners. I wasn't surprised to see that every girl was white. The announcer, whom I'd seen back-stage, was a lumpy-looking man with shifty eyes and a black mustache. Why did these creeps get involved with kids' pageants, anyway?

On second thought, I didn't want to know.

The man strolled to the front of the stage and took the microphone. "Good evening!" he exclaimed. Several members of the audience lamely shouted back. Still, it was a better response than Mr. Beck had ever received. "Welcome to the tri-county pageant! My name is Mr. Ferber. I'm over-joyed to be here, and I'm sure you all feel the same way."

"Notice he's not speaking to the contestants," I said.

Momma glanced at me. "What did you say?"

"And now I'll introduce our little princesses one by one: the superstars of the tri-county area." Mr. Ferber motioned with one fat hand. "First, we have Miss DeeDee Kemble!"

DeeDee, a blonde with enormous eyes and a wreath of flowers in her hair, marched across the stage, grinning and blowing kisses. No trace of her backstage tears.

"Miss Rosemary Birmingham!"

Rosemary, a pigtailed brunette, crossed with her thumb in her mouth.

"Miss Kayla-Ann Green!"

The tiny girl with the poofy dress, who I'd observed making faces in the mirror. I glanced at Momma. She looked concerned. I didn't know what she was so worried about. The other girls were adorable, a tribe of glittering pixies, but none had my sister's voice. And I'd bet my entire rock collection not a single girl could sing in Italian.

"Miss Frederica Jones!" Mr. Ferber continued. "Miss Madison Matthews!"

And then I heard my name.

"Grace Carpenter!"

I jolted around in my seat and searched the room. A multitude of unfriendly faces stared back. I turned to the front again, admonishing my imagination.

"Miss Lily Morehouse!"

The red-lipsticked redhead flounced across the stage. She did have a figure. Possibly better than mine.

"Gracey, come on! Let's go!"

This time, the voice was unmistakable.

I stood, frantically scanning the crowd. A gray-haired woman across the cafeteria table complained that I was blocking her view, but I didn't care. At last I spied Mandarin tucked into the nook of a closet doorway. She waved her hands wildly.

My heart soared. Mandarin had come for me! All the way to the tri-county pageant at the Benton High School cafeteria. Of course, I didn't know *why* she'd come, but it had to be for something exciting.

"Grace!" It was Momma this time. "Grace, sit down! What are you doing?"

"I'm sorry, Momma . . . I have to go."

"You have to go where? What are you talking about?"

"I'll be home later tonight, okay?"

"You will not! You —"

"Miss Serena Bond!" the announcer called.

Momma, distraught, glanced at the stage, and then back at me, and then back at the stage again. The grumbles around us amplified into quiet curses as I hovered there, half in and half out of my seat. Finally, Momma gestured me away.

"Fine! Just go, go! Get on out of here!"

I clambered over the tangled legs of the angry crowd, to the aisle where Mandarin waited. "Took you long enough," she said, grabbing my hand. Together, we rushed along the dim corridor toward freedom.

"Miss Taffeta Carpenter!"

My hand slipped from Mandarin's. I caught the door before it shut between us, and turned to look.

Taffeta stepped out of the row of little girls. Her grin seemed to catch the light and send it back at me, like sunshine zinging off a car windshield. I couldn't tell if she was sucking in, but it didn't matter. She was beautiful. I watched the tilt of her head as she gazed out at the audience, scanning, searching.

And suddenly, she was looking straight at me.

I doubted she could see me all the way in the back of the room, where I hunkered like a fugitive. But then her grin faltered. Her eyes widened.

My fingers slid a few inches down the door.

"Come on, Gracey! Let's go!"

Ducking my head, I followed Mandarin into the evening outside.

24

the quarry

"Look," Mandarin said. "Heat lightning."

We stood in the parking lot of Benton High, on either side of her father's truck. Far across the badlands, the evening sky faded into a gradient of flashing light. The whole earth seemed to rumble faintly, as if something were awakening.

"What causes it, anyway?" I asked as Mandarin stuck her key into the driver's-side door.

"Dragons," she said.

There was a shudder of wind right as she said it. Wild-winds. Or maybe not. I pulled the cuffs of my cardigan over my hands and shivered. Mandarin reached across and unlocked my door. I hopped in and slammed the door behind me.

"So . . . I see your dad let you use his truck again."

"It's my truck now." Mandarin patted the steering wheel. *"Really?"*

"I still got to pay him back. But how'd you think we were going to leave town in the first place?"

The wind quaked against the sides of the truck, and the heat lightning seemed to crackle into the cavity of my chest. I suddenly became aware of the tiniest details: the flimsy fabric between my hands and my thighs, the expansion of my lungs, the way my dry tongue seemed to fill my whole mouth.

Is this it?

This very night? Without any warning at all. Would she? Of course she would—it was just like her. I commanded my heart: *Careful, now.*

"Leave town? You mean . . . Now? Like, this is it?"

Mandarin stared at me. Her face was dangerous. "What if it was?"

I tried as hard as I could to hold her stare. But fear won. I dropped my eyes. Just for a second, but it was enough.

Knowingly, Mandarin nodded.

But she didn't look angry. Only resolute—maybe even self-satisfied. Probably because I'd proved her right. Silently, she thrust the key into the ignition. The engine vibrated but didn't start. She tried again. Nothing.

"So where are we really going?" I asked when I found my voice.

"You'll see."

Mandarin twisted the key a third time, pumping the accelerator. At last the engine grunted to life. She slammed her foot down again and the truck shot onto the road.

❋   ❋   ❋

Despite my shame, it didn't take long for the drive to in-
fect me. We were miles from home, halfway across the county.
The radio sputtered out classic rock. Shadows the color of ripe
plums pockmarked the landscape. I saw the occasional glow
of far-off house lights, like solitary fireflies stuck fast in the
darkness. The truck's windows were rolled down, and the
wind agitated our hair like playful fingers.

I felt ultra-conscious, hyperalert. And for the first time,
I began to feel like maybe I *could* leave with Mandarin, just
maybe. If this was what it entailed, I really could.

Maybe if the Scotsman truck didn't rattle so much as
Mandarin sped down the old highway. I could hardly imagine it taking us all the way to the coast.

"What a fucking gorgeous night!" I exclaimed. "On a
night like this, doesn't it feel like anything's possible?"

"Anything," Mandarin replied.

She watched as I pulled a cigarette from the pack on the
dash. I stuck it into my mouth, then realized it wasn't lit, and
that I didn't know how to smoke, anyway. I returned it to the
pack. We crested a hill, and the wind gusted against the sides
of the truck like sheets swinging from a clothesline. I caught
a whiff of manure.

"Oh, gross." Mandarin wrinkled her nose and reached for
the crank handle. "Roll up your window, quick."

I obliged, momentarily disenchanted.

The truck rumbled down the slope of the hill and into a

vast, flat valley. Outside my window, the landscape grew rockier, thousands of years of geology sculpted by wildwinds and ancient seas. Because of the darkness, I didn't recognize the terrain until I noticed a smear of light ahead.

"Wait," I said. "That's Washokey. Isn't it?"

"Bingo," Mandarin replied.

"Are we going back?" I tried to hide the disappointment in my voice. Nothing would kill my exhilaration more quickly than going home.

Mandarin checked her side mirror. "Eventually."

"Well then, where are we going *now?*"

She didn't answer. But then, unexpectedly, she swerved off the highway.

I held back a shriek as the truck bumped and banged for several yards before grinding to a stop. Although I hadn't noticed them from the road, now I saw all the parked cars and pickup trucks. Beyond them, the land dropped away in some kind of canyon or gorge.

"We're here," Mandarin announced.

"Where's here?"

"The quarry."

"The quarry?" I had never been there before, though I'd heard of it. "What's at the quarry?"

Mandarin flicked on the overhead light, making it hard to see out the windows. She reached across me and unlatched the glove compartment.

"What's at the quarry?" I asked again as she pulled out a black cosmetic bag. She withdrew a compact, flipped it open, and handed it to me. I glanced at the brand name on the back of it: Femme Fatale Cosmetics, Inc. Had she taken it from my house, or bought it from Momma? I didn't want to ask.

"Washokey's in the quarry," she said. "Washokey, in the flesh."

"What's that supposed to mean?"

She handed me a black eyeliner pencil, then a tube of mascara. I cradled everything in the folds of my dress.

"Don't just stare at everything. Put it on. We're gonna whore you out tonight."

I paused, then laughed uncertainly. "What are we *really* doing?"

"I'm being serious. I know you'd like to meet a guy, and this is the best place I know to catch one. Besides the bar, of course." She handed me a makeup brush.

"But . . ."

But what? I knew I couldn't protest after I'd worked so hard to be like Mandarin. I'd told myself a million times I'd follow her lead anyplace, any which way, if only she'd agree to lead me. "It's just . . . ," I began again. "You know I've never . . ."

"Obviously."

"That's not what I meant. I've never even *kissed* a guy."

"No big deal. Although . . ." Mandarin looked at me, her expression intense. "Do you want to practice first?"

I stared at her a little too long. Then she laughed, and I looked away.

"You'll be fine!" she said. "Quit worrying. Just ditch that idiotic bumblebee sash."

❀ ❀ ❀

The story behind the Washokey quarry was another one of those local legends, like the Virgin Mary rock, documented in self-published books available at Wyoming souvenir shops.

The quarry, so the story went, had been carved sixty years earlier by a single obsessive-compulsive man with a desire to dig. What he'd expected to find wasn't clear. Some people claimed diamonds. Others said gold, oil, or dinosaur bones. After a decade and a half of digging, the man suffered a heart attack. It took weeks for his son to find his body, still propped atop his shovel. Since he had never found whatever substance he'd sought, he was said to haunt the quarry forever after, et cetera, et cetera.

All his work had been futile, anyway. The only substance worth mining in the Washokey Badlands Basin was boring old bentonite—mineral rubbish used as a filler in candy and lipstick. Probably including Frisky Flamingo and What in Carnation.

Nature had since reclaimed the quarry. Because it collected rainwater and winter melt, it served as a sort of badlands oasis. Its edges were crowded with cottonwoods and scraggly shrubs. The center was perfect for beer bashes.

Or so I'd heard.

Music echoed off the walls as Mandarin and I descended the hand-carved steps running down the quarry's side. Shadows cast by the twin bonfires flickered all around us. I concentrated on placing my ill-fitting high heels on rocks I hoped wouldn't dislodge, willing myself to look at my feet instead of the people below.

Once we reached the bottom, Mandarin led me through the crowd. Everybody from school was there. Or at least, all the upperclassmen. I glimpsed a few freshmen and sophomores and was thankful Alexis & Co. seemed to be missing, though I did see Brandi Shelmerdine. I recognized Kate Cunningham, and Peter Shaw, and Joshua Mickelson, and Tag Leeland, and other juniors and seniors from homeroom.

It was so *bizarre* that parties like this existed—and had always existed. All these everyday faces congregating and having the time of their lives, without my even knowing.

There were strangers, too. "Kids from other towns," Mandarin told me. "They come all the way from Worland and Thermopolis and Benton. Our quarry's the best."

I wondered if I should feel proud.

Everybody stared as Mandarin walked by. But how could they not? Her skin looked flawless in the dark, her hair impossibly black. The firelight made her hazel eyes flash. I wouldn't have been surprised if she'd crouched on all fours and roared, her true primal self revealed.

Meanwhile, I clung to her finger as if it were a twig on a cliffside, the only thing anchoring me above a bottomless pit. Without the sash, my dress looked like a skanky nightgown, swishing around my bare legs. I tried to saunter, but my heels snagged on the uneven ground. Every time I blinked, Mandarin's mascara threatened to fasten my eyes shut.

I felt like at any minute, somebody would call me out: "What is *she* doing here?"

It seemed like forever until we emerged from the far side

of the crowd. Mandarin pulled me closer. "Want me to get you a beer?"

I'd never tasted beer before. I'd never even had the chance to. Momma didn't keep alcohol in the house, and though I suspected that Alexis & Co. had sampled their share, they'd never invited me to partake.

"Only if you're having one," I said.

"Maybe just one. Remember, I'm driving. I'm a responsible drinker. But we're here for you. Get drunk! Live it up!"

I smiled weakly.

Mandarin nudged me through the space between the two bonfires. For a second, my entire body seemed to erupt into flames. On the other side sat the kegs, so old and dented they looked like discarded oil barrels. A lengthy line of people trailed from each. I began walking toward the back of the lines, but Mandarin caught my arm.

"I need some brewskies, boys," she announced. "Who'll pour?"

Instantly, three eager guys each filled a red plastic cup from the three respective kegs, practically slobbering with disbelief that Mandarin Ramey had deigned to speak to them. The two guys who finished first shoved their cups toward us. The third guy glanced at his cup, then took a swallow and wandered away.

I kept my eyes on Mandarin as I took my first sip of beer. I'd imagined a taste like root beer, but what filled my mouth was soapy and thick, with a bland and vaguely bitter flavor. I choked down a second swallow, because Mandarin was watching me and drinking more quickly. I didn't want her to think I couldn't keep up, so I took another swallow, then another.

Mandarin seemed to speed up even more.

I forced myself to relax my throat, swallowing hugely, my eyes locked on Mandarin's, hers locked on mine.

"Whoa . . ." One of the guys beside us elbowed his friend. "Check out these bitches. They're suckin' down that beer like they ache for it. I'll bet they're wishin' it was—"

Mandarin flung her cup at him. It clunked against his chest, flowers of beer darkening his shirt.

"Hey, man," he shouted. "What the hell!"

"I'm not a man, dickface," Mandarin said, "and I'm not a bitch, either."

The guy held up his hands and backed off.

"There's nothing to see!" another guy called to the gathering crowd. I recognized him—Joshua Mickelson, the crooked-nosed lifeguard who'd approached me in the cafeteria line with Tyler Worley. "What an asshole," he said to us.

"Thanks," Mandarin said unsmilingly.

Joshua edged closer to her. "Great party, huh? So when did you get here?"

I swallowed the last of my beer, feeling even more out of place. I was obviously not meant to be part of their conversation.

"Hey, Grace!"

I almost jumped. I needed to get used to hearing my name in improbable settings.

On the other side of the bonfires, Davey Miller waved enthusiastically. He looked as out of place as I probably did, in his tapered black jeans and oversized white sneakers. After a nod from Mandarin, I wound through the crowd in his direction, feeling unreasonably relieved.

"Davey! What's up? What are you doing here?"

He wore a T-shirt featuring a David Bowie album cover. Probably not the best choice for this crowd. But it was far better than his usual shirts, which featured bad paintings of Indian maidens playing pan flutes, or wolves howling before the aurora borealis.

"I came with my next-door neighbor," he replied. "You know Ricky. As soon as we got here, though, he ran off with some girl. He told our moms we were going to a movie. . . . I should have known I was just a decoy. Guess you came with Mandarin?"

"Of course," I said smugly. I hoped I'd never grow used to it, being Mandarin Ramey's friend. "So where'd you get that shirt?"

He looked sheepish. "It was Ricky's idea. I guess I was trying to fit in or something. Dumb, huh? As if it were that easy."

"Oh, I know! That's why I'm glad Mandarin and I are different from everyone else."

"Different? How so?"

I squinted at him. "Well, I mean, *obviously*. We're not like them. Just look at us."

"I guess," Davey said, but he still appeared unconvinced.

I was about to ask him what his deal was. But suddenly, there was a hot mouth at my ear, speaking so low that I felt rather than heard the words.

"Need a refill?"

I cupped a hand over my ear involuntarily and turned to face Tyler Worley.

He had floppy brown hair and an unshaved jaw and stood at least eight inches taller than me. I had never been close to so much male at once. I breathed deep, bonfire smoke heating me from the inside out. Davey was forgotten as Tyler took my hand.

At the keg, he filled my cup like an expert. "Did you see that? A perfect pour. Not any head at all."

I had no idea what he meant, and didn't want to ask. "Um, beautiful."

"That's why they call me Pourmaster. Naw, but seriously, I'd make a great bartender, don't you think?"

"If that's what you want to be," I said, thinking of Solomon Ramey.

"Why not? It's, like, the perfect job. I could sleep during the daytime. At night I'd get to serve myself for free, plus any sexy ladies that come wandering in." He winked and knocked me with his hip. I brought one hand to my face, trying to cover my flushed cheeks. I'd never thought flirting would be so . . . *embarrassing.*

"Well, I won't be twenty-one for ages."

"You think that'd stop me from serving you? Didn't I just?"

I spotted Mandarin through the gap between the fires. Joshua stood beside her, his lips still moving, but her eyes were on me. I raised my beer in salute.

"Earth to Grace," Tyler said. "What're you staring at?"

I looked at him, surprised. "I didn't think I told you my name."

He took a swallow of beer before speaking. "We go to the same school, don't we?"

"Oh," I said. "Right."

I raised my cup again, tapping it against his. This time, I didn't mind the taste so much. A new song came on and people cheered, including Tyler.

"Hell yeah! This is a great song. Dance with me?"

Without waiting for an answer, he grabbed my hand and pulled me away from the kegs and fires, into the surging forest of silhouettes. Before I knew it, we were dancing—or, more accurately, swaying together, as the crowd made it difficult to do much more than that.

All of a sudden, Earl Barnaby staggered into us, arms flailing. I squealed, then clapped a hand to my mouth, shocked that such a sound had come from my own vocal cords.

"What the hell's your deal?" Tyler demanded.

"It's okay," Earl slurred, his words thick and wet. "It's okay, buddy. I'm all right. Look here, I got somethin' for you an' your girl." He held out a thin metal flask.

Without questioning the contents, Tyler unscrewed the tiny cap and drank. "You want?" he said to me, wiping his mouth.

I stared at the flask. I'd never seen one up close. It was one of those foreign objects of adulthood, like condoms or marijuana pipes. The reflections of the dancers around us crawled on the metal surface. "It's just that . . . I've never . . ."

"Just swallow fast. It's apple juice, all right?"

Still, I hesitated. Beer was one thing. Mystery liquid from Earl Barnaby's flask was another landscape entirely. And what was old Earl doing at a quarry party, anyway? I glanced over my shoulder, but I couldn't find Mandarin. I was on my own.

What would Mandarin do?

Well, of course. And suddenly, I knew why she'd brought me to this party in the first place: she was testing me, yet again. I was sure of it. She was probably watching right that second, camouflaged among the drunken faces, anticipating my reaction.

I accepted the flask. It felt heavy in my hand, and the mystery liquid sloshed when I shook it. I took a deep breath, tipped my head, and poured. Forget apple juice. It was like drinking molten bonfire, the taste and the burn.

"How about we get out of here?" Tyler suggested.

Instead of answering, I took another swallow.

25

dark places

The clamor of the party sounded muffled and tinny, as if piped in from a distant radio. Louder were the sounds of crickets, the rush of the river, and the night wind disturbing pebbles and sending them tickling off the surface of the Tombs. Against the largest boulder, Tyler had me caged, his mouth shoved wetly into mine.

Once we had finished Earl Barnaby's flask, Tyler had led me to his pickup truck. "My first!" he'd declared.

It struck me as hilarious that he was so certain he'd own a succession of pickups throughout the rest of his life. Classic Washokey.

A prehistoric country song wailed from the speakers as soon as he turned on the engine, which made me laugh a second time. Garth Brooks, or Willie Nelson. I never knew the difference. Actually, almost everything seemed funny: the way Tyler yawned before snaking his arm over the top of the seat. The briefness of our journey: just a minute on the highway, and we arrived at the Tombs, much closer to the quarry than I'd imagined. How comical that I'd never known.

I wasn't laughing now.

I'd long since lost track of the minutes that had passed since Tyler had brought me to the Tombs, no more than fifteen feet from my personal Someplace Magic. It seemed like hours before he released me, wiping his brow with his wrist. I slipped beneath his arm and staggered away. The world swayed in the opposite direction. My cheeks were numb, my chin scraped raw from his stubble. I could scarcely feel my lips at all. My head felt stuffed with cotton and my mouth was sour with the acidic after-tang of Earl's whiskey. I would have spit if I could have moved my lips.

I wanted to crawl beneath my comforter, to pull my sheet over my ear, to forget Mandarin's test, to forget everything.

But then Tyler reeled me in again. This time, his rough palm crept under the hem of my dress, sliding up my thigh.

"Tyler . . . ," I protested from the corner of my mouth.

"Shhh," he said.

I pulled back an inch. *"Tyler . . ."*

"Shhh . . . Just relax. It's all right."

If I can just get through this, I told myself, *I'll be all right.* I thought of the Virgin Mary rock, somewhere in the jumble of boulders above me. I tried to picture her face, but I couldn't. My memory was blurry, as if someone had smudged the ancient paint.

"It's getting late. Let's go back, all right?" I begged.

"Come on, girl. You wanna be like your friend Mandarin, don't you?"

He was right. But I wrenched away anyway, stumbling the last few feet to the edge of the river.

Escape! Dive in and swim for the other shore!

Instead, I knelt on the bank, my shoulders tensing in expectation of Tyler's hands. When they didn't come, I pushed back my sweaty bangs, feeling the base of my palm smear Mandarin's eyeliner. I wanted to throw up, but the sick taste in my mouth didn't seem to be connected to the commotion in my stomach.

I stared in the water, hoping for a reflection.

I saw nothing. But I knew exactly what I looked like: a little girl playing dress-up. Like I'd never outgrown my pageant days, after all.

Tyler's arms curved around my middle and pulled me upright. I tried to pry them off. "I need to find Mandarin!" I meant to sound forceful, but my voice cracked.

"Calm down. We'll go find her, all right? In just a minute." He yanked me closer and pressed his body against mine, bunching my dress around my hips. I dropped my arms to cover my underwear, but he caught them and didn't let go.

Grab, kiss, pull away. An endless cycle. I'd never even kissed a boy before—and now this? This wasn't romance. This wasn't what it was supposed to be like.

And yet Mandarin did this and more, all the time, over and over again. While already I felt like I'd been there forever, numb-faced and slobbered on, in the dark places of the Tombs.

Maybe this was my purgatory.

"No!" I shouted. I wedged my arm between our chests and pushed Tyler as hard as I could. He slammed into the ground. I hesitated, amazed by my own strength. That gave him time to jump up again, like someone had jabbed a rewind button.

"You little bitch," he snarled, lunging for me.

I hit the ground without any awareness of my fall. My vision shifted, then righted again. I tried to scream, but Tyler cut it short by collapsing on top of me. Now I was choking on sobs, and his hands were everywhere. Beyond him, the stunted trees seemed to shudder and twist.

Then I heard a crack somewhere just outside my closed eyes. Tyler rolled off me, cursing furiously.

I peeled my eyes open.

Mandarin was crouched on a ledge above us, her face contorted with rage, one arm slung back to hurl another rock. When it slammed into Tyler's shoulder, I scrambled away on my hands and knees. From the edge of the river, I watched dazedly as Mandarin savaged him with stones, slamming them into his neck, his back, his forehead. She had great aim. I shouldn't have been surprised. Tyler tried to shield his face, but I saw blood leaking between his fingers.

"For fuck's sake, knock it off, you crazy bitch!"

"Then get the fuck out of here, you creep!" she screamed. "You fucking maniac. You know how old she is? Barely fourteen years old. You're fucking sick!"

Fourteen?

Tyler took advantage of the pause in her attack to hop

to his feet. "You're insane! What the hell's wrong with you? Why'd you tell me to bring her out here in the first place?"

Why'd you tell me . . .

It took a moment for me to understand. I looked up at Mandarin still crouched on the ledge. Her eyes caught mine, then darted away. Just like mine had earlier, in the parking lot of the Benton High auditorium, when she'd feigned leaving town for real and *I'd* been found out.

"Just . . . get the hell out of here," she ordered Tyler, the fury draining from her voice. "Or I'll tell everyone at school you're a fucking rapist."

With his arms still wrapped around his head, Tyler turned and lurched off toward his truck. He flung open the door and dived into the front seat. The tires scraped over the gravel as he backed into the road, then took off in the direction of the party.

Mandarin came over and stood a few feet from me. Her knee was freshly skinned, probably from climbing down the boulder. I stared at her knee instead of her face.

"Gracey . . . ," she began.

"Take me home," I told her knee.

❊ ❊ ❊

I sat in the passenger seat of Mandarin's truck, leaning as far from her as possible. She was driving much more slowly than usual, but I didn't comment. Washokey passed outside my window, the same stores, the same dreary, monotonous houses. When we passed Solomon's, I closed my eyes.

When I opened them, I discovered that Mandarin had pulled to the side of the road. She'd left the truck running. I could tell she was waiting for me to speak.

Finally, she cleared her throat. "Gracey, he didn't . . ."

"No," I said.

"Thank God." She sounded genuinely relieved. "Because I *told* him . . ."

She cleared her throat a second time. When she spoke again, her tone had changed. And she sounded—of all things—self-righteous.

"Y'know, Gracey, if you hadn't—"

"I don't want to hear it," I said, interrupting her. "I heard enough. All I needed to hear was that you *planned* this, Mandarin!"

She took a cigarette from the pack on the dash. Instead of lighting it, she picked at it with her thumbnail, shaving off tobacco flakes. "I didn't plan for it to go that far," she said quietly.

"A real friend wouldn't have planned anything at all."

"I would never let anything happen to you. You know that."

"Just a second ago, you weren't sure if anything *had*. What were you thinking—that handing me over to some Washokey creep would make me trust you? Why couldn't you have just explained it all to me? I didn't need to experience it myself. You should have told me. I would have listened!"

"You wouldn't have."

"I would!" I kicked the dashboard, like a little kid throwing a tantrum. Mandarin's pack of cigarettes fell to the floor.

Mandarin sighed and steered back onto the road. We drove the last few blocks to my house in silence. When she pulled into the bottom of my driveway, she turned off the engine and looked at me.

"Gracey, listen. . . . You've got to let me explain."

I opened the passenger door and started to climb out.

"I needed you to leave with me," she continued anyway. "I still need you. But I always felt like there was something keeping you here, some reason you couldn't let go. And so I knew I had to show you how Washokey really is. How the people here, the guys . . ." With one hand, she folded the cigarette over her index finger, tearing it in half.

"I knew you needed to see for yourself."

I shook my head. Her explanations were empty. Meaningless. Nothing but mosquito noise. Because that night, I had learned the third truth about Mandarin Ramey.

Sleeping with men she hated wasn't ironic. It wasn't one of her carefree fuck-yous, flipping off the people she claimed to hate. She wasn't in control. Not her. Not really. Some deeper, damaging part of her was in charge. A part so intent on filling her empty spaces it was destroying her. And that night, it had come close to destroying me.

It was ugly and appalling. It was pathetic.

Why hadn't I seen that before?

"Well, your plan backfired, didn't it?" I slid all the way out and slammed the door. Then I screwed up my face and, through the open window, shouted words I thought would feel good—but in reality, they felt like knife pangs, not in her chest, but mine.

"Because you're nothing but a goddamn selfish liar, Mandarin. And now I won't go *anywhere* with you!"

Mandarin stared blankly back.

❉ ❉ ❉

I didn't shower, or wash my face, or even wipe the mud from my calves. I peed with the light off so I wouldn't have to look in the mirror. I stuffed my dirty dress into the trash. Then I crawled into bed without pulling down the covers, curling up with my knees against my chest. I squinched my eyes shut.

But I couldn't sleep.

I rolled out of bed, knelt beside my shoe box of rocks, and pried the lid open. I unfolded the paper bundle and dumped Mandarin's arrowhead into my hand. Or rather, Mandarin's *mother's* arrowhead, regifted to me.

I went to my window. For a moment, I stood there, recalling the time I'd climbed out and let go, weeks earlier, millions and millions of years before.

And then, although I knew it was melodramatic, I hurled the arrowhead outside. I hadn't aimed for the baby pool, but it fell right in, scarcely making a splash in the circle of murky water.

how good my life could be

When I woke the next morning, I felt like I'd been stomped on by a giant cement jackalope. I had to unglue my mud-caked legs from the top of my comforter. The back of my head ached and my elbows stung—probably from when Tyler had knocked me down. My brains seemed to overflow in my skull.

The worst pain, however, was the one in my chest. It throbbed with my heartbeat, blurred my eyes. It made me want to roll over and sleep forever.

But my headache drove me from bed at last. I pulled on my longest sweatpants and padded downstairs.

"Momma, do we have any aspirin?" I called blearily.

"I just want an *explanation*."

My stomach sank, which made me feel even more nauseous. "What do you mean?" I asked as I rounded the corner into the kitchen, where I discovered that Momma wasn't speaking to me at all—her words were directed at my sister.

Taffeta sat on the kitchen counter with her arms crossed, her head bowed. She scowled so ferociously she looked like a little old woman. Ghosts of the past night's makeup still haunted her face, faint lipstick staining her mouth as if she'd been slurping a red Popsicle.

We probably look like sisters, I realized, remembering the mascara smudges circling my own eyes. But I didn't want to think about it. Thinking hurt.

"Aspirin?" I asked again, turning to Momma.

She wore her baggy blue muumuu and had her fists on her hips, so the satin ballooned in an hourglass shape around her. Her face was makeup free, and she'd pulled back her hair in a sloppy ponytail. Her eyes were narrowed. The vein in her forehead throbbed.

Momma was at the end of her rope.

"Taffeta, *how could you?* After all the time and money we put into your pageants—*how?* After everything I've done for you?"

"Tylenol would be fine," I said. "Or Excedrin."

"The pantry," Momma replied without looking my way.

Ducking to remain out of striking distance, I found a bottle of aspirin on the top shelf of the pantry. I tipped too many tablets into my palm. When I tried to cram them back into the bottle, several spilled through my fingers and pinged on the floor.

"All I want is an explanation." Momma turned to me. "You won't believe what she did!"

I was suddenly positively, absolutely certain Taffeta had

sung a dirty song, just like I'd suggested during Candy Land. "What happened?"

"She didn't sing! She got up there, and just . . . didn't sing."

I glanced at Taffeta. Her chin was wrinkled like a dried-up fruit. Tears leaked from her immense brown eyes. So she hadn't sung. That wasn't like taunting the judges with a dirty song, or flipping up her dress and mooning the crowd.

All of a sudden, I remembered the way she'd seemed to pick me out of the audience as I'd followed Mandarin out of the Benton High cafeteria.

I had abandoned her.

Taffeta's throwing the pageant was all my fault.

I placed a pair of aspirin tablets in my mouth and tried to swallow. I didn't think I could feel any worse. I should have known: no matter how bad you felt, you could *always* feel worse.

Momma was still ranting. "I've put every ounce of energy I have into your looks, your voice. Making you beautiful, making you important. You *knew* how hard I'd worked. Last night was a slap in the face, Taffeta, a slap in my face! This pageant was going to be it for us, the real beginning, and you ruined everything.

"How could you *do* that to me?"

For a moment, I didn't know who I pitied more—Momma or Taffeta. Then Momma turned on me.

"I thought Taffeta was going to be different," she said, "but the two of you are exactly alike. And now there's no chance left! None!"

Without thinking, I hurled the bottle of aspirin.

It hit Momma's chest, right in the center of a fuchsia hibiscus. The white pills ricocheted off the countertops like tiny bullets, bouncing all over the floor.

Momma gaped at me, stunned.

"Taffeta's not a *doll*, Momma. She's a real person. She may be six years old, but she's got a mind of her own. . . ." I trailed off when I remembered the quarry party. How mindlessly I'd walked into Mandarin's scheme. Who was I to talk?

"Grace Carpenter," Momma sputtered, "I didn't ask for your opinion!"

"Well, she needs somebody to speak up for her." I went over to Taffeta and held out my arms. "Let's go play Candy Land. I'll even let you make the rules—"

"*No!*" Taffeta screamed.

I reeled in my arms as if she'd slapped them. She hopped off the counter and kicked the empty aspirin bottle as she ran from the room.

Momma and I stared at each other, both of us too thunderstruck to speak.

❋   ❋   ❋

School emerged like a pirate ship from a bank of storm clouds. I had no choice but to face it, even if it meant walking the plank.

I spent extra time getting ready Monday morning. I couldn't wear one of Mandarin's undershirts, or my jeans slung too low, because it would disregard all that had happened. But if I wore my normal clothes, everybody would suspect that my friendship with Mandarin was over. In the end, I wore my jeans at half-mast, under a simple gray T-shirt.

Fortunately, Mandarin didn't show up to math.

She didn't show up on Tuesday, either.

On Wednesday, Ms. Ingle asked me to stay after history. She had a new poster behind her desk: Rosie the Riveter in a red bandana, flexing her bicep. *We Can Do It!*

Do what? I wanted to ask.

"I hate to bring this up with you, Grace," Ms. Ingle said. "But I don't know who else would know. Have you any idea what's going on with Mandarin?"

I tried to look nonchalant. "No. Why?"

"This is the third day this week Mandarin has missed history. And I had a talk with Mrs. Cleary this morning." I pictured the two of them gossiping in the teachers' lounge, Mrs. Cleary tapping her yellow nails on a chipped mug of coffee. "Mrs. Cleary says she hasn't been showing up to math, either. And finals are next week."

I stalled, rolling my palm over a wooden apple on Ms. Ingle's desk until I realized what I was doing. I put my hands behind my back.

"I'm just concerned about her," she said. "Mandarin's missed some of the most critical prep sessions. And you're the closest thing to a friend she's got."

How does she *know?*

"Small town," Ms. Ingle explained, as if reading my mind. "Everybody knows."

I tried to concentrate on maintaining a straight face. I wasn't sure if I was about to burst into tears or hysterical laughter.

"Have you talked to her father?" I asked.

Ms. Ingle just looked at me.

"Never mind," I said. "I guess it wouldn't make any difference."

"Then there's the service project." Ms. Ingle tipped her head to the side. "Is there anything you'd like to tell me?"

I thought of all the times I'd tried to initiate choosing a project with Mandarin, especially that time in her room, right before our fight. She'd always wanted to put it off. And now? There were ten days left until graduation. Without my assistance, Mandarin would never complete the project in time to graduate.

I knew I could defend her. I could lie and say she was working on something top secret, give her one last chance. In that moment, I had the ability to save her.

I closed my eyes when I spoke.

"Mandarin hasn't even picked a service project. I don't think she ever planned on doing one."

The next day, Mandarin showed up to geometry. I knew she'd arrived when I sensed some subtle shift in the atmosphere, but I never turned to look. For once, Mrs. Cleary didn't call her out for being tardy. Maybe she had some compassion after all.

At lunch, I headed for the end bathroom stall, like I had all week. No one was inside the bathroom when I knocked my English textbook to the floor. As I leaned over to pick it

up, I noticed the red words scrawled along the very bottom
of the stall door.

School is Horseshit.

Despite the hours I'd spent in the stall, I had forgotten
about it. A person could only read the phrase from ground
level—sprawled out on the tile, or leaning over, like me. For
some reason, it bothered me like it never had before. I rum-
maged around in my tote bag until I found a pen. I leaned forward and drew a fat black line over the first word. Then I
hesitated, my hand hovering uncertainly. I wasn't sure what
to write.

Before I could make up my mind, I heard the outer door
creak open.

I froze, trying my best to remain silent and motionless. I
waited for the intruder to go into one of the stalls beside me.

Instead, the faucet turned on. I heard intermittent splashes
and, indistinctly, a low humming. Strangely familiar.

Prince's "Little Red Corvette."

Every day after school that week, I'd been forced to avoid
the places Mandarin and I used to frequent—which made up
practically our whole town. I couldn't grab a milk shake at
the A&W or brood in the empty school yard. I didn't go to
the Sundrop Quik Stop, because it was across the street from
Solomon's. What if I passed Mandarin outside while she was
on a cigarette break? The library was too close as well. And
after what had happened with Tyler, I didn't want to go to the
Tombs. Maybe someday I'd be ready to return. But not yet.

All Mandarin's fault.

If it was really her humming out there, I should fling open

the door of the bathroom stall, confront her, tell her everything I was thinking.

But even after all this time, I was still too much of a coward.

At last, the faucet shut off. I heard paper towels cranking from the dispenser. Then nothing, for a moment, as the person seemed to hesitate.

I held my breath.

Then the outer door creaked open and shut. Silence. I exhaled shakily, lowering my crossed arms to my knees.

Life, I wrote above my fat black line. I stared at it, frowning.

Every moment of that endless week, I had to live with the awareness that somewhere within the confines of Washokey, Mandarin existed without me. And the return to my ordinary life without her, to the lonesome, solitary Grace I'd been stuck with for years and years, was almost debilitating.

As angry as I was at Mandarin, most of all, I missed her.

I missed the childlike Mandarin, who twirled in the cotton, danced through the grocery store aisles, flew across the empty football field with both arms open. I missed the passionate Mandarin, who looked into the glass eyes of a trophy and saw the wild animal it used to be. I even missed the impulsive, dangerous Mandarin, who pulled me into the murky canal waters, drove her ancient truck way too fast, painted my eyes and led me toward the bonfires. Because even as she terrified me, it was that Mandarin who finally woke me up.

Until our friendship, I'd never known how good my life could be.

That was her fault too.

27

way back when

Early on Saturday, I took a walk in the badlands.

I brought my English notes, although I didn't plan to study much. If finals were anything like midterms, I had nothing to worry about.

I followed one of the water trails tapering into the hills. The only sounds were the crunching of my shoes, the occasional low-pitched buzz of an insect, and the hush of a gentle wind—not the slightest bit wild—ruffling the dry grasses and shrubs. As I stopped at a crest, gazing out at the gradients of blue hills, brown hills, gray hills, I thought, *Mandarin would have loved it out here.*

Because despite the silence, the badlands didn't only contain dead things. On my walks, I'd seen ground squirrels and jackrabbits, rattlesnakes, and hawks soaring over prairies of salt sage, the kind we used to chew as little kids. I'd seen oases, where the water burbled up from underground and green things grew. And summer grasshoppers that popped away from my feet like water tossed onto a hot skillet.

I'd been so cautious about sharing my magic places, I hadn't showed Mandarin any. Not the badlands. And not the Tombs. Not the Virgin Mary rock. Or any of my rocks.

I had called Mandarin selfish. But maybe in my own way, I was selfish too.

I didn't start back until the midday sun became so hot my blood practically simmered in my ears. Although home life had rarely been pleasant, after the fiasco at the tri-county pageant, an uneasy cloud had seemed to envelop our entire house.

Without pageants pending, Momma didn't know what to do with herself. She wandered from room to room, up the stairs and down. She drank so much coffee I wondered why she didn't go into cardiac arrest. She started meals but didn't finish them, leaving the ingredients all over the counter. When we passed each other in the kitchen, it was hard to tell who was giving the silent treatment to whom.

Really, Momma and I were just stalling. Like boxers in their respective corners before a match began, each waiting for the other to make the first move. If there had been just the two of us, the dance could have gone on forever. But there was a third contestant in the ring neither of us had anticipated.

❋   ❋   ❋

I had just climbed out of the shower when I heard a splashing sound. At first, I thought I had water in my ears. Then I glanced out the bathroom window and spied Taffeta in the backyard, which was strange for several reasons.

First, our backyard was a disaster: an overgrown wasteland of broken toys and weeds. My sister seldom played out there, especially since the Millers had a swing set complete with monkey bars and a faux rock-climbing wall.

Second, she was wearing her tri-county pageant dress, along with her Little Miss Washokey tiara.

Third, she was sitting in the baby pool.

I wasn't sure whether I should be concerned or delighted. In my room, I pulled on a T-shirt and underpants. Then I flew down the stairs, jerked open the sliding glass door, and stepped outside.

"Taffeta! What the heck's going on?"

My sister didn't answer. She sat with her chin on her fist, like that sculpture *The Thinker*. Her uncombed hair straggled down her back. The murky rainwater from the baby pool had soaked into her dress, staining it the color of grease.

"Did you put all that on yourself?"

She still didn't answer.

"I didn't think you had it in you." I knelt beside her. "Guess I shouldn't have underestimated you. When you want to, you can be a real stubborn brat."

No reply.

"I mean that in a good way." I offered her my hand. "Look, Taffeta. I'm sorry I left your pageant early. Truly sorry. So you've made your point. Will you get out now?"

She shook her head. At least it was a response.

I prodded the earth in front of me until I found a stone. With my thumbnail, I began to scrape away the dirt.

"This reminds me of last winter, when you begged me to push you on the swings. Remember? I didn't want to, because it was so windy. But you kept whining, so I finally gave in."

My sister shifted in the water. I could tell she was listening.

"So I pushed you. And soon the wind picked up, just like I said it would, and you started swinging all crooked. You wanted off. But your mittens stuck to the chains. Don't you remember? We had to leave them there. Momma was so mad. . . ."

I heard the sliding door open. Momma, wearing her infamous muumuu, stood in the doorway.

"Oh," she said.

Like it was *perfectly normal* for her daughters to congregate in and around an old baby pool that hadn't budged through two winters, one daughter in her underwear, the other wrecking the pageant dress into which she'd sewn all her superficial hopes and dreams.

"You didn't even know she was out here," I said accusingly, scrambling to my feet.

"Don't be silly. Of course I did."

"That's not true, Momma! You couldn't have known— you'd be freaking out!"

Even though I was yelling, for once Momma didn't raise her voice. She looked at me and said quietly, "I always know where you girls are."

You girls? I shook my head, thinking of all the far-flung

nooks and crannies where Mandarin and I had assembled. "No you don't. You have no *idea* where I go."

"I know more than you think."

"How?" I demanded. "How do you know?"

"I have my ways."

Thinking of Polly Bunker, I narrowed my eyes. "Gossip."

"That, and other methods."

"You could have just asked."

"You never would have told me."

She was right. "But it would have meant something," I said. "The asking."

At last, Momma came over and stood in front of us. Her eyes wandered from one daughter to the other. I could tell it took her every milligram of willpower not to swoop Taffeta out of the baby pool and dunk her, pageant dress and all, in a soapy bath. But she just stood there with her arms crossed.

"I know I'm not a good mother," she said at last. "But I know I'm not a terrible mother either."

I sighed. Did she expect me to be thankful? In my opinion, there were far too many mediocre mothers, and fathers, and not nearly enough good ones. In Washokey, at least. Maybe my sample was too small.

"You know, Grace, I didn't mean to be pregnant with you," Momma began.

"Momma . . ." I glanced at Taffeta.

"Just let me finish. Things like that don't necessarily happen when you're ready. Hell, I wasn't much older than Mandarin. Eighteen's just a number. I wasn't anything near an adult . . . It was the hardest thing I ever had to do, growing up that fast."

"Then why, Momma? Why'd you have me in the first place?"

The question shot out before I could stop it, burning my eyes, my throat. I ordered myself not to cry. Not now. Not worth it.

Momma shrugged helplessly. "You were my baby."

She took a step closer.

"After everything I went through, I promised myself I'd make life easy for you girls. That's what the pageants were about. I wanted the world to fall down at your feet. When you wrecked your Little Miss Washokey . . . it was like you were flipping me off. All that time I'd spent—I thought it was *our* time."

"The road trips," I said. "Not the pageants. The pageants were *your* time."

It felt strange saying them out loud, the words I hadn't been able to articulate for years and years. They came easier than I'd have ever believed.

Just words. Nothing more.

"I guess it was how I knew to be close to you," Momma said. "And we were close, way back when. Weren't we?"

"We were," I agreed quietly.

Neither of us said what should have followed: *Maybe we can become close again.* But I knew we both were thinking it.

We stood there for a while longer, our eyes flickering away from each other's. Finally, Momma reached down and lifted up Taffeta. She didn't resist. Brown water streamed from her dress, seeping onto Momma's muumuu.

"You don't have to be in pageants anymore," Momma

said to Taffeta. "You don't ever have to sing again, if you don't want to."

"But I *want* to."

"*Really?*" Momma and I exclaimed at once. I felt like my brain was about to spontaneously combust. All my memories of pageants were tinged with irritation. It had never occurred to me that my sister had actually enjoyed some part of them.

"I just get to choose the songs I sing," she said. "Songs I like singing. How about that?"

"Sure, honey!" Momma's eyes looked misty. "Like what songs?"

Taffeta thought for a moment. "Maybe something disco."

❀　❀　❀

I waited until Momma was busy in the kitchen making Hawaiian salad and Taffeta was getting dressed after a much-needed bath. Then I dug through the scum in the baby pool until I found what I was looking for.

I kept it in my hand as I dialed Mandarin's number.

28

someplace magic

I followed the back road west of town, the one used mainly by farmers driving sheep or riding horses. It was a dirt road, but years of animal droppings made it look paved in cakey hay asphalt, mashed by animal hooves and pickup truck tires. Every once in a while, I'd come across a new pile of crap. Some were huge.

By the time I reached the river, it was almost sunset. The wind picked up, but I couldn't tell if it was a normal wind or otherwise. I put a hand over my mouth and breathed through my fingers, attempting to keep my head clear.

I had no idea which Mandarin I would encounter that night: happy, angry, somber, or hysterical. I needed to be ready for any of them.

When I arrived, she was standing at the base of the

Tombs, dressed in her lavender sweater, with the ridge of her clavicle jutting out over the neckline. It was the first time I'd ever seen her without black eyeliner. She held the jackalope head against her thigh, her fingers wrapped around the antlers. "So this is your place, huh?"

"Someplace magic," I replied.

She glanced at the spot where she'd besieged Tyler with stones. "I didn't know," she said. "I promise."

I shrugged and turned away, leading her up the boulders to my cave in the Tombs.

Once inside, I sat with my legs crossed. Mandarin didn't sit right away, though. She circled the space, stooped over, one hand flat on the stone walls. When she reached the cave painting, she paused and looked at it for a long time.

"It's the Virgin Mary," I said. "Supposedly. Remember the stories?"

"She isn't, though."

"Isn't what?"

"Mary."

She sat at last, with her back against the wall, the jackalope head in her lap. The smudgy black eyes of the painted woman peered over her shoulder.

"So why'd you want to meet?" she asked warily.

I cleared my throat. She was going to find out anyway, but I knew I should be the one to tell her. "I told Ms. Ingle you didn't do a service project."

Her reaction was right on target.

"But school's not over till next week!" The jackalope tumbled from her lap. "Why'd you have to go and tell her that?"

"She asked."

"Why didn't you lie?" She rose to her knees, but I didn't budge. "You had no right to do that, Grace. That was *our* fucking project."

Any other time, I would have backed down. But not that night. If I'd stood up to Momma after fifteen years, I could handle Mandarin Ramey. "Wrong," I said. "You couldn't even choose a topic. My project was helping *you* out."

"Well, you didn't, Grace. You ruined everything!"

"You mean graduating? Are you honestly going to tell me you think you'll pass every final next week? That's not my fault. You ruined that for yourself, Mandarin."

We glared at each other.

And after one, two, three beats, Mandarin dropped her eyes. She picked up the jackalope and set it in her lap facing up. "I know," she said.

I thought I might feel happy about this tiny victory. I didn't.

"I just . . . I don't know what stops me. Everybody knows I'm screwed up on the outside—all the stuff I do, I mean. They don't know how I'm screwed up on the inside. Only the people who get close."

"You solve that easy enough," I said. "You don't get close to anybody."

"Well, you. And I had friends in elementary school too, y'know. Sarah Cooper at the A&W wasn't all bad. And there was this one girl . . ."

"Sophie Brawls."

Mandarin raised her eyebrows. "I guess you heard about the fight. And what happened after. It got so blown out of proportion. Not the fight, I mean—that was huge. For us.

But it was ours to settle. When Mr. Beck got involved, and then the cops . . . Sophie didn't even try to stop it all from happening.

"And then there's my mother. . . ."

She paused, as if to catch her breath.

"We used to make dolls out of cottonwood down. Her and me. We'd cut shapes from old shirts and sew them up. I once heard you can't truly hate a person until you've cared about them. Until you've loved them. And boy, do I ever know about that. It happened with Sophie Brawls. It happened with my mother—"

"Why don't you contact her?" I said, interrupting her, afraid my name was next. "She lives so close. Riverton's just a few hours away."

Mandarin snorted. "She abandoned me when I needed her. So now that she wants me, why should I make it easy for her? She deserves to wait."

I ran my fingers over the gritty surface of the stone floor, thinking about Momma. After the incident that morning, I could no longer deny it: she had tried to reach out to me over the years, in various, mostly misguided ways. But I'd ignored her efforts. I'd wanted to punish her, just like Mandarin did her mother.

"But for how long?" I wondered.

Mandarin shrugged impatiently. "She could make more of an effort than *arrowheads*. What the fuck's that about? Like, embracing my maternal heritage?"

"Maybe," I said. "Or maybe it's about how you've hurt each other. They're weapons, after all."

"When did you get so damn wise about mother-daughter relationships?"

My turn to shrug.

"That reminds me." Shifting forward, I reached into my back pocket and withdrew the arrowhead I'd salvaged from the baby pool. "I shouldn't keep this—it's not right."

Mandarin accepted it. She held it up, but there wasn't enough light to make it glow.

"I don't want her to know how messed up I am," she whispered.

And then it all made sense.

Mandarin wasn't just afraid of failing herself. She didn't want to fail her mother.

That was what kept her in school. That was why she clung to her hopes of graduating, as impossible as she made it for herself.

I knew her failing wasn't my fault. It would have taken someone a thousand times stronger to force Mandarin to finish a single math assignment on her own, let alone complete a service project for the community she hated. But even so, my chest ached for her. Like the first time I'd seen her with a man, I wished for the power to destroy whatever monster made her sabotage herself.

If one even existed. Maybe it was Mandarin's official mythological creature.

"Mandarin . . ." I hesitated, not knowing what to say. "It's getting kind of stuffy in here. Want to go out on top?"

When she nodded, I led the way, following a staircase of boulders to my lookout above the Tombs. The river reflected the colors of the sky. It looked like a gulch of molten lava. I heard the high-pitched whoop of night birds in the snarled vegetation bordering both banks. Beside me, Mandarin tapped the head of her jackalope.

"Where do you think those other animal heads went?"

"Maybe they're tangled up in the tree roots somewhere, or stuck up against a beaver dam. Or maybe they sank. . . ." I glanced at Mandarin's face. "But I'm sure they made it. Round the bend to the Missouri River."

"The Missouri? I thought the Bighorn went into the Colorado River."

"Apparently the Bighorn flows north," I explained. "I read it in my history book. That almost never happens— most rivers flow south. It's actually pretty amazing. So they'd end up in the Atlantic instead of the Pacific. But who cares, right? An ocean's an ocean."

Though when I pictured the elk head bobbing out at sea, slapped by waves, it wasn't a much better image than it being jammed among the other heads in the brush downriver. At least that way it wouldn't be alone.

"Mandarin," I began. "There's something I just don't get. You say the people here are one of the main reasons you want to escape. If not the only reason. But do you really think people are different outside of Washokey? What if you leave, only to find more of the same? Where's there to go after that?"

Mandarin stared out at the river.

"Maybe it's just your way of looking at them," I added.

"Maybe you're right." Her voice shook. "Maybe I can't be happy anywhere."

Her tears looked like garnets in the light of the sunset.

My heart broke. I closed the space between us, pressing myself up against her, placing my hand atop hers. It felt fragile, like a broken bird. For how strong she could be, how angry, how violent, how *manipulative,* she could also be the complete opposite. Not just somebody I admired, wanted to be like—but somebody who needed me.

I took a deep breath. Maybe that was my mistake. Because at that moment, the wind increased. I felt my throat capture it, my lungs swell with it.

And all of a sudden, I longed to pretend that nothing had happened. To pretend Mandarin had never betrayed me, and I had never betrayed her back. To pretend that this was one of our spangled, breathless, fucking-gorgeous nights, like the one we spent at the canal, or the one when we liberated the trophies, or even the night of the tri-county pageant, before everything went sour. I needed to hold our magic just a little longer. Whatever it took.

"Mandarin." I grabbed both her hands. "Let's go."

"Where?"

"Away. Let's leave town. Tonight."

She shook her head. "You're crazy."

"You don't have to work later, do you? Will anyone miss you?"

She glanced down at our entwined fingers.

"I'm serious, Mandarin! I really want to go this time, I mean it. You can count on me. I haven't got the modeling pictures back from where I sent the film, but I'll bring my camera and we can take new ones. On the beach—the beach in California. Or in the strawberry fields. Come and get me at midnight. That'll give us enough time to pack."

Despite her tears, I thought I saw the trembling begin-
nings of a smile.

"Really?"

"Yeah really. We can do this! And not for the people here,
but for us. We just made too big of a deal out of it, made it
seem harder than it really is. When it's really just about—"

"Taking that first step," Mandarin finished.

"Exactly!" I exclaimed. "Look—I'll wait on my front
porch at midnight. With two bowls of strawberry ice cream
for the road." I squeezed her hands more tightly. Her wet eyelashes looked like stars. "Will you go?"

"Yes," she said, nodding, smiling at last.

Her smile made me want to dance. Maybe I would have
if I hadn't been balanced at the very top of the Tombs, dizzy
with adrenaline, the Bighorn River slogging along many feet
below. When I stood, the earth appeared to drop another ten
feet. "Are you ready to go?"

"I'm going to stay here a bit." She paused. "Grace?"

I caught my balance at the edge of the boulder before I
glanced back.

"Thanks," Mandarin said. "For everything."

I noticed she was gripping her mother's arrowhead. For
some strange reason, her words plucked at my spine like a
winter chill. But I chose to ignore them.

"So I'll see you at midnight, all right?" I lowered my feet
onto the next rock. "Forget this stupid river. We're going to
see the ocean!"

When I crawled into the cave, I found it almost entirely
dark. I'd never stayed out at the Tombs so late. I could barely

make out the Virgin Mary, or the nameless Indian mother, or whoever she was.

For a second I paused, squinting at the twin black splotches of her eyes, recalling how I used to consider her the perfect mother. Now, in the dark, she just looked creepy. I had an urge to smear my hand across the stone surface. But I didn't want some prehistoric Native American curse to thunder down upon me. I scrambled out. The wildwinds thrust against me until my feet hit the ground.

29

a shock in the silence

Forty minutes after midnight, I sat with my back against the front door of my house. I had nothing with me but two bowls of melted pink ice cream, cradled on my lap.

I heard the drone of the summer cicadas, a few crickets, the tick-tick-flutter of someone's sprinklers. Far off, a dog bayed forlornly. Or maybe a coyote. I didn't hear what I was listening for: the hum of an engine, the rasp of tires on Pioneer Ridge's patchy asphalt.

The street was empty.

Earlier, after Momma had gone to bed, I'd opened the closet and stared at my clothes. Then I shut the door and paced around, looking at my room from different angles. The stack of shoe boxes containing every worthy rock I'd ever found. The stupid swans peeling from my walls. Grandma's musty pillows. My camera. My old computer, and the books on my shelves. I could place each one: where and when I'd gotten it, what I'd been doing when I read it.

At eleven-forty-five, when I'd finally brought the bowls of ice cream outside and sat atop the porch steps, I was ready.

Not ready to go.

But ready to betray her again.

And if it was possible, considering her criteria, ready for her to hate me.

When I'd made that difficult decision to leave my shoes in my closet and my camera on my desk, it had never occurred to me that Mandarin wouldn't come. I felt hurt by it, despite the circumstances. But as the minutes passed, ticking toward the end of the hour, I also felt afraid.

Maybe I can't be happy anywhere, she had said.

And that night of my birthday, at the football field: *It feels like I'm disconnected.*

And at the river, after the trophy liberation: *I'd want to float away.*

I had left her on top of the Tombs, overlooking the river, in that mood. She hadn't wanted to accompany me down. I should have insisted. Wasn't Mandarin capable of anything?

I was so lost in my thoughts, I became aware of the rumbling only gradually, as if it had begun somewhere deep underground and was rising to the surface. I strained against it, prayed for it to quit, but it only grew louder. I scanned the street one last time. Then, cradling both bowls in the crook of my arm, I wrangled open the front door, squeezed through the gap, and kicked it shut.

In the dark hall, I leaned against the other side of the

door with my cheek against the wood, listening to the roar of the mosquito truck. I could smell it, the toxic stink entering my lungs, my blood vessels, and then the truck receded and the roar faded away.

The phone rang, a shock in the silence.

Startled, I almost dropped the ice cream bowls, juggling them for a precarious instant before setting them on the floor. I grabbed the phone before it could ring a second time.

"Hello?" I whispered.

When I heard her voice, I slid down the front door until I was crouching, my face and fingers and knees folded around the receiver, as she explained what she was doing, and why she had to do it, alone. I tried to convince her otherwise. But already the rumbling was beginning again: the mosquito truck's second coming. The sound approached faster this time, as if the driver had made a wrong turn and was speeding to correct it, louder and louder, until I could hardly hear her words, or my own reply, my weak effort to change her mind.

By the time I hung up the phone, the roar had died completely.

The night was so silent I could hear the motor of the refrigerator. I picked up the ice cream bowls and followed the sound to the kitchen.

I turned the faucet to hot, held the bowls up high, and poured, watching the twin pink rivers fold into the running water. I stacked the bowls and stuck my hands, then my arms, under the water as I breathed in the steam, purifying my body of fifteen years of wildwinds and mosquito poison.

"Grace? Are you all right?"

Momma stood in the doorway. She wore a pale yellow terry cloth bathrobe. Her muumuu was probably still rancid from baby pool water.

"Who was that on the phone?"

I turned off the faucet, feeling a weak little flare of that familiar annoyance. *Lie*, habit compelled me. *Deny. She doesn't deserve to know.* But that would take too much energy. "She's gone," I said.

"Gone? Who's gone?"

"Mandarin."

"But . . . what . . ." Momma stumbled over her words. "I don't understand. Gone? Should we get the police? If there's still a chance—"

"It's too late."

I felt hot tears soaking my cheeks, but I wasn't sobbing. Telling Momma the truth was more of a relief than I ever would have dreamed. Even better than standing up to her. It felt like a giant sigh, a sweet gulp of air after centuries of submersion.

She had asked, and I had told her.

For now, that was all I needed.

As I passed through the living room, the sky in the window seemed to glow slightly, as if radioactive, like some momentous event had unfolded just beyond my scope of sight. The cicadas were silent. But like a solitary violinist, one lucky cricket began to play.

3Ø

personal kaleidoscopes

Everybody gaped as I unfolded Davey's note in homeroom. Kids in Washokey would never learn to stare with subtlety.

The news of Mandarin's disappearance had infiltrated the town by Monday. By Friday, the other students seemed to believe my silence was the indicator of some profound information—even though I'd always been that quiet in class. But if I'd discovered anything these past few weeks, it was that a person's actions could be interpreted in a number of ways, depending on who was watching. Their viewpoints were simply skewed by their beliefs, their prejudices, and their private desires.

Their personal kaleidoscopes.

I couldn't judge them, of course. I was the same way.

Not bothering to conceal it, I read Davey's note: *I'm sorry about the phone calls.* He'd called several times that week, but I hadn't gone to the phone.

"That's okay," I replied out loud. "Thanks, though."

He nodded at me, then scribbled in his notebook again. He ripped out the page and handed it to me without folding it.

I just wanted to be sure you're all right, it read. *Are you?*

The loudspeaker beeped. I toyed with the piece of petrified wood in my pocket as Mr. Beck began the final announcements of my sophomore year—which was also sort of my freshman year, but who was counting?

"May I have your attention, please," Mr. Beck said. There was a definite catch in his voice. "Good morning, everyone, on this . . . Friday, June fifteenth. It's a fine day, with the temperature in the low eighties. This is your principal, Mr. Beck, on the last day of school. As you all know, commencement will take place on the football field at four. Seniors should be dismissed following homeroom for rehearsal."

He paused, as if searching for something to say. "I hope you all have a splendid summer vacation."

As soon as the loudspeaker clicked off, the door to the classroom creaked open. Samantha Dent's timid face appeared in the gap. Volunteering as an office aide had been her service project.

"Um, excuse me," she said. "Mr. Beck would like to see Grace in his office."

I glanced at Ms. Ingle. She stood before an old yellow flag, the one with the coiled snake: *Don't Tread on Me.* "Go ahead," she said.

I dropped my reply to Davey's note on his desk. Then I squeezed by Alexis. Her hair was pulled back with a headband I remembered from elementary school. For a second, I expected her to smile, or smirk, or even grimace—to acknowledge our history, our years of friendship, inhibited as they might have been. Some demonstration that despite our differences, she cared. But she just looked away.

I hesitated beside Ms. Ingle's desk. I'd considered what I was about to do a hundred times in the past week, but I hadn't actually decided until I set my piece of petrified wood in front of her.

"You know my service project didn't turn out the way I'd planned . . . ," I began.

Ms. Ingle looked at me quizzically. "Grace, it's not a problem. You put in far more than ten hours' effort."

"I guess. But . . . I've been thinking. I've got this whole entire rock collection, just gathering dust in my room. Maybe I could sort them and label them in a display case, or something. I could give it to Mrs. Mack. Or you could keep it in here. Rocks are history too, aren't they?"

"They sure are," Ms. Ingle replied.

As I followed Samantha out of the classroom, I pictured Davey blinking at my note. *No, I'm not*, I'd written in reply. And then, in smaller letters: *But I will be.*

❀   ❀   ❀

Samantha and I walked in silence until we reached the office door. Then, all of a sudden, she stopped and turned to me. "I'm sorry," she said.

"Thanks," I said. "It's not what everybody thinks, though. She had a good reason for—"

"Not about Mandarin. About . . . you know. The way we've acted. Me and Paige and Alexis. To tell you the truth, I'm kind of over them. Ever since Alexis lost Miss Teen Bighorn, she won't stop bitching about it. I mean, who really gives a shit?"

That was the most I'd ever heard Samantha say at once. "I sure don't," I replied.

Samantha smiled at my feet. "Hey, so they've promoted me to waitress at the restaurant. If you're looking for a job, we need a hostess. If that's not too weird."

Elk heads flashed before my eyes. *Weirder than you know.* "Yeah," I said. "Maybe."

Samantha headed back down the hall. I heard voices inside Mr. Beck's office, so I sat in one of the vinyl chairs outside, inspecting the bulletin board in front of me.

It was covered in butcher paper, faded pink. Card stock borders decorated with dancing pencils lined the edges. Like a proud parent, Mr. Beck had stapled up kindergarten artworks, photos of student athletes at play, reports bound by plastic hinges with red A-pluses on the covers. And right at my eye level hung my All-American essay.

I stared at it in wonder.

I recognized the font, the shapes of the paragraphs, as if it had been photographed somewhere inside my brain. Leaning forward, I skimmed it, mouthing the phrases I'd labored to get right. As I read them now, they sounded all wrong.

We've got to take that first step off into the future by ourselves. What had I been thinking?

The door opened, and a twosome of beaming parents stepped out, followed by Mr. Beck. I noticed he had dyed his white roots black, probably for graduation. The cheap pigment had stained his forehead in several places.

"Good morning, Grace," he said.

"You wanted to talk to me?"

He nodded. "Yes, but I thought instead of talking in the office, we could take a walk. How does that sound?"

It sounded pretty embarrassing, if anybody saw us. But then I glanced again at Mr. Beck's ridiculous bulletin board: the photographs, the dancing pencils, my essay. And I thought of the time I'd seen him eating alone at the Buffalo Grill. And I decided I was sick of being embarrassed.

"It sounds fine," I told him. "Just one thing first . . ."

I reached out and ripped my essay from the wall.

We passed through the empty halls in silence, stopping by an open window that overlooked the playground. I spotted Taffeta, wearing a white sailor dress. She and the other kindergartners were lined up in two rows on the sunny lawn, arms linked.

They were playing Red Rover.

I felt pressure building behind my eyes, so I turned to Mr. Beck.

"Before anything else," he began, "I was wondering . . . would you like to talk about Mandarin?"

"With *you?*"

It took Mr. Beck a moment to regain composure. He smoothed his tie, his ponytail, his mustache. "Yes, yes, I see why you wouldn't," he said at last.

"No offense."

"We do our best, you know," he said. "But . . . we just don't have the resources of a larger, city school. It's not the first time this has happened."

"Not the first time what has happened?"

"That a Washokey student's run away."

Run away?

Mandarin had run away. I supposed she had—but the words had the wrong connotation. Mr. Beck probably suspected her of fleeing an abusive father, or running off with some man she'd met at the bar. To escape a stifling town. He'd be right about the last part.

"Red Rover, Red Rover! Send Annabelle over!"

I glanced back out the window. Far beyond the kindergartners, the seniors had started to congregate on the football field for graduation rehearsal.

"The other matter I wanted to discuss . . ." Mr. Beck cleared his throat. "You didn't send in your paperwork for the leadership conference."

I bit my lip. Momma had signed the papers the day after my birthday. But instead of sending them in, I'd stashed them between the pages of my pageant album. "How did you know?"

"The conference directors called me yesterday. There was a waiting list to attend the conference, you see. They had to fill your spot with a student from a different school."

"Oh," I said. It stung a bit. But I had to admit— "Leadership: the Musical" just wasn't for me. "You mean Becky Pepper's not going?"

"Well, Becky Pepper wasn't the winner. . . ."

"Red Rover, Red Rover! Send Christopher over!" A

round little boy ran at the opposite side but couldn't break through the other kids' arms. He latched on to the outermost of their ranks.

". . . and so, the grant's still yours," Mr. Beck was saying.

I glanced at him. "The grant?"

"From Kiwanis and 4-H. It was supposed to fund the conference. But since it's too late for you to attend, we can gift it to you in a savings bond, like your other one. Or maybe they'd let you use the funds for a different trip. It'd have to be educational, of course, to fit the criteria. In the meantime, you might start thinking about where you'd like to go. You'll need a chaperone, of course. I'm sure Ms. Ingle would be interested."

Mr. Beck reached out as if to pat me on the back, but wavered. I saved him by catching his hand where it hung in the air and shaking it.

"Are you sure you can't tell us where Mandarin went?" he asked hopefully.

I shook my head. "I'm sorry."

The ends of his mustache appeared to droop.

"Red Rover, Red Rover! Send Taffeta over!"

I looked out the window as my sister flung herself into the barricade of children. For a moment I thought she wouldn't break through, but she did. Cheering, she grabbed the hand of another little girl, and together they ran and rejoined Taffeta's side.

Maybe Mandarin had never completed a community service project. But she'd definitely left an impression on our town. Some of it good, some of it bad. All of it transcendent.

I saw it now, watching the children laugh as they threw themselves at the other side in an attempt to burst through, break free. Nothing could be more Mandarin than that.

"But I can tell you *why* she left," I said.

She had asked me to give her a head start before I told anyone. I didn't know whether she feared somebody tracking her down, or whether she wanted to give her father a chance to fully absorb the note she said she'd taped to the refrigerator.

Or whether it was because she wanted to maintain her image just a few days longer, before everybody knew the real truth—that out of all the crazy places she could have run off to, of all the boys and girls and men with whom she could have gone, of all the infinite reasons to escape Washokey, Mandarin chose to find her mother.

after

"Look!" Momma exclaimed. "Pronghorns."

She braked and pulled over to the shoulder of the road. Right away, I spotted them: about a dozen russet antelopes with splotches of white on their chests. They strolled through the autumn-colored grasslands, seemingly undisturbed by our car. I tried not to think about the three new replacement trophies I'd seen at the Buffalo Grill, along with the two recovered from a riverbend a couple of miles north.

"There's a baby, Grace! Look."

Momma pointed at a tiny fawn balanced on spindly legs, staying close to his parent.

"When they sense a predator and there's no time to run, they drop," she said. "Did you know? They just lie there, perfectly still, blended in with the grass. You can even approach them, stand right over them. They don't budge until their mother comes back."

We'd only been on the road a few hours. But the change in Momma had begun as soon as we'd merged onto the interstate. Like in the photos in the manila envelope on my lap, somebody had amped up the saturation of her face, the hue and contrast of her eyes and hair.

"It's strange," she had said. "I'd forgotten what it's like."

She couldn't keep quiet, which wasn't unusual for Momma, especially since she'd started working on "that cookbook I always wanted to write." But instead of nervous prattling, her words were colored by amazement.

"Do you remember that time outside of the reservation in Riverton, when we saw that band of Indians crossing the road? They were all wrapped up in blankets, on horses. You were pretty small, Grace. I know you don't remember much from back then—"

"I remember," I said.

Momma was quiet for a moment. "Oops," she said. "We just went over the state line. The sign's behind us. Now we're in South Dakota."

"Just like that?"

"Just like that."

I shook my head in wonder. No malicious spirits had halted our departure. No force field or cosmic electric fence. Not even the whirl and whoop of an alarm, like I'd imagined the day I ditched school with Mandarin. No barricade of Wyomingites with linked arms, protecting the border Red Rover–style.

"We're getting close now," Momma said. "We'll reach the monument in an hour and a half."

"President heads." Taffeta spoke up from the backseat.

Momma and I glanced at each other. We thought she'd

been napping. "We should have woken her up for the prong-horns," I said.

"I saw the anter-lopes."

"Then why didn't you say anything?"

Taffeta shrugged. "I like listening."

"So I thought we'd drive back up to Rapid City for sup-per," Momma said. "We can get a motel in town. And in the morning . . . Where to next, Grace? It's your trip."

I looked out the window. So far, South Dakota didn't look that different from Wyoming. "Keep heading east," I said, putting my knees up against the dash.

I used to wonder what it would look like if all my foot-steps were painted red: all the steps I'd ever taken in all the places I'd ever been. There would be one long tendril way out to Seattle, reflecting the time I'd visited my aunt. Scribbles all over Wyoming, from our assorted pageant trips. Every-thing would converge in Washokey, Wyoming. Footsteps traced and retraced so many times they'd become a dollop of red paint, or a heart in a rib cage of hills.

Maybe it sounded kind of creepy, but I liked the idea—that we left pieces of ourselves everywhere we went, coloring all our important places.

Even if Washokey was the center of them all.

Not long after we passed the state line, we pulled over at a gas station so my sister could use the bathroom. From the car, I snapped a photo as Taffeta reached for Momma's hand.

Once they disappeared, I climbed out of the car and en-tered the station. It was exactly like the Sundrop Quik Stop in Washokey, except the key chains and lighters all said South Dakota.

I set the manila envelope on the counter and pried it open. It already bore the address Mandarin had given me on the phone a few days after school had ended.

"Would you like to mail that?" asked the man behind the counter.

"Just one sec."

As I sifted through the photos—Mandarin lying in the grassy pasture with her hair spread out, hanging off the fence with her elbows on her thighs, wearing the contraband cowboy outfit in the shadowy barn—I wondered yet again where she'd go if it didn't work out with her mother.

She was always west in my fantasies. Sometimes I pictured her in Hollywood, waiting tables between auditions. Or I imagined her modeling in San Francisco, posing against a postcard background of bridges and fog. In my darker daydreams, I envisioned her standing under streetlights in Las Vegas, leaning against doorways and into cars. Briefly, I had even imagined her lifeless body shattered by waves, or lost in some remoteness of the badlands.

But I didn't believe it.

Because ever since my last beauty pageant, when Mandarin had caught my wayward lilac bloom and twisted it between her fingers, we'd been linked together. Now I felt her distance, but not her absence. And someday, we might be able to close that gap.

Before I tucked it back inside the manila envelope with the photos, I unfolded the revised version of my essay and skimmed it one last time.

*Everybody says the winds in Washokey, Wyoming, make peo-
ple go crazy. But Washokey isn't the only place with crazy-making
winds.*

*In California, they're called the Santa Anas, and they scoop
the heat from the high desert and fling it at the coast. In France,
they're called the Mistrals, and they drove Vincent Van Gogh to
cut off his ear.*

*Some people say the ozone gets stirred up or reduced, and
we're breathing in the wrong sort of oxygen as a result. Maybe it's
this wildwind psychosis that makes us do things like put pronghorn
antlers on jackrabbit heads and lipstick on little girls.*

*But whether they're crazy-making or just annoying, it's not
just the winds that make us crazy to leave. From pioneers setting
out across the prairie to mustangs fleeing their Spanish masters, the
most American thing about us is our itchy feet. We're always itch-
ing to go, to move on, to escape. We convince ourselves we could
truly be happy if only we were somewhere else. Or somebody else.*

*While it's smart to plan for the future, we won't find real hap-
piness if our eyes never leave the horizon. When we're all rush-
ing off in different directions, we miss the worthwhile places, and
worthwhile people, already around us.*

*But we can't wait for them to chase us down—we've got to
seek them out. Because for two people to meet in the middle, both
have to take that first step.*

acknowledgments

First and most, this book is for and because of my mother, Marcia, Californian and Wyomingite, who helped me find Grace (as well as armloads of rocks) in the Wyoming badlands.

I'd like to thank my twin sister, Danielle: muse, inexorable critic, and womb/soul mate. Michelle Haft, best friend and constant inspiration. The rest of my family, Hubbards and Allens and Cummingses, and my friends, who love me even when I'm being a writing recluse who doesn't return calls for a month.

My brilliant agent, Michelle Andelman, who wanted more of "edgy, longing, magnetic" Mandarin half an hour after I crept into her slush pile.

My team at Delacorte Press, especially my editors, Michelle Poploff and Rebecca Short, expert story shapers who helped perfect my novel beyond its wildwindiest dreams.

For support, honest critiques, and hysterical laugher, my *alces alces* superwomen: Amanda Hannah, Kristin Miller, Kaitlin Ward, and Michelle Schusterman. Also, Hannah Wydey, Kristin Otts, Kody Keplinger, and the rest of the YA Highway girls.

My UCSD writing mentors Michael Krekorian, Brian Root, Eileen Myles, and Harriet Dodge, one of Mandarin's earliest advocates.

Annie Proulx, for reawakening the landscapes of my own young adulthood and beckoning me back.

And last but never least, Bryson, love of my life, who doesn't understand all this insanity but supports me anyway.

about the author

A travel writer and young adult author, Kirsten Hubbard
has hiked ancient ruins in Cambodia, dived with wild
dolphins in Belize (one totally looked her in the eye), slept
in a Slovenian jail cell, and navigated the Wyoming
badlands (without a compass) in search of transcendent
backdrops for her novels. She lives in San Diego. Visit her
website at kirstenhubbard.com.